W9-BFE-374

MURDER IN CHINATOWN

MURDER IN CHINATOWN

A Gaslight Mystery

Victoria Thompson

BERKLEY PRIME CRIME, NEW YORK

THE BERKLEY PUBLISHING GROUP
Published by the Penguin Group
Penguin Group (USA) Inc.
375 Hudson Street, New York, New York 10014, USA
Penguin Group (Canada), 90 Eglinton Avenue East, Suite 700, Toronto, Ontario M4P 2Y3, Canada
(a division of Pearson Penguin Canada Inc.)
Penguin Books Ltd., 80 Strand, London WC2R 0RL, England
Penguin Group Ireland, 25 St. Stephen's Green, Dublin 2, Ireland (a division of Penguin Books Ltd.)
Penguin Group (Australia), 250 Camberwell Road, Camberwell, Victoria 3124, Australia
(a division of Pearson Australia Group Pty. Ltd.)
Penguin Books India Pvt. Ltd., 11 Community Centre, Panchsheel Park, New Delhi—110 017, India
Penguin Group (NZ), 67 Apollo Drive, Rosedale, North Shore 0745, Auckland, New Zealand
(a division of Pearson New Zealand Ltd.)
Penguin Books (South Africa) (Pty.) Ltd., 24 Sturdee Avenue, Rosebank, Johannesburg 2196, South Africa

Penguin Books Ltd., Registered Offices: 80 Strand, London WC2R 0RL, England

This book is an original publication of The Berkley Publishing Group.

This is a work of fiction. Names, characters, places, and incidents either are the product of the author's imagination or are used fictitiously, and any resemblance to actual persons, living or dead, business establishments, events, or locales is entirely coincidental. The publisher does not have any control over and does not assume any responsibility for author or third-party websites or their content.

Copyright © 2007 by Victoria Thompson.
The Edgar® name is a registered service mark of the Mystery Writers of America, Inc.

All rights reserved.
No part of this book may be reproduced, scanned, or distributed in any printed or electronic form without permission. Please do not participate in or encourage piracy of copyrighted materials in violation of the author's rights. Purchase only authorized editions.
The name BERKLEY PRIME CRIME and the BERKLEY PRIME CRIME design are trademarks belonging to Penguin Group (USA) Inc.

First edition: June 2007

Library of Congress Cataloging-in-Publication Data

Thompson, Victoria (Victoria E.)
    Murder in Chinatown / Victoria Thompson.—1st ed.
        p.   cm.—(Gaslight mysteries)
    ISBN 978-0-425-21531-9
        1. Brandt, Sarah (Fictitious character)—Fiction.   2. Women detectives—New York (State)—New York—Fiction.   3. Malloy, Frank (Fictitious character)—Fiction.   4. Police—New York (State)—New York—Fiction.   5. Midwives—Fiction.   6. Racially mixed children—Fiction.   7. Chinatown (New York, N.Y.)—Fiction.   I. Title.

PS3570.H6442M864 2007
813'.54—dc22

                                                                                                2006052669

PRINTED IN THE UNITED STATES OF AMERICA

10   9   8   7   6   5   4   3   2   1

To my mother for being my biggest fan!

MURDER IN
CHINATOWN

I

"I'M NOT IN LABOR, AM I?" CORA LEE ASKED.

Midwife Sarah Brandt shook her head. "I'm afraid not." She'd been sitting in Cora's comfortable parlor for over an hour, her hand on Cora's swollen stomach while they waited for the labor pains to come and go. "Real labor pains get stronger and closer together. These are . . ." Sarah shrugged apologetically.

"I know," Cora sighed. "They stopped completely. But I was so sure!"

"False labor can feel like the real thing," Sarah assured her. "Especially when it's your first baby, and you don't know what they're supposed to feel like."

Cora groaned dramatically and let her head fall back against the well-stuffed sofa. She was a strapping Irish girl whose generous curves had been enhanced by pregnancy.

Although she would never be termed pretty, her condition gave her a glow that surpassed beauty. Even her untamed russet curls seemed deliberately disheveled.

"Don't be too disappointed," Sarah said. "You aren't even due for two more weeks yet."

"Thirteen days," Cora corrected her. "And you said the baby might come two weeks *early*."

"What I *actually* said," Sarah corrected her right back, "is that the due date is just an estimate. The baby could come as much as two weeks earlier or two weeks *later*."

Sarah smiled when Cora groaned again. "I can't last four more weeks. I can hardly get out of a chair as it is!"

"You might try some ginger tea," Sarah suggested.

"Does that work?" Cora asked hopefully.

"Sometimes," Sarah said. "And sometimes not. Babies come when they're ready, and there's not much we can do to hurry them along."

"I just want to see him," Cora complained, lovingly massaging her stomach. "I've been waiting so long!"

"I know, it always seems like forever, but believe me, babies are a lot less trouble when they're inside than they are when they're outside."

"I won't mind!"

"I'll remind you of that when your baby keeps you awake all night," Sarah said with a smile. She rose from where she'd been sitting beside Cora and began to gather up her things. She certainly wasn't needed here, so she might as well be on her way. "Is your husband getting anxious, too?"

"Oh, yes. I think he's more excited than I am."

Before Sarah could respond, the door to Cora's flat burst open, and a girl rushed into the room.

"Auntie Cora, you have to help me!" the girl cried.

"Help you do what?" Cora asked in surprise as the girl practically threw herself at Cora's feet and clasped her aunt's knees.

"I won't marry him! He's old and ugly, and he doesn't even speak English!" She gazed up at Cora with pleading eyes.

Sarah stared at her in surprise. She looked far too young to be marrying anyone at all. She still wore her long, raven hair in pigtails, and her clothes were that of a schoolgirl. Sarah guessed her age at not more than fourteen.

"What on earth are you talking about, Angel?" Cora asked, affectionately stroking stray wisps of hair away from the girl's flushed face.

"Mr. Wong, the one who owns the restaurants," she said, near tears. "Papa wants me to marry him!"

"Angel," a voice chided from the doorway. "I told you not to bother Auntie Cora."

Sarah looked over and saw a well-dressed woman entering the door that the girl had left hanging open. Like Cora, she was Irish, and older than Cora by at least a decade. Her red hair was starting to fade, but it still betrayed her heritage.

"She's not bothering me, Minnie," Cora assured her.

The woman took a few more steps into the room and stopped when she noticed Sarah. Her eyes widened in alarm. "You're the midwife, aren't you?"

"Yes, I am," Sarah said.

Her gaze went back to Cora hopefully. "Is it time?"

"No, it's not," Cora said, not bothering to hide her disappointment. "I called poor Mrs. Brandt out for nothing. The pains stopped."

The moment Sarah had spoken, the girl had jumped to her feet, looking chagrined at having behaved so emotionally in front of a stranger. Now Sarah could see her face clearly.

Her eyes were only slightly turned up, but like her hair, they were black and shining. In another part of town, Sarah might not have even noticed, but *here* there could be only one explanation for her exotic beauty. Like so many children in this neighborhood, she was half-Chinese.

Minnie, like Cora and many other Irish women, had married a Chinese man.

"Are you sure you're not in labor?" Minnie asked.

"Very sure," Cora said. "Aren't we, Mrs. Brandt?"

"I'm afraid so," Sarah said.

"Oh, where are my manners?" Cora asked of no one in particular. "Mrs. Brandt, this is my mother-in-law, Minnie Mae Lee, and her daughter, Angel."

The two women exchanged sly grins, telling Sarah they shared a secret joke.

"Pleased to meet you, Mrs. Lee," Sarah said.

"Likewise," Minnie Mae Lee said. "But don't pay Cora no mind. I'm only her 'paper' mother-in-law."

"Paper?" Sarah echoed.

"Minnie thinks she's too young to be my mother-in-law," Cora explained, still grinning.

"I *am* too young," Minnie insisted good-naturedly. "George is only eight years younger than me!"

"But Georgie son of wifey number one in Chin-ee," Cora said with a grin, using the sing-song cadence that mimicked a Chinese accent.

"Papa only has one wife," Angel insisted indignantly. "And she's my mama!"

"Of course she is, dear," Cora said. "We're just teasing poor Mrs. Brandt."

"And George isn't really my papa's son," Angel informed Sarah.

"Don't let the immigration people hear you say that," her mother warned, still teasing.

Angel didn't seem to realize her mother wasn't serious. She clapped a hand over her mouth, then lowered it slowly. "Would they send George back to China?" she asked, horrified.

"They could," Minnie said. Then she noticed Sarah's confused frown. "Don't mind us, Mrs. Brandt. You see, George—Cora's husband—couldn't get into America because of the Exclusion Act."

"That's a law that says nobody from China can come to America," Angel explained quickly, equally proud that she knew and outraged that such a law existed.

"They passed it back in 'eighty-two," Cora added.

"How awful," Sarah said. She had no reason to be familiar with the Chinese immigration laws, but she shouldn't have been surprised that they were harsh. She knew how much most white people hated the Chinese in New York. It must be the same all over the country.

"The Chinese found a way around it, though," Minnie said with a trace of pride. "Turns out that if a man who was already here had children back in China, they could come over and join him."

"So Charlie—that's Minnie's husband—he sort of adopted George so he could get in," Cora explained.

"Oh," Sarah said, finally understanding. "So George is Charlie's son *on paper.*"

"That's right," Cora said. "A paper son."

"Which makes me a paper mother-in-law," Minnie said with a laugh.

"Lots of people claimed they had children in China when they didn't, even though it's against the law," Angel offered defensively. "It was the only way they could come over. And why would you stay in China if you could come to America?"

A very good question, Sarah thought, and one she couldn't answer. "I'm sure you're glad your father came over," she said diplomatically.

To her surprise, Angel's lovely face collapsed into tears.

"I'm sorry!" Sarah exclaimed in dismay. "I didn't mean . . ."

But no one was paying her any attention.

"I won't marry him! He's old and he's ugly and he doesn't speak English!" Angel was crying again.

Minnie wrapped her arms around her daughter, who began to sob against her ample bosom. "He speaks perfectly good English," Minnie said, patting the girl on the back.

"He's still old!" the girl wailed.

"Now's not the time to talk about this," Minnie said meaningfully. "Mrs. Brandt doesn't care nothing about our troubles."

"I was just leaving," Sarah said, not wanting to intrude in a family argument. She turned to Cora. "Don't be too discouraged. You still might go into labor today."

"Or in four weeks," Cora said darkly.

Sarah tried an encouraging smile. "Whenever it is, send for me."

The women wished her farewell as Sarah took her leave. Angel looked up long enough to bid her good-bye before returning to the comfort of her mother's bosom to bewail her fate.

As Sarah made her way out of the building and onto the street, she considered the lives these women had chosen. Most of the white people she knew would despise them for marrying Chinese men. Prejudice ran high against many ethnic groups, of course, and the Irish had certainly suffered their share, but the Chinese experienced a special kind of hatred because they were truly a different race. They also had the effrontery to worship different gods, eat strange food, wear strange clothing, and use a language with letters that bore no resemblance to "real" writing.

Unlike European immigrants, who could learn English and wear American clothing and eventually fit in, the Chinese were forever marked as foreigners by their slanted eyes and yellow skin. White women who married them had to endure discrimination and ostracism, even from their own families.

On the other hand, Sarah thought as she looked up at the building she'd just left, how many Irish women lived in such a comfortable flat with lace curtains at the windows and carpets on the floor? Chinese men who could afford to marry had worked hard and provided well for their families. Perhaps Cora and Minnie's decisions to marry Chinese men hadn't been so remarkable after all.

Sarah couldn't help wondering what Irish *men* thought of their women taking up with the Chinese, though. She knew one Irish man she could ask, although she was pretty sure she knew what he would say. His job as a New York City police detective brought him into contact with the worst elements of every ethnic group in the city. Frank Malloy would never see how well men like George and Charlie Lee provided for their families. He would know only the hopheads in the opium dens and the criminal element who happened to cross his path.

Still, she felt a strong urge to discuss the matter with him. During the year that she'd known him, they'd talked over many serious issues, including issues of life and death. Sometimes she'd changed his views, and sometimes he'd changed hers. They probably wouldn't discuss his thoughts on this matter, though. Not unless somebody in Chinatown happened to get murdered.

D ETECTIVE S ERGEANT F RANK M ALLOY HAD BEEN BONE tired when he entered the building where he lived. He'd been chasing down the members of a pesky gang of the homeless children known as street Arabs all day, crawling through drainage pipes and lumbering down alleys and even climbing a fence or two. The gang members were as smart and evil as adults when it came to committing crimes, but their criminal minds still lived in children's bodies. Those young and agile bodies were a definite advantage when trying to elude a police force composed entirely of adults. Frank was getting much too old for that kind of work.

As he started up the stairs to his second-floor flat, however, he heard a door open and the clatter of small feet, and his weariness dropped away. When he looked up, he saw his son Brian fairly flying down the stairs to meet him. The boy probably would have cried "Papa!" in his joyous excitement, but he couldn't speak. He'd never be able to speak, at least with his voice. Born deaf, he was also mute, except for the incomprehensible sounds he made without realizing it. In his excitement at seeing his father, he was making them now.

Brian flung himself into Frank's arms, nearly knocking his father off his feet. Frank gave him a fierce hug. Not too long ago, he'd never expected to see his son walk, much less run. He had Sarah Brandt to thank for that. She'd sent him to her friend, a surgeon who had fixed the boy's club foot.

After returning his father's hug, Brian pushed himself back so he could see Frank's face, or rather so Frank could see his hands. Then Brian began moving those little hands rapidly, speaking in a language Frank couldn't understand. For too many years, he'd believed that his son's silence was a defect of his mind and not his ears. Watching him now, as he demonstrated what he'd learned at the School for the Deaf, Frank understood just how wrong he'd been. Brian's mind was as quick as any child's.

"Wait," Frank said with a grin, knowing Brian couldn't hear him but unable to stop himself from speaking to his deaf son. He set the boy on his feet a few steps above him so they were almost eye to eye. "I need your granny to tell me what you're saying," he explained, making the sign that represented his mother. It was one of the very few Frank knew.

Brian nodded vigorously and grabbed Frank's hand, urging him to climb the stairs more quickly. When they reached the landing, they found Frank's mother standing in the doorway, waiting for them.

A small woman with a face like a dried-up potato, she was wiping her hands on her apron and looking like she'd just sucked on a lemon. It was her usual expression.

" 'Evening, Ma," Frank said.

"I suppose you'll be wanting something to eat," she replied sourly.

He knew better than to refuse. She didn't *want* him to say he'd already eaten to spare her the work. She wanted to pretend to be put upon that she had to prepare his supper. "First tell me what he's saying," he said, pointing to Brian, who was still signing frantically.

"Simple enough," she said, barely sparing the boy a glance to interpret his rapid motions. "Says he learned to write his name today."

Frank felt the impact of her words like a blow to his chest. *"Write his name?"* he echoed in amazement. He could hardly breathe.

"Much as you're paying that school, he should be writing whole books by now," the old woman huffed, pretending she wasn't as excited as Frank and about to burst with pride. She signed something back to the boy, and he darted by her, through the doorway and back into their flat.

"I guess you'll be teaching at that school pretty soon," Frank observed.

She quickly tucked her hands beneath her apron, as if she'd been caught doing something she shouldn't. "It ain't that hard to learn. Somebody's got to be able to understand what the boy says." She'd made the argument often, and it was true enough, but Frank knew there was much more to it than that.

At first she'd insisted on going with Brian to the school because he was so young and she didn't trust them to look after him properly. Somehow she'd been recruited to assist with the students, though, and now she was learning sign language right along with Brian. It was quite an accomplishment for a woman her age, but he knew better than to compliment her outright. He wasn't sure if it had something to do with pride going before a fall or being afraid of drawing attention to something good for fear the devil would snatch it away. Whatever it was, his mother didn't appreciate flattery and wouldn't tolerate it.

"Well, don't stand out here all night. Come on inside so the boy can show you," she snapped.

Later, after Frank had eaten and Brian had laboriously drawn the letters of his name on every inch of the paper he'd brought home from school, over and over again, before finally being carried off to bed, exhausted, Frank studied the paper in wonder. The boy was only four. How he wished Kathleen could see her son, the child she'd died giving life to. Maybe, if there really was a heaven, she would know somehow.

"Are you gonna sit up half the night again, looking at them papers?" his mother asked when she came out of the kitchen.

Frank glanced over at the stack of folders sitting on a table in the corner. Reading them again would do no good. He knew them almost by heart. "No, I'm too tired tonight."

"I don't see why you've got to leave them here. They're always in my way."

Frank doubted this very much, but he wasn't going to argue. "I told you, it's a special case I'm working on. I don't want the files to get lost down at Headquarters."

"*Special case,*" she scoffed. "It's that woman what makes it *special.* You're always working on some *special* case for her."

"Her name is Mrs. Brandt, as you know perfectly well," he reminded her irritably. "You also know it's her husband's murder, and yes, I'm working on it for her. We owe her, Ma, for what she did for Brian."

He saw it then, the briefest flash of fear flickering across her face. He'd never been able to understand why she was afraid of Sarah Brandt, who'd only ever shown her kindness.

"She'll only bring you trouble, Francis," his mother warned. "She's not like us."

Frank considered that a recommendation in Sarah's favor, but he didn't say so to his mother. "Go to bed, Ma," he said wearily.

"What about you? You need your rest," she asked anxiously.

"I think I will take another look at the files, after all," he said, more to annoy her than because he really wanted to. "I won't be long."

He ignored her snort of disapproval as he reached for the stack of files. He didn't open them, though. When his mother had gone, he set them down again with a disgusted sigh.

What had ever made him think he could solve Tom Brandt's murder? Four long years had passed, and the evidence had been slim even back when it happened. True, he'd found a witness and learned some interesting new facts about some of Dr. Brandt's patients. He'd developed a theory about the case, and he'd even gotten permission from Police Commissioner Theodore Roosevelt himself to work on it . . . *in his spare time.* Trouble was, he didn't have any spare time. He needed more information, the kind that took lots of digging and hunting people down and getting them to talk about things they'd forgotten long ago or didn't want to remember at all. That kind of investigation took weeks, and Frank didn't have weeks to devote to it. He didn't even have hours to devote to it.

Unless he got some help, Tom Brandt's murder would never be solved. Frank knew where to get that help, too. Trouble was, he'd rather cut off his arm than ask for it. Then he glanced down at the sheet of paper with Brian's name scrawled all over it, and he remembered all he owed Sarah Brandt. That was when he knew he'd do whatever it took to bring her husband's killer to justice.

CORA LEE DIDN'T HAVE TO WAIT FOUR MORE WEEKS FOR her baby. He arrived on the very day Sarah had guessed he would. Cora's labor lasted only five hours and ended in the late afternoon. No all-night vigil for Sarah. She hadn't even been called out of bed. All in all, a very satisfactory experience for everyone.

She and Minnie Mae Lee were sitting with the new mother while she nursed her son for the first time.

"You're doing real good, Cora," Minnie assured her. "He's a fine boy. Look how fat! George'll be that proud of him!"

"Have you picked a name yet?" Sarah asked.

"Oh, yes," Cora replied. "Daniel, after my father."

Minnie shook her head. "The Chinese don't name a baby after a close relative like that. George'll take a fit."

"George is in America now," Cora said. "He took an American name, just like Charlie and all the other businessmen do. He needs to name his son like an American, too."

"Speaking of George, where's he got to?" Minnie asked. "I thought he'd be up the minute he heard." Minnie and her family lived upstairs, and she had sent her son Harry out to find the new father and deliver the news.

"He won't come 'til Mrs. Brandt is gone. He's bashful," Cora explained to Sarah.

"Bashful," Minnie echoed with a laugh. "That's one way to say it."

"How would you say it?" Cora challenged her.

"Private," Minnie said after a moment's thought. "Chinese men, they don't go around with their women in public, not like white men," she told Sarah. "They leave us pretty much to ourselves."

"Which is fine with me," Cora said. "George never tells me what to do or where to go, not like an Irish man would."

"Don't think they ignore us, though," Minnie hastened to add. "They're the kindest men alive. Always polite, never a cross word."

"And nothing's too good for us, either," Cora said. "Well, you can see for yourself how it is."

Sarah could. A quick glance around the beautifully furnished bedroom of the flat Cora shared with her husband showed her every comfort a woman could wish for.

"I think he's asleep," Cora said, gazing adoringly down at her child.

"Probably just needs to burp," Minnie said. "Let me have him."

She took the child from his mother and hoisted his tiny body up to her shoulder with practiced ease. Settling him there, she began to pat his back and murmur sweet nothings to him. Sarah busied herself with straightening up the room, while Cora leaned back against a bank of feather pillows and sighed with satisfaction.

"Ma!" a voice called from the front room. "Ma! Come quick!"

"That boy," Minnie muttered, making her way to the bedroom door without missing a pat on the baby's back. "What is it, Harry? Couldn't you find George and your pa?" She shifted the baby to the crook of her arm and opened the door with her free hand.

On the other side of the door stood a gangly boy of about seventeen. To Sarah's surprise, he was dressed in the loose-fitting silk shirt and linen trousers that Chinese men wore. They looked odd on him, because his features were even less Oriental than his sister's.

"It's Angel," he said with a worried frown. "I can't find her."

Minnie didn't seem too concerned. "What do you mean, you can't find her?"

"I mean, after I told Papa and George about the baby, I

went back up to tell Angel. She went into her room after she got home from school, but when I looked in just now, she wasn't there."

"She probably went out to play with her friends while you were gone," Minnie said reasonably.

"That's what I would've thought, too, except . . ." His young face creased into a frown, and he wrung his hands nervously.

Sarah noticed Cora had sat up straight again. She was listening attentively to every word, her face creased in a worried frown.

"Except what?" Minnie prodded.

"Her wardrobe door was hanging open."

"What of it?" his mother asked impatiently.

"All her clothes are gone!" Harry nearly wailed.

Cora gasped, but Minnie just made a sound of annoyance.

"All her clothes can't be gone. That's impossible."

"See for yourself," Harry said. "Her clothes are gone, and so is she!"

Minnie muttered something and started to push past Harry.

"The baby!" Cora cried, and Minnie stopped abruptly, remembering she still held him. She passed him to Sarah and then hurried out of the room, with Harry close behind her.

As soon as they were gone, Cora moaned. "She's run away. I was afraid of this. I tried to tell Minnie, but she wouldn't listen."

Sarah looked down at the infant in her arms. He really was fast asleep. She took him over to the elaborately carved cradle his parents had provided for him and laid him gently down in it.

"Surely, she wouldn't have really run away," Sarah offered by way of comfort.

"Oh, yes, she would," Cora said in dismay. "She's a stubborn girl, too much like her mother, and she had a good reason. Or at least she thought she did."

"I know she was upset the last time I was here," Sarah said diplomatically, wanting to ask outright about the forced marriage Angel had been protesting but not wanting to offend.

"Oh, I forgot you heard all that," Cora said. "Yes, Charlie wants her to marry his friend, John Wong. He's a good man and very rich, but Angel is just a girl. She's got all these romantic notions about falling in love."

"She seems a bit young for marriage," Sarah observed.

"She'll be sixteen next month," Cora said. "In China that's plenty old enough, and Charlie's still Chinese, even if he's been in America over twenty-five years."

Sarah didn't know what to say to that, so she held her tongue.

"Silly girl! I told her I'd help her," Cora said, half to herself.

"I'm sure she won't get far," Sarah assured her. "Someone will see her and send word to her family."

"She won't go near anybody who knows her," Cora said, a tear running down her cheek. She brushed it away absently. "She'll know they'd send her home again. But where else could she have gone?"

Sarah shared her concern. The New York City streets were no place for a young girl all alone. Danger lurked on every corner when a pretty young girl could be taken into an alley and raped and then sold to a brothel or worse. No one would ever see her again or even know what had become of her.

They heard someone running down the corridor outside

the flat, and then Minnie burst through the front door and rushed into the bedroom. Her eyes were wide and her face scarlet. "Cora, she's gone! She took everything she could carry. I've got to find Charlie so we can start looking for her."

"Go on," Cora said. "Hurry."

"But I don't want to leave you alone," Minnie protested.

"Don't worry about me. Mrs. Brandt will stay, won't you?"

"As long as necessary," Sarah assured them both. "Don't worry about a thing."

"God bless you," Minnie cried, and then she was gone.

Frank Malloy didn't have an appointment, so he was prepared to wait. Felix Decker was one of the wealthiest and most powerful men in the city, and he would have no reason to waste his valuable time on a lowly police detective.

Except, of course, that Felix Decker was Sarah Brandt's father, and he would know Frank was there because of her.

Decker's secretary looked up when Frank entered the office. His face registered recognition and surprise. "Detective Sergeant Malloy," he said, surprising Frank that he'd remembered him. "Is Mr. Decker expecting you?" He glanced anxiously at what must have been Decker's appointment book, probably concerned that he'd made an error in Decker's schedule.

"No, he's not. If he doesn't have time to see me now, I can wait for a while or come back later."

"Please, have a seat," the secretary said. "I'll see if he's free."

To Frank's surprise, the great man summoned him at once. When he saw Decker's face, he realized why.

"Is something wrong?" Decker asked, half rising from his chair. "Is it my daughter?" His face had gone pale.

"No, nothing like that," Frank assured him hastily. He had no love for Felix Decker, but he hadn't meant to frighten the man half to death. "She's fine, as far as I know. I haven't seen her for a couple weeks."

Decker's relief was obvious. He sank back into his chair and took a moment to compose himself. But only a moment. When his gaze met Frank's again, he was in complete control and his usual mask of reserve had slid back into place.

"Sit down, Mr. Malloy, and tell me why you've come."

Frank seated himself in one of the two comfortably worn leather chairs placed in front of Decker's desk. Once again he was struck by how unpretentious the office was. He'd investigated murders that concerned several wealthy businessmen in the city, and all of them had held court behind massive desks in lavishly furnished rooms draped in velvet and carpeted with handwoven rugs. Decker's desk was large but plain, and the furnishings comfortable but not ostentatious.

"It's about Tom Brandt's death," Frank said.

"You've found his killer," Decker guessed. Frank couldn't tell if he was pleased at the thought or not. His patrician face betrayed no expression. He and Decker had disagreed before on whether it was in Sarah's best interest to solve Dr. Brandt's murder.

"No," Frank said, the word burning his throat, but that wasn't the worst thing he had to admit today. "And I'm not going to be able to solve it, either."

Decker raised one eyebrow at this. "Why not?"

"Because I don't have the time it's going to take to track down everyone I need to talk to."

"I thought Commissioner Roosevelt had given you permission to work on the case."

Sarah had taken care of that. "He said I could work on it if I didn't neglect my other duties. At least one of the women's families has left the city. It could take weeks to find all of them." Before his death, Tom Brandt had taken a deep interest in the cases of several young women who had developed a mysterious form of insanity that made them believe the good doctor had seduced them. At least Frank hoped it was just their insanity that made them believe it.

"You're convinced that one of these women is connected to Brandt's death?" It was more a challenge than a question.

"They're the best lead I have," he said, not really answering.

"What do you want me to do?"

Frank managed not to sigh. He didn't *want* Decker to do anything, but he had no choice. "Hire a Pinkerton again," he said, referring to the private detectives employed by Allan Pinkerton's agency. "Have him locate all the families and find out which of the women have fathers who were alive at the time Brandt was killed."

"If I'm going to all that trouble, I could simply ask the Pinkerton to solve the case," Decker pointed out.

"*No,*" Frank said without thinking, making Decker raise his eyebrow again. "I mean, I don't trust them to do the job right. We only have one chance to question these people. If your Pinkerton asks the wrong question or misses a clue, we might never find the real killer."

"You want to question them yourself," Decker said skeptically. "You think you're the only one who can do the job right."

Frank didn't bat an eye. "I *am* the only one who can do it right."

Decker considered him for a long moment. Maybe he was remembering how Frank had handled other cases. Maybe he was remembering how Frank had found the truth when no one believed he could. Or maybe he was certain Frank would fail and lose Sarah Brandt's respect forever. Whatever he was thinking, he said, "All right, Mr. Malloy. I will hire a Pinkerton to get your information."

2

"No one in Chinatown would hide her from her family," Cora said, not for the first time.

Night had fallen, and Sarah had lit the gaslights in the flat and prepared supper for both of them. They'd eaten in silence, and now they were waiting.

"Does she have friends outside of Chinatown? Maybe someone from school," Sarah suggested.

"Angel wouldn't be welcome, being half-Chinese."

"That's such a pretty name," Sarah remarked, trying to take Cora's mind off the crisis if only for a moment. "It really suits her."

"Minnie's last name is Angel. Minnie Mae Angel. When they saw how pretty their baby was, like she came straight from heaven, Minnie got the idea to call her Angel. She's that innocent, too. She won't know somebody might mean her harm. She'd probably go with anybody who was nice to her." Cora's voice broke, and she wiped her eyes with the corner of the sheet.

"What about Minnie's family?" Sarah asked. "Would they take her in?"

"Minnie doesn't have any family here. She left them all in Ireland."

"She came over alone?" Sarah asked in surprise.

"Sure, lots of girls did. Their families died, and everybody else was starving. In America they could find work and maybe even a husband, so they came over here."

"Is that what you did?" Sarah asked.

Cora smiled slightly. "Didn't have much choice, did I?" She rubbed her head absently, as if it ached.

"You should get some rest," Sarah suggested. "The baby will probably be awake most of the night. While he's asleep, you should at least try to take a nap."

"I couldn't sleep," Cora protested, "not with Angel out there someplace, all alone."

"You can't help her by staying awake. You've got to think of your baby," Sarah argued. "And Minnie will need your support, too, especially if they can't find Angel."

More tears leaked out, spilling down her cheeks. Sarah went to her and helped rearrange the pillows so she could lie down. "What if the baby wakes up?" she asked as Sarah tucked her in.

"You'll hear him, I promise," Sarah said.

"But—"

"I'll be right here."

"I'll just close my eyes for a few minutes then."

Within seconds, exhaustion claimed her. Sarah turned

down the gas jets in the bedroom and went out into the parlor to wait.

The baby woke up a little later, and Cora fed him again. Sarah convinced Cora the waiting would go much more quickly if she slept, so she consented again. Sarah had dozed off herself when Minnie returned to the flat.

Sarah started awake at the sound of the door opening, and one look at Minnie's face told her they hadn't found the missing girl.

"Cora?" Minnie asked.

"Asleep," Sarah reported. "They're both doing fine. Did you find out anything at all?"

Minnie shook her head as she sank wearily onto Cora's comfortable sofa. "Someone saw her walking down the street. She was carrying a bundle, but no one thought anything about it. Figured it was laundry or something. Nobody noticed where she went."

"You checked with her friends?"

"She didn't go to any of them, and they all swear they don't know where she did go." Minnie seemed to have aged a decade since this afternoon. "Charlie and George and everybody we know is still out searching, in case she tried to hide in an alley or something."

"Have you called in the police?" Sarah asked.

Minnie looked at her as if she'd suddenly gone insane. "The *police*?" she echoed in amazement. "Why would we call in the police?"

"They . . . they could help look for her," she tried.

Minnie made a rude noise. "The police don't come to Chinatown unless they want to arrest somebody. They won't care a lick that Angel is missing unless she stole something or killed somebody. Even then, they won't care unless she stole from a white person."

"Maybe if you offered a reward," Sarah said, hating herself for having to say it. The police seldom investigated a crime unless a "reward" was offered. In their defense, they could hardly survive on the salary the city paid them. On the other hand, the poor had little hope of justice if it had to be purchased.

Minnie rubbed her forehead wearily. "Charlie won't offer no reward to the police. He hates them like the devil."

Sarah had no answer for that. "I'll stay with Cora for the rest of the night. You should probably try to get some rest yourself."

"I couldn't sleep, not with my girl out there someplace all alone. I just came back to see if she'd changed her mind and come home. I'm going right out again."

Sarah tried unsuccessfully to get her to eat something, then wished her good luck as she left again. She found herself wishing for Frank Malloy. He'd know what to do. He'd know how to search for Angel. Or so she told herself. The truth was, no one would be able to find Angel if she didn't want to be found—or if someone else didn't want her to be found. Girls disappeared in New York every day. Sometimes their bodies floated up in the harbor, but most times they simply vanished.

Time was when Sarah could only imagine the heartbreak of losing a child. Now she had a child of her own. She'd found little Catherine at the Prodigal Son Mission. She'd simply appeared on the Mission's doorstep one morning, and she either couldn't or wouldn't speak, so no one knew where she'd come from.

Did a mother somewhere weep for the child she'd lost?

The child Sarah had found? Sarah could easily imagine that mother's pain and Minnie's, too. Losing Catherine would be like having her heart ripped from her chest. She whispered a prayer for Angel's safety and settled in for the rest of the night to wait.

SARAH ACHED IN EVERY MUSCLE AS SHE APPROACHED her home on Bank Street late the next afternoon. No one had found any sign of Angel, and Minnie had finally returned home. She'd insisted she could look after Cora and the baby herself. It would keep her mind off her own troubles, she'd said, and sent Sarah home for some much-needed rest.

She automatically glanced over at her neighbor's front porch. Years of experience had taught her that Mrs. Ellsworth would be out, sweeping her front steps while she kept an eye on everything that happened on Bank Street. But Mrs. Ellsworth's steps had gone unswept most days in the months since Sarah had brought Catherine home from the Mission. Mrs. Ellsworth now had better ways to spend her time.

The moment Sarah pushed open her front door, she heard the sound of running feet. Catherine appeared almost instantly, running full tilt from the back of the house, through the front room that Sarah used as her office, and straight into Sarah's arms. Hugging Catherine's small body tightly, Sarah once again understood Minnie's desperate fear. She inhaled the sweet scent of the child's hair and brushed her lips across the satiny cheek. How could a mother bear the pain of losing a child? Surely, nothing else could be so terrible.

"We were about to give you up," Mrs. Ellsworth said good-naturedly.

Sarah looked up to see that her neighbor had followed Catherine at a more sedate pace. Maeve, the girl who served as Catherine's nursemaid, was behind her, smiling a greeting. They had most likely been working on something in the kitchen. Mrs. Ellsworth was teaching them the fine art of homemaking.

"Is everything all right?" Mrs. Ellsworth added. Sarah saw the unspoken question in the older woman's eyes. When Sarah was gone for a long time on a delivery, it usually meant something had gone wrong.

"Oh, yes," Sarah assured her, still holding on to Catherine's hands as she straightened. "A healthy baby boy. I stayed because there was some trouble in the family. A young girl went missing, and they all went to look for her, so there was no one to take care of the new mother."

"They found the girl then?" Mrs. Ellsworth asked.

"No, they didn't."

"Was she a little girl?" Maeve asked, her young face clouded. She, too, had been a resident of the Prodigal Son Mission when Sarah recruited her. Her parents had put her out on the streets when they'd deemed her able to fend for herself. Sarah had never asked what she'd been forced to do to stay alive until she'd found the safety of the Mission.

Catherine squeezed Sarah's hands, and Sarah looked down to see the concern in her eyes, too. Catherine was no more than five years old herself, but she'd also known the terror of being alone. It had made her mute.

"The girl is almost your age, Maeve," Sarah said. "She'll be sixteen next month."

"Well, now, you can tell us all about it in a minute," Mrs. Ellsworth said brusquely. "But first, come on into the kitchen where we can get some food into you. You look wrung out."

"I am," Sarah agreed and allowed Catherine to take her by the hand and lead her back the way they'd come, into the warm comfort of the kitchen.

They'd been making pastry. Several empty pie shells awaited filling, and flour and sticky dough covered the entire tabletop. Maeve quickly cleaned a spot at the table, and Catherine brushed flour off one of the chairs for Sarah to sit.

"I can scramble up some eggs, if that's all right," Mrs. Ellsworth was saying. "Not fancy, but it's quick."

"That's fine. I don't know how much longer I can stay awake," Sarah said, sinking down into the chair Catherine had prepared for her. Catherine climbed up into her lap and laid her head against Sarah's shoulder. Sarah held her close, reveling in the feel of her small body.

Mrs. Ellsworth started preparing the eggs while Maeve continued to clean off the table. She scrubbed a little harder than necessary, Sarah noted, and her face was fixed in a troubled frown.

"What is it, Maeve?" she asked.

The girl looked up, stopping her work for just a moment before returning to it with a vengeance. "I was just thinking about that girl. Why'd she run off, anyway? Did they beat her or something?"

"No, they didn't beat her," Sarah said. She couldn't be sure, of course, but she remembered the way Minnie had held her daughter. She cherished the child. "It seemed like they treated her very well, in fact."

"Then why'd she leave?" Maeve seemed actually angry at this unknown girl.

"Probably because her father wanted her to marry an older man," Sarah said.

"Why? Did he owe him money or something?"

"Not that I know of, although he could have, I guess." Her mother seemed to think it was a good idea, though, and she loves the girl very much. The man makes a good living. She probably thought he'd be a good husband for her."

Maeve's frown deepened as she continued to concentrate on scrubbing the last bits of dough off the table.

What was she thinking? Sarah wondered. And why was she so angry?

Maeve muttered something under her breath.

"What was that?" Sarah asked.

Maeve looked up in surprise. "What?"

"You said something," Sarah said, even though she knew Maeve hadn't intended for her to hear. "I didn't hear it."

"I just . . . I said she was stupid," she admitted reluctantly.

Sarah nodded. "Running away was a foolish thing to do. Dangerous, too."

"You said her family was looking for her," Maeve said.

"Yes, everyone was out, even the neighbors."

Maeve shook her head. "They didn't want her to leave. It don't make sense."

"Doesn't," Sarah corrected her.

"Doesn't make sense," Maeve repeated obediently. "She's got a family what loves her and wants her, and she runs away because she don't . . . doesn't want to get married to some rich man? That's just crazy."

Sarah figured Maeve would have loved to find herself in a position like that. "I know. She isn't the kind of girl who would know how to survive on her own, either. That's why her parents are so frightened."

Now Maeve's frown turned thoughtful. "A girl like that . . ."

Sarah waited, but she didn't go on. "What about a girl like that?" she prodded.

"She ain't likely to go off alone, is she? I mean, really run away. She's used to somebody taking care of her. She'd be too scared to be on her own."

"That's what her parents thought, too, but they checked with all her friends. She isn't staying with any of them."

"*Girl* friends," Maeve said dismissively.

"What do you mean?"

"I mean her girl friends are probably just like her. They'd be afraid to hide her. She'd never go to them."

Sarah was beginning to understand. "You're right, her friends aren't hiding her, and she'd be too scared to go off alone. You think she's found someone else to take care of her, don't you?"

"A man," Maeve said with certainty. "You'll see. She's with some man."

This was what Sarah had feared, of course, but perhaps it wasn't quite as bad as she'd imagined. "Do you think it's a man who cares about her?"

Maeve shrugged. "They always say that, don't they?"

Sarah's heart sank. Of course they did. Angel Lee might have run off with a man she loved, a man she thought loved her in return, but that didn't mean he really did. He could still have sold her to a brothel or even to a rich man whose perversion ran to violating the innocent. Many young men in the city made a living doing just that. They were called "cadets." "I wonder if her parents have considered the fact that she might have had an admirer."

"Maybe you should suggest it to them, Mrs. Brandt," Mrs. Ellsworth said, looking up from her cooking.

Catherine raised her head, turned Sarah's face toward her own, and nodded vigorously.

"Can you hurry with those eggs, Mrs. Ellsworth?" Sarah asked wryly. "I'll be needing some coffee, too, since it looks like I'll be heading back to Chinatown."

SARAH HAD BEEN HOPING THAT ANGEL HAD RETURNED or been found, but she was disappointed. The neighbors were still clustered in the street outside, discussing the sad situation. Sarah made her way through them with a heavy heart.

"Oh, Mrs. Brandt, did you forget something?" Minnie Lee asked when she opened the door to find Sarah in the hallway outside Cora's flat. She looked haggard and haunted.

"No, I just happened to think of something, so I came back to tell you."

"Something about Cora?" Minnie asked, stepping aside to silently invite Sarah in. "Or the baby?"

"No, about Angel."

"Have you seen her?" Minnie asked eagerly. Her hope was painful to witness.

"No, no, nothing like that," Sarah said quickly. She tried not to watch the hope dying in Minnie's eyes. "But I was telling my daughter's nursemaid about Angel, and she said . . . Well, maybe you've already thought of it, but she thought that Angel would have been too scared to run away all by herself, and—"

"I know, we thought that, too," Minnie said, her voice thick with unshed tears. "But nobody's seen her. We already asked all her friends. That was the first thing we thought of."

"Mrs. Lee, I don't know if you've considered this or not, but maybe Angel had another friend, one you didn't know about."

"We know everybody she knows," Minnie insisted.

Sarah took a deep breath, knowing how defensive Minnie would be and how protective of her daughter. "You might not know if she had a friend who was a man."

Minnie's eyes widened. "A man? She never . . . How could she? She doesn't even know any men."

"She'd keep it a secret, wouldn't she?" Sarah said. "She wouldn't want you to know, because you wouldn't approve."

Minnie reached up and rubbed her temple. "I don't know . . ." Tears welled in her eyes, and she swayed slightly. Sarah caught her arm and led her over to sit on Cora's comfortable sofa.

"Have you eaten anything at all?" Sarah asked.

Minnie waved away her question. "How could Angel have met a man? A man who would steal her away from her family?"

"I don't know that she did," Sarah said. "But it would explain why none of her friends know where she is. It would explain why she was brave enough to run away. She'd believe he would take care of her. How else would she know where to go or how to hide from you?"

Minnie knuckled tears from her eyes. "I almost hope you're right," she admitted. "As bad as that would be, it's better than what I've been imagining."

"Minnie!" Cora called from the bedroom. "Who's out there? Did they find Angel?"

Minnie pushed herself off the sofa and hurried into the bedroom, with Sarah following closely behind. "It's Mrs.

Brandt," she said. "She came to . . . She was asking about Angel."

"How are you doing, Cora?" Sarah asked.

Cora smiled sadly. "I'd be fine if Angel was home safe. Little Danny, he's the sweetest thing." She nodded to where the baby slept peacefully in his cradle. "I'm so lucky."

"You are that," Minnie said softly.

"You didn't come all the way back here just to ask me how I am, did you, Mrs. Brandt?" Cora asked.

"No, I . . ." She glanced at Minnie, but she offered no objection. "I was telling Mrs. Lee that my daughter's nursemaid thought perhaps Angel had been lured away by a man."

"A man? How would Angel meet a man?" Cora asked, much as Minnie had. "She's still a child. She never goes anyplace except to school and church. Minnie watches her real close."

"Harry looks after her, too," Minnie added. "He don't let nobody even speak to his sister unless he approves."

"He's the best chaperone a girl ever had," Cora agreed.

"Maybe he let down his guard for someone he didn't think was particularly threatening," Sarah suggested. "Someone charming and kind."

"I don't know," Minnie said, rubbing her head again. "Why would he?"

"I don't know, either," Cora said, "but it's something to think about at least. It's something you haven't thought of before, too. Why don't you ask Harry if he can think of anybody who maybe paid attention to Angel or got a little too friendly."

"Angel wouldn't just go off with somebody," Minnie insisted. "She's a good girl."

"Of course she is," Sarah said. "But innocent girls are also easy to fool. A man who was handsome and nice—she would never suspect him of having evil intentions. You've probably protected her from evil all of her life. That's what loving parents do, but it would make her easy prey."

Minnie moaned in despair, but Cora nodded vigorously. "She's right, Minnie. At least I hope she is. It would mean we have a chance of finding her."

"Mother of God," Minnie said. Her face was ashen, and Sarah took her by the arm and led her to a chair in the corner of the bedroom.

"You're going to drop over if you don't get some rest," Cora scolded her in exasperation. "Tell her, Mrs. Brandt."

"I'm sure she doesn't need me to tell her," Sarah said. "Sit right here. I'm going to make some tea, and you're going to drink it."

"I don't know what's in the kitchen, but get her something to eat, too. She hasn't had a thing all day," Cora called after her.

A few minutes later, Sarah had tea brewing, and she buttered some bread. She knew from experience that a person in a crisis often could not bear to even swallow food. Maybe Minnie could manage a few bites, at least.

Minnie turned up her nose at the bread, but to Sarah's relief, she did drink some of the tea.

"You should ask Harry if he remembers anybody looking at Angel," Cora said. "Mrs. Brandt will stay with me while you go up. He's upstairs with Charlie and George in your flat, isn't he?"

"No, I can't ask him anything in front of Charlie," Minnie said. "Even if he does know something, he'd never admit it in front of his father."

Cora nodded her understanding. "Bring him down here, then. Tell him you need him to do something for me."

Plainly, Minnie's exhaustion and terror rendered her almost incapable of making a decision. She just stared back at Cora numbly.

"I can go get him," Sarah offered.

"Oh, I couldn't ask you to do that," Minnie protested.

"I can," Cora said. "Thank you, Mrs. Brandt. It's one flight up, the first door on the right."

Sarah left before Minnie could change her mind. Unlike apartment buildings in other parts of the city, this one was clean and well kept. Sarah supposed it was the fact that the residents here didn't have to worry about basic survival. They had the luxury of knowing they would eat three good meals every day and have a warm place to sleep every night. Freed of the desperate daily struggle so many faced each morning just to ensure they would survive that day, the people in this building had the energy to take pride in their surroundings.

Sarah knocked on the door Cora had directed her to. It opened quickly, and Sarah saw the boy Harry, who had first delivered the news that his sister was missing. He looked as haggard as his mother, and his Chinese clothing was soiled and wrinkled. His red-rimmed eyes narrowed to make out Sarah's identity in the shadows of the hallway.

"Who . . . ?" he asked.

"Who is there?" a voice called sharply.

"A lady," Harry replied.

"I'm Mrs. Brandt," Sarah reminded him, speaking loudly enough for those inside to hear her. "The midwife. Your mother asked me to get you. She needs you to do something for her."

"Ma needs me," he called over his shoulder and stepped quickly out into the hallway, pulling the door shut behind him. Sarah had the impression he was making an escape as much as answering a summons. She remembered what Minnie had said a moment ago, of how Harry wouldn't admit anything in front of his father, and wondered what kind of relationship Harry had with Charlie Lee.

"What does she want me to do?" he asked as Sarah led the way back down the stairs.

"I'm not sure," Sarah lied. They made their way carefully in the dim stairwell, and he followed her into Cora's flat. "They're in the bedroom," she told him when they were inside.

Harry hurried in, his young face drawn with worry. "Ma, what is it?" he asked as he entered the room. "Is something wrong?"

Minnie stood up, clutching her hands tightly in front of her. "No, dear, I just wanted to ask you something . . . about Angel."

He frowned. "I already told you, I don't know where she went. Why doesn't anybody believe me?"

"We believe you," Cora assured him quickly. "It's just . . . Mrs. Brandt here thinks maybe you might've seen something and not realize it."

"How could I not realize it?" he asked, turning to Sarah, who had followed him into the bedroom and stood in the doorway. She saw the defensiveness in every line of his body. He was a slender lad, his wiry body taut with the strain of Angel's disappearance.

"Your sister is very innocent, and it doesn't seem likely she would've been brave enough to just run away," Sarah began.

"Someone asked me if she could have had an admirer who might have lured her away."

"You mean a man?" Harry asked in amazement. "Angel would never go off with a strange man."

"Maybe he's not a stranger," Sarah said. "Maybe it's someone she knows or sees often. He'd be friendly and nice to her. She might have met him in the neighborhood. It could be someone she sees every day, in a shop or on the way to school."

But Harry was shaking his head. "We checked with all her friends."

"It wouldn't be one of her friends," Minnie said, her voice thin with desperation. "It would be someone else, someone older, who would know how to hide her so we couldn't find her."

"You might have seen him watching her," Sarah suggested. "Or talking to her. Did anyone ever give her a gift?"

"George always buys her candy," Harry said doubtfully.

"Someone not in our family," Cora said in exasperation. "Did you ever think somebody was getting too friendly with her?"

"Not when I was with her. I don't let strangers talk to her," Harry claimed belligerently.

"Are you *always* with her?" Sarah asked.

Everyone looked at her in surprise. Harry frowned. "No, not *always*," he admitted reluctantly.

"When aren't you with her?"

He looked straight at Sarah, and she noticed his eyes were light brown, not black like his sister's. Once again she was struck by how Irish he looked. Not Chinese at all except for his clothing. "I . . . She gets out of school earlier than me. She walks home with her friends."

"Then she could have met someone after school, and you wouldn't know," Sarah prodded.

"I guess so."

Before anyone could think of another question, they heard the door opening in the front room. Sara looked out to see a Chinese man coming into the flat. He paused for a moment, looking around, and then he saw Sarah standing in the bedroom doorway. She couldn't guess his age, but he seemed young, perhaps not even thirty.

"Cora?" he called.

"George?" Cora called back. "We're all in here."

He came forward slowly, reminding Sarah what the women had said about their men being private. Or shy. He wore Western clothing, a dark suit and white shirt, although he'd removed the collar and tie and the neck of the shirt was open for comfort. He was a smallish man, thin and not very tall, but his face was open and handsome, although he looked as weary as the others who had been searching for Angel all day.

Sarah stepped back so he could enter the bedroom. He looked around the room, his gaze touching each person there. When he turned to his wife, he said, "Why you want Harry and not me?"

"We wanted to ask him some questions about Angel," she said.

Plainly, this didn't answer his query. "What question?"

"Mrs. Brandt thought Angel might have run away with a man," Cora explained.

George turned to Harry, suddenly furious. "You know this and do not say?"

"No!" Harry cried. "I don't know anything about Angel and some man!"

"We just thought he might've seen someone being friendly to her," Cora quickly explained. "But he didn't."

George's hands had closed into fists, and now his anger turned on Sarah. "Why do you say this about Angel?"

"She's just trying to help, George," Minnie said wearily. "She thought maybe some man might've tricked her into running away with him."

"We were hoping that was it," Cora added. "If she's with some man, she's alive and well, and we might be able to find her."

George looked as if he wasn't sure whether to remain angry at Sarah or not. Cora rescued her.

"Come and look at the baby. You've hardly had a chance to admire your son."

George needed no further encouragement. He went directly to the cradle.

"Can I go now?" Harry asked with a hint of desperation.

"Yes, go," his mother said in resignation. He hurried past Sarah and slammed out of the flat.

"I should go, too," Sarah said, not wanting to intrude any longer. She hadn't helped at all and had only managed to cause everyone more pain. "I'm sorry I disturbed you."

"You were just trying to help," Cora repeated.

But she hadn't. She left the bedroom, and Minnie followed to see her out.

"I'm so sorry," Sarah said when they reached the front door. "I was hoping I could help you find Angel."

"I know. I wish you were right about the man," she admitted. "If she was with somebody who loves her . . ."

Sarah reached out and touched her arm when her voice broke. "I have a friend who's a detective sergeant with the police," she said. "Maybe he could—"

"No police," Minnie said firmly. "Charlie would never have it. Besides, what could they do that we didn't?"

Sarah didn't know. That wouldn't stop her from at least asking Frank Malloy, however.

3

Frank didn't know whether to be pleased or annoyed that Sarah had summoned him. She wouldn't send for him unless it was something important. Her note, delivered to his house, had said she needed his advice to help one of her clients. He couldn't imagine what kind of advice she'd need from him, but since he hadn't heard about any murders today, he wasn't worried. At least not much. In the past, he'd too often drawn her into a murder investigation. But not today.

At Sarah's house, Maeve opened the door and greeted him with a big smile.

"Mr. Malloy, come right in. Catherine's been waiting for you all day."

"Cath—?" he started to ask but caught himself. He'd almost forgotten that the little girl he'd first known as Aggie had revealed her real name. "Where is she?" he asked instead as he stepped into the house.

"She's pretending to be shy," Maeve said with a wink.

Frank pulled off his hat and looked around. "Catherine? Where are you?" he called.

A giggle drew his attention to the stairway, where the little girl peered out from behind the door.

"There you are," he said, and she laughed in delight. "Aren't you going to come see me?"

She darted out of the stairwell and straight into his arms. "You're getting big," he marveled, picking her up. "I can hardly lift you anymore."

This pleased her, and she giggled again. She didn't speak, though. Something had frightened her into silence before she'd turned up on the Mission's doorstep several months ago, and she still didn't trust the world enough to end that silence.

"Malloy," a familiar voice said. Sarah was coming from the kitchen, smiling the way she always did when she saw him, as if she had been waiting forever for the pleasure. He knew that wasn't true, but his heart lifted just the same. "Thank you for coming."

"How could I refuse?" he asked slyly. "I don't think you ever asked for my advice before."

"That hasn't stopped you from giving it often enough," she replied just as slyly. "Come on into the kitchen. Mrs. Ellsworth taught the girls to make a Sally Lund cake this morning. We've been waiting for you to cut it."

The cake was delicious, and the coffee hot. When they were finished and the dishes cleared away, Sarah sent the girls upstairs to play.

"I really appreciate your coming on such short notice," she said, refilling his coffee cup.

"Your note said it was important," he reminded her, wondering if she knew he would have come whether it was or not. "It's not a murder, is it?"

"Oh, no," she assured him with a small smile. "I'm trying very hard to avoid getting involved in any more murder investigations."

"I'm glad to hear it." He didn't return her smile. He really didn't want her put in danger ever again. "So, what is it?"

"A girl is missing. She's related to a woman whose baby I delivered two days ago."

"What do you mean, missing?"

"She came home from school, as usual. She's fifteen, almost sixteen. Her brother saw her go into her room. Her mother was with me downstairs, delivering the baby. After the baby was born, she sent the brother out to find the new father and tell him. While he was gone, the girl disappeared. This was the day before yesterday."

"Could she have gone to visit a friend?"

"That's the first thing they did, check with all her friends. She wasn't with any of them, though, and she'd taken all her clothes, too. Someone saw her going down the street, carrying a bundle. They assumed it was laundry and didn't think anything of it."

"Sounds like her family wants to find her." They both knew that not all families would. Lots of girls went missing in New York City, and their families were often relieved to have one less mouth to feed.

"They're frantic. They had all the neighbors helping them look for her. They searched most of the night and the next day, but of course they couldn't find any trace of her."

"What's this girl like? What kind of a family does she have?"

"Her family is respectable, and she's completely innocent. They can't imagine where she could've gone. Maeve thought . . ."

"What did Maeve think?" Frank prodded, intrigued.

"She thought Angel must have a lover."

Frank straightened in surprise. "Maeve is pretty smart."

"You agree?"

"If you said the girl—did you say her name is *Angel*?"

"Yes. It's her mother's maiden name."

"If you told me she just didn't come home from school one day or went to the store and nobody saw her again, then I'd think she was kidnapped. Happens a lot. Girl like that would bring a premium price in a brothel."

He saw her flinch and hated having to remind her of the harsh realities of life in the city.

"Girls don't pack their clothes if they're being kidnapped into a brothel," she reminded him.

"She might not have known that's where she was going," he reminded her.

"Of course she didn't. She would've thought she was eloping. But if she did go off with a man, he might not have had romance on his mind. I've been hoping that wasn't the case, but even if it was, we have a better chance of finding her if somebody did lure her away."

"*We?*" he echoed in disapproval. "Are you looking for her, too?"

Her cheeks grew pink, making her look like a girl for a second or two. "I'm not getting involved, Malloy," she said defensively. "I'm just trying to help her family, if I can."

Frank sighed. He knew her too well. She'd do whatever

she could to find this girl, even if it meant barging into every brothel in the city looking for her. "If somebody bought her, you'll never find her, Sarah. Nobody will."

"I know," she insisted. She probably did, but he didn't think that would stop her from trying.

"What do you want me to do?" he asked in resignation.

"How can they find out who she ran off with? They've already asked all her friends. None of them know."

He resisted the urge to sigh again. "I guess I could give it a try."

"Oh, I'm not asking you to do that!" she said quickly. "They don't want the police involved."

"Why not?" he asked in surprise.

She gave him an apologetic smile. "It's Chinatown."

"*Chinatown?* You deliver babies in Chinatown?" he asked in amazement.

"I deliver babies wherever I can," she said.

He shouldn't have been surprised. "So the girl is Chinese?"

"Half-Chinese and half-Irish, on her mother's side." She seemed to take a perverse pleasure in informing him of that.

He should have guessed. He knew Chinese women weren't allowed into the country. He also knew most of the wives in Chinatown were Irish. "So an innocent, half-Chinese girl packs up her clothes and runs away while her mother is too busy to notice. Sounds like she might've planned it."

"I thought so, too. She was probably just waiting for the baby to come and everyone to be distracted. Oh, I almost forgot, she was also upset because her father was arranging a marriage for her, to a much older man."

"Another Chinaman, I guess," Frank said.

"Yes. He owns some restaurants, I think. He's wealthy,

but that didn't mean anything to Angel. She thought he was old and ugly."

"That changes things. She might've run off to get away from the ugly old husband," Frank mused.

"I can't imagine a girl like Angel taking a risk like that. She had no money, or at least not much. Where would she go? Where would she stay?"

"She might not have thought about that. Kids can be really stupid."

She sighed in dismay. "Maybe, but I still don't think she would've gone off alone. Someone had to help her, and if we find that someone, we'll find Angel."

Frank wasn't so sure. The girl could be anywhere by now, and if someone had her, they'd take great pains to hide her.

He saw the anger flash in her eyes when he didn't reply. "There must be something we can do," she insisted.

"There's something her *family* can do," Frank said meaningfully.

"What?" she asked anxiously.

"A girl like that wouldn't go off without telling somebody. You said she has friends. They wouldn't be able to hide her, because that's the first place her family would look, but they might keep her secret. If she ran off with somebody, she was in love, or thought she was. Girls tell their friends when they fall in love. Somebody knows. Maybe all of them do."

"Oh, for heaven's sake, why didn't I think of that? Of course she would tell her friends if she had a boyfriend!"

"The girls would think this Angel is safe because she's with her lover, so they'd never tell her family and ruin the romance."

"So we have to convince them Angel might be in danger," she said.

"Why do you keep saying *we?*" Frank asked in annoyance. "I thought you said you weren't going to get involved."

"I'm not!" she insisted. "But I *will* tell her family what you think. I'm sure they'll be able to find out the truth from her friends. Thank you, Malloy."

"I haven't done anything," he said, uncomfortable with her gratitude. "Thank me when you find the girl."

He didn't add what he was really thinking: *If* you find the girl.

MINNIE OPENED THE DOOR TO CORA'S FLAT. SHE LOOKED as if she hadn't slept since Sarah last saw her, but she managed a polite smile of greeting. "Mrs. Brandt, how nice to see you. Please, come in."

"I don't suppose you've heard from Angel," Sarah said as she stepped inside.

A spasm of pain crossed Minnie's weary face. "Not a word."

"I'm so sorry. How are Cora and the baby doing?"

"Fine as can be," Minnie said with forced cheer. "Come on in. She'll be that glad to see you."

Sarah greeted Cora, who was still in bed as Sarah had instructed. Sarah didn't subscribe to the theory that women who had given birth should be treated like invalids, but she knew that restricting them to bed for a week or so would ensure they wouldn't overdo and end up truly ill.

Cora had been burping the baby over her shoulder, and she took him down so Sarah could admire him. "He's doing so well," she marveled. "Sleeps all the time except when he's hungry. Couldn't ask for a better baby."

Little Daniel gazed back at Sarah through his almond-shaped eyes with the intensity of the newly born. After a second, he smiled, as if enjoying being the center of attention, and the women laughed in delight.

When Sarah felt she had spent enough time admiring him, she turned to Minnie. "I think I told you that I have a friend who's a detective sergeant with the police," she began, hurrying on when she saw Minnie instinctively recoil from the thought of the police. "I know you don't want them involved, but I asked him for some advice about what he'd do if he was trying to find a missing girl."

Minnie was shaking her head. "Oh, Mrs. Brandt, you really shouldn't concern yourself with—"

"Don't be a fool, Minnie," Cora scolded. "At least find out what he had to say!"

Sarah hurried on before Minnie could object again. "He said that young girls like Angel usually don't just run off without telling someone about their plans. He said she probably confided in at least one of her friends."

"But that's the first thing we thought of," Minnie protested. "The girls didn't know anything."

"They told you they weren't hiding her," Sarah corrected her. "But they might have lied when you asked if they knew where she was. If she eloped with a boyfriend, they wouldn't betray her to her family, who wanted her to marry a man she didn't love. They'd think it was all very romantic and that she's safe someplace with someone who loves her."

"*Boyfriend,*" Cora scoffed. "That's such a funny word. I know that's what the girls call their suitors, but who'd want to run off with a *boy?*"

"A girl who's too young to know better," Sarah said. She

looked at Minnie, who frowned thoughtfully. "We can't be sure that's what happened, but it's worth talking to her friends again, just to be sure. If we can frighten them a little and they do know where she went, they might tell us."

"I don't know," Minnie murmured, shaking her head.

"It's worth a try," Cora argued. "You know how girls are with their secrets. Mrs. Brandt is right, I can't imagine Angel didn't tell *somebody* that she was going to run away."

"But if the girls didn't tell us before, why would they tell us now?" Minnie asked.

"Like I said, you'll have to frighten them. Make them think that Angel might be in danger."

Minnie's face was gray with fatigue, and she stared blankly back at Sarah. "I can't," she said wearily. "I just . . . I don't know what to do."

"Mrs. Brandt, you'll help her, won't you?" Cora asked, but she didn't wait for an answer. "Minnie, take Mrs. Brandt upstairs to see Biddy and Una. They'll be home from school by now. They'll be surprised to see a stranger. Tell them . . . tell them Mrs. Brandt works for the police or something. They won't know any different. Tell them they have to talk to her or she'll take them off to jail. That will scare them."

Minnie's eyes glistened with tears. "What if they really don't know where she is?"

Now Sarah understood. Minnie couldn't bear one more disappointment. "They'll know something," Sarah promised rashly. "If you take me to them, I'll find it out."

"I'd go with you if I could," Cora said. "Please, Minnie. You've got to at least try."

"You'll talk to them?" Minnie asked Sarah.

"Yes," Sarah said, recalling her promise to Malloy not to get involved. Of course, he'd never have to know.

Minnie drew a deep breath, as if for strength. "All right." Hastily, she wiped the tears from her eyes with her fingertips and squared her shoulders. Sarah followed her as she made her way out of Cora's flat, into the hallway, and up the stairs. They went up two flights, to the floor above the one where Minnie and her family lived. They could hear the sounds of families living their lives behind the closed doors. Minnie knocked on one of them.

The woman who answered was instantly solicitous when she saw her visitor. "Hello, Minnie. Have you found her yet?"

"No," Minnie said, her voice nearly breaking. "I was wondering, I'd like to see Una again. She might've remembered something new by now."

"She would've said something," the woman protested.

"Not if she promised Angel not to tell," Sarah offered when Minnie made no reply.

"Who's this?" the woman asked with a worried frown as she peered at Sarah in the shadows of the hallway.

"Mrs. Brandt," Minnie said. "She's—"

"Helping the family," Sarah supplied. "Is Una home?"

The woman frowned uncertainly, but she said, "She's across the hall with Biddy."

"Thank you," Sarah said, using the official tone she'd heard Malloy use so often. He had the authority to go along with it, but this woman wouldn't know Sarah carried none.

Sarah turned and went to the door the woman had indicated. She rapped sharply before looking back at Minnie and silently inviting her to join her. Minnie reached her side just as the door opened. This woman also asked about Angel, and Sarah answered before Minnie could.

"We haven't heard anything yet, and we'd like to ask Una and Biddy a few more questions, if you don't mind."

The woman blinked in surprise. "I'm sure they already told Mr. Lee everything they know," she said.

"We just want to make sure," Sarah replied.

The woman looked back and forth between Minnie and Sarah. "Minnie?" she asked.

"Mrs. Brandt is helping us. Please let her see the girls," she pleaded.

"Well, I don't see why not," the woman said uncertainly and stepped aside for them to enter. Una's mother had joined them, and she stepped in behind them, still wearing her apron and looking concerned.

This flat, like Cora's, was well furnished and comfortable. Both of the mothers wore serviceable dresses of good quality. Their husbands provided well for them.

"Biddy, you and Una come out here," Biddy's mother called.

The girls appeared in the doorway and stopped dead when they saw the four women waiting for them. They'd been sharing a confidence that had them smiling, but the smiles vanished as they stepped into the front room.

"What is it, Mama?" one of the girls asked the woman who lived there.

"I'd like to ask you some questions," Sarah said, glad to hear her voice still held that air of authority. "Are you Biddy?"

She nodded uncertainly.

"I'll need to speak with the girls alone," Sarah informed the mothers. "They'll be more honest if you're not in the room."

"Mama, what's going on?" Una asked.

"We're trying to find Angel," Minnie said, having found her confidence again. She cleared the remaining tears out of her voice. "Mrs. Brandt here is helping us."

The girls stared at Sarah with wide-eyed apprehension.

"I don't think—" one of the mothers began to protest, but Sarah cut her off.

"Let's go into the kitchen, girls." She moved purposefully toward the doorway in which the girls stood, then looked back over her shoulder at the mothers. "This won't take long."

As she'd hoped, they were intimidated enough to stay where they were. The girls backed into the other room, as if afraid to let Sarah out of their sight. They were holding hands.

"Sit down, girls," Sarah said, motioning to the well-scrubbed wooden table.

They sat, still not taking their eyes off Sarah, who took a chair opposite them.

"I know that Angel confided in you," Sarah began bravely and was rewarded by the expressions of surprise on the two girls' faces. "You promised you wouldn't tell on her, and that's all very well and good, but you're going to have to break your promise to her, because she could be in danger."

She waited, giving the girls a chance to digest this piece of information. Biddy finally broke the silence. "What kind of danger?"

Biddy was the larger of the two girls. Like Angel, they both wore their dark hair in braids. Also like Angel, their eyes betrayed their Chinese heritage. Except for her eyes and her coal black hair, Biddy looked just like her mother, though. Her plain Irish face was broad and open, and her figure would be full.

"The boy she ran away with might not really want to marry her," Sarah said, taking another risk.

"But he loves her!" Una cried, then immediately slapped

a hand over her mouth as Biddy elbowed her viciously in the ribs. Una probably took after her father, with her birdlike delicacy. A smattering of freckles stood out starkly across her nose as her face paled.

"Maybe he does love her," Sarah said. "I hope so. I hope they're happily married by now, too. But I'm afraid there are young men in the city who trick girls like Angel—girls like both of you, too—into thinking they're in love. They get the girls to run off with them, and when they're away from their families, they sell them to . . ." How to explain this? Would the girls even know what a brothel was? "To evil men who make them do terrible things and mistreat them."

Now both girls had gone pale. "But she said . . ." Biddy began, then caught herself.

"I know you don't want to break your promise to Angel," Sarah said, "but if she's been tricked, she'll be very glad you did. We might be able to find her and rescue her if you help us."

"But what if she wasn't tricked?" Una wanted to know.

"If she's married, that's fine. There's nothing her parents can do, but at least they'll know she's safe. Her mother is very worried about her. You can see how upset she is. You wouldn't want your own mother to be that worried about you, would you?"

The girls exchanged a glance, silently debating.

"But if Angel is being held prisoner by evil men, she'll be terrified. If you were being held prisoner, wouldn't you want someone to help you?"

"But we promised," Biddy said. "Angel made us swear!"

"She's probably praying that you'll break your promise and tell someone what happened to her. If we know who she was meeting, we'll have a chance of finding her. If not . . . you may never see her again." Sarah tried to make it sound even more ominous than it was.

"You mean . . . she might die?" Una asked in a whisper.

Sarah thought that was not the worst fate that could befall the girl, but she said, "Yes, she could."

This time the look the girls exchanged was horrified.

"We . . . we don't know where she went," Biddy confessed.

"Do you know the boy's name?" Sarah asked.

"Quinn," Una said, earning another elbow from Biddy. "I don't care," Una told her friend defiantly. "I don't want nothing bad to happen to Angel."

"What's his first name?" Sarah asked.

"That *is* his first name," Biddy said, angry with her friend but determined to set the record straight. "Quinn O'Neal. But he loves her. They're getting married. You'll see."

"I hope so," Sarah said fervently. "Where did she meet this boy?"

"He ain't no boy," Biddy said. "He's twenty."

Sarah's heart sank. Why would a twenty-year-old man want to marry a child like Angel? "Do you know where he lives?"

They shook their heads.

"Where did Angel meet him?"

"At the market," Una said quickly, before Biddy could. She wanted to be as helpful as her friend.

"The market? You mean the Gansevoort Market?" Sarah asked, naming the area on the West Side of the city where farmers brought their wares to sell.

"Yes, he works there," Biddy said.

"He's not a farmer, though," Una added importantly. "He unloads wagons and things like that."

"How did you meet him?" Sarah asked, thinking that a job like that would be a good way to spot young girls.

"We go to the market all the time," Una said.

"With our mothers," Biddy added.

Like hundreds of other girls, Sarah thought.

"One day we went off by ourselves, looking at things," Una continued. "He called out to us, asked was we lost."

"He's handsome," Biddy said, "and real friendly, so we stopped to talk to him."

"He only wanted to talk to Angel, though," Una said with just the slightest trace of bitterness. "Because she's so pretty."

"What did they talk about?" Sarah asked.

"Nothing much," Biddy said, wrinkling her face as she tried to remember.

"Silly things," Una added. "Like did our mothers know where we were."

"He didn't know we're Chinese," Biddy said. "Not at first."

"Angel told him," Una said. "He wanted to know why we looked so different."

"How long ago did you first meet him?" Sarah asked.

They didn't remember exactly. "Back in the fall, I think," Una recalled. "When there was still vegetables at the market."

"How often did you see him?"

"*We* didn't see him much at all," Biddy said, and this time she also sounded bitter. "He was only interested in Angel."

This was sounding worse and worse. "How did she manage to see him?"

"At first she just went to the market, but she couldn't always get away from her mother, and then the weather turned cold," Biddy explained. "So she started saying she was going upstairs with us after school, and she'd climb down the fire escape and sneak off."

"No one ever suspected?" Sarah asked in surprise.

"Why should they?"

Why, indeed. Angel was an obedient girl who'd never given her parents a reason to distrust her.

"Do you know where they met?" Sarah asked. "Was it at the market?"

"No, that was too far. She wouldn't have time to get there and back," Una said. "They'd meet someplace nearby, but she never told us where."

"Are you sure you don't know? Did she say anything about it at all?"

"I don't remember anything," Biddy said.

"Try hard. It's very important," Sarah urged.

"I think . . ." Una mused.

"What?"

"I think it was behind a store," she said.

"Why do you think that?"

"She said one time that she wasn't afraid somebody would see her, because she'd just go in and out the front of the store, like she was shopping."

"I don't remember that," Biddy protested.

"Did she say anything about what kind of a store it was?"

Una tried to remember. "I can't think of anything. Just that she'd go into the back of the store and meet Quinn."

"Do you think he worked at the store?"

Una shrugged. "She never said."

"We already told you, he worked at the market," Biddy reminded her.

"Do you remember what part of the market he was working in?" Sarah asked.

Biddy described the location to her. Sarah knew the market well. It wasn't too far from her home on Bank Street.

"Can you think of anything else she told you about Quinn? Anything about his family? Anything at all?"

"He wanted to marry her," Biddy said crossly.

"Especially when she told him her parents wanted her to marry Mr. Wong," added Una.

"How did you feel about that?" Sarah asked them.

They exchanged another glance, probably wondering if it was safe to tell Sarah their true feelings on the subject.

"I didn't blame her for running away," Biddy admitted.

"Mr. Wong is old," Una added, as if that settled everything.

"Don't tell Angel we told you what happened," Biddy said. "Please, don't. She'll be mad at us."

"I won't," Sarah promised.

"Are you going to tell our mothers?" Una asked. "They'll be mad that we lied to Mr. Lee."

"I won't say anything to them, but they're bound to find out. If you tell them yourselves, they won't be as mad at you."

They frowned, not certain they trusted her logic.

Sarah took two of her calling cards from her purse and laid them on the table in front of the girls. "If you think of anything else that might help, please let me know. Or you can tell Angel's mother or her auntie Cora. You can even leave a message for me at the Prodigal Son Mission on Mulberry Street."

Una picked up the card and stared at it for a moment. "Do you really think Angel is in trouble?"

"I think there's a good chance that she is."

"She's not," Biddy said with certainty. "She's married, and she's happy."

Sarah smiled. "I pray you're right."

Sarah thanked the two mothers when she returned to the front room.

"Did they help you at all?" Biddy's mother asked.

"I'm not sure," Sarah hedged. "They were able to answer a few questions, at least." She turned to Minnie. "We should be going."

Before the other two could protest, Sarah thanked them again and ushered Minnie out into the hallway. Minnie waited until they had walked down the first flight of stairs before stopping Sarah. "What did they say?" she asked in a whisper.

"Angel was seeing a young man named Quinn O'Neal."

Minnie gasped. "How? When?"

Sarah briefly explained.

"I don't believe it! Angel never . . . I never knew her to lie!"

"Young love is a powerful force," Sarah reminded her.

"What can we do now?" Minnie asked helplessly.

"That's up to you," Sarah said. "I wish I had more information about this Quinn fellow, but Angel was very discreet, and the girls apparently weren't interested in learning a lot of details."

"You think he sold her, don't you?" Minnie asked, her face ashen.

Sarah could feel her anguish. "I honestly don't know. Maybe he really did elope with her, like the girls said. Either way, finding this Quinn is your best chance of finding Angel."

"I need to tell Charlie," Minnie said. "He'll want to know the whole story. Will you come with me? I'll never remember everything."

For an instant, Sarah imagined what Malloy would say about this, but only for an instant. "Of course," she replied.

4

CHARLIE LEE WAS AT THE LAUNDRY HE OWNED. MINNIE sent one of the children playing around the front stoop for him, then took Sarah up to her flat to wait, after they'd checked on Cora and brought her up to date. Minnie made them some tea, more to keep busy than to be a good hostess, and Sarah was enjoying the fragrant brew in the kitchen with her when they heard the front door open. Minnie hurried out to meet her husband, and Sarah could hear her explaining the situation to him in the other room. A few moments later, Mr. Lee appeared in the kitchen doorway.

Sarah wasn't sure exactly what she had expected. The only Chinese men she'd encountered with any frequency were the ones who operated the chop suey restaurants that had sprung up around the city. Charlie Lee was nothing like them. Although he wasn't a large man, his presence filled the room. He wore a tailored business suit with a boiled white shirt and neat tie. A gold watch chain stretched across his trim waistline, and a diamond ring winked on his finger. His dark eyes took in Sarah with a glance, seeing everything he needed to know about her in those few seconds.

"You are Mrs. Brandt?" he asked. His accent was noticeable but not heavy.

"Yes," she said. "I'm so sorry about your daughter, Mr. Lee."

His expression didn't waver, but she thought she detected the slightest flinch at the mention of the girl.

"Why do you care what happen to her?" he asked in challenge.

"I care what happens to every young girl in the city," she said quite honestly. "I can't protect all of them, but I do what I can. I've been helping at the Prodigal Son Mission for several months. I even hired one of the girls from there to work at my house."

"My daughter not like the girls at Mission," he said, his anger evident.

"I know, which is why we need to find her as quickly as possible."

"Charlie," Minnie said from where she stood behind him, but he silenced her with a gesture.

"What do you know about my daughter?"

Sarah told him, going into much more detail than she had with Minnie. She told him about Quinn O'Neal and how they'd met and what the girls had told her about how Angel had sneaked out to see him. Mr. Lee continued to stand ramrod straight as he listened intently to every word. Only the color rising in his face betrayed his fury.

"These girls, they lie to me," he said when she was finished.

"They're young and foolish and romantic. They thought they were helping Angel elope."

"That is no excuse."

He was right, of course. "I told Minnie that I have a friend who's a detective sergeant on the police force," Sarah said. "I'm sure he'd—"

"No police," Mr. Lee snapped. "I will find Quinn O'Neal myself."

Sarah didn't know what to say to that. She certainly wished him success, but it seemed inappropriate to say so. She rose from where she still sat at the kitchen table. "I guess I should be going. If I can be of any more help, please let me know."

Mr. Lee stepped aside to let her pass into the front room, where Minnie still stood, wringing her hands and looking distraught. "Thank you so much, Mrs. Brandt. If you hadn't come, we might never have found out about this Quinn fellow."

"I certainly hope it helps you find Angel," Sarah said.

As she left the building, she had an odd feeling of failure. True, she'd uncovered information Angel's family might not have found without her help, but would it be enough? For once, she understood Malloy's warnings about getting involved. When she'd helped him solve murders in the past, they had worked together until the killer was found and punished. This time . . . this time, in spite of her efforts, they might never even know what happened to Angel. How would Minnie bear it?

SARAH ORDINARILY WOULDN'T HAVE BEEN SURPRISED TO see a young man at her door. Young men were most frequently the ones sent to fetch her to a delivery. This fellow was Chinese, however, right down to his thick-soled slippers, and although he looked vaguely familiar, she knew he wasn't Cora Lee's husband. He also seemed more angry than anxious, the way young men usually were when they came to get her.

"Mrs. Brandt, my mother sent me to ask you . . ." He glanced past her, to where Maeve and Catherine hovered in the kitchen doorway, and hesitated.

"Is your mother having a baby?" Sarah asked.

"No!" he yelped, then caught himself and managed to regain his dignity. "It's about my sister, Angel."

Oh! Now she knew him. He was Harry Lee, Minnie's son. "Have you found Angel?"

His face hardened and, with it, his anger. "Yes," he said through gritted teeth.

"Is she all right?"

"No," he said. "She's dead."

"Dead?" Sarah's heart seemed to contract. "I'm so sorry! What on earth happened?"

"Somebody choked her," he said baldly.

They heard a strangled cry, and Sarah turned to see Maeve covering her mouth. Her eyes glistened with tears. Catherine was staring, wide-eyed, and it was impossible to know how much of this she understood. "Maeve, will you take Catherine back to the kitchen?" Sarah asked gently.

Maeve could only nod, but she quickly obeyed. Sarah hoped Catherine hadn't comprehended what Harry had been saying. The child had already seen too much ugliness in her short life. When they were gone, Sarah turned back to Harry.

"Why did your mother send you to me?"

"She said . . . she said you know somebody on the police," he explained reluctantly. "My father, he won't want the police, but my mother says they'll come anyway, because Angel was murdered, so we might as well try to get somebody who can help."

"Tell me what happened," Sarah said.

He drew a deep breath, as if he had to calm himself a bit before he spoke of his sister. "We found Angel a few days ago. She was alive then, and with that man, O'Neal." Sarah tried to judge why he was so angry, but everything he said just seemed to make him angrier instead of distracting him, as it should have.

"The one who had eloped with her," Sarah clarified.

"Yeah, they got married."

"Oh, my!" Sarah exclaimed in surprise. "I never thought . . ."

"Neither did my parents," he said bitterly. "We couldn't believe she was really married, but they had a license and went to a priest and everything."

That must have been such a relief to Minnie, to know her daughter was safe, at least. And now she was dead! "What happened? When did she die?"

"Today. I mean, they think it was today. They found her in the alley behind the tenement where she lives . . . lived with O'Neal. Somebody ran to tell my mother right away. When she saw what had happened, she said to get you because you'd know what to do."

Sarah knew exactly what to do. "Maeve, I have to go out," she called. By the time Maeve and Catherine had emerged from the kitchen, she had on her cloak. She kissed a worried-looking Catherine good-bye and reassured her that everything would be fine. Then she gave Maeve instructions for the evening. Mrs. Ellsworth would undoubtedly check on them, too. She nearly always came by after supper.

When she and Harry were out on the sidewalk, she asked, "Where did your sister live?"

He gave her an address on the Lower East Side. It was only a few blocks from Chinatown, but it might as well have been in another country for as much as the people in the two neighborhoods would have mixed. The whole city was like that, each neighborhood like a country unto itself. "Let's start there."

"Aren't you going to get that policeman?" he asked doubtfully.

"Let's worry about that when we get there, shall we?" she suggested and hurried off, leaving him to keep up as best he could. Sarah knew she was unlikely to catch Malloy at Police Headquarters. Her best bet was to have the officers who had been called to Angel's murder send for Malloy directly. Even if another detective had already been assigned to the case, she could appeal to him to send for Malloy, too.

As they hurried down Bank Street, Sarah mentally went over the various routes they might take to the Lower East Side. She quickly determined that the Sixth Avenue Elevated Train would be the best choice. The trains that ran on rails two stories above the hopeless traffic of the city streets would carry them swiftly down to that portion of Manhattan Island. They'd have to walk across town from there, but the train would probably cut an hour from their trip.

Harry Lee preceded Sarah up the stairs on Sixth Avenue that led up to the waiting area. She couldn't help but notice the way people stared at him as they passed. He did look very different, with his dome-shaped hat, his brightly colored silk shirt, and the long pigtail hanging down his back.

Fortunately, they didn't have to wait long for a train, and Sarah paid the fare for both of them. The train lurched into motion before they were seated, and Sarah half fell into a seat. With apparent reluctance, Harry sat down beside her. This elicited some disapproving looks from the other passengers, but Sarah ignored them.

Grateful for a chance to ask him a few questions, she said, "How long ago did you find out where your sister was?"

She saw the muscles in his jaw working in the moments that passed before he replied. "Three days, I think. About that."

"Did you see her?"

His gaze cut sharply to Sarah for an instant before he looked away again. Sarah noticed that his eyes were light brown, almost honey-colored, not dark like his sister's. "No, I didn't see her."

"Who finally found her then?"

"My father. He . . . he'd been looking for her. He found the man she'd been meeting, and she was with him."

"You said they were married."

"That's what they told him. Angel . . . She always was a bad girl."

"What do you mean by that?" Sarah asked in surprise. Minnie had insisted she was always sweet and obedient.

His jaws worked again, and the color rose in his neck. "She has no respect, no honor."

"Because she was sneaking out to meet this man, you mean?"

"Because she has no respect!" he repeated more vehemently. "She doesn't respect her family. She has shamed us all!"

"Because she ran away?"

"Because she refused to obey my father," he snapped, as if Sarah were simpleminded not to understand.

"When he wanted her to marry his friend," Sarah guessed.

"Yes. She embarrassed us, and then she ran away with a stinking Irishman."

Sarah could have reminded him that his mother was Irish, but she didn't. She found his contempt interesting. The Irishman in question would likely have called Harry a stinking Chinaman in turn. Prejudice was an interesting phenomenon.

They rode in silence for a while, and Sarah watched the buildings that seemed to be moving along beside the train. She could see into the windows, catching a glimpse of the lives being lived in full view of everyone who rode this train.

"Do you really know a police detective?" Harry asked suddenly.

She heard the challenge in his voice. Why would a respectable lady know a police detective? Most people considered the police little better than the criminals they arrested, and truthfully, few of them were. Frank Malloy was a rare exception, although she knew he did make compromises that he wouldn't want her to know about. "Yes, I do."

"My father won't pay the police," he informed her. Another challenge.

Few crimes in New York were solved unless a "reward" was paid. "That won't matter. Detective Sergeant Malloy will still investigate your sister's murder."

He frowned, and Sarah understood his skepticism. Still, she had confidence in Malloy. She only hoped she could get him assigned to the case.

After what seemed an eternity, they finally descended the stairs from the station into the teeming streets again. After walking a few blocks east, they were in the heart of the Lower East Side, where immigrants of all types mixed and mingled. The people they passed spoke a variety of languages and wore a strange mix of clothing, some reflecting ethnic origins and others simply reflecting extreme poverty. The aroma of foods from the street vendors mingled with odors from the manure on the cobblestones, garbage piled on the corners, and unwashed bodies clogging the sidewalks.

"It's down here," Harry said when they'd made their way cautiously across yet another busy street. He pointed to an alley running between two tenement buildings. Sarah followed him down, past piles of refuse and battered ashcans, and they came out into the area behind the rows of tenements that faced opposite streets. Above them hung a mass of crisscrossing clotheslines suspended between the buildings. Porches and fire escapes ran up the backs of the tenements, and all were littered with piles of belongings from the residents—extra furniture and bedding that would be brought in at night, when the floor would provide sleeping space for the people who crowded the small rooms beyond capacity.

A crowd had gathered in the yard behind the building closest to them. They were intently watching the group of people standing on the back porch of that building. Sarah saw that one of the individuals on the porch wore a police uniform. If it was someone she knew, she'd have less trouble getting him to send for Malloy. Luckily, many officers knew her, even though she didn't always know them. She had become something of a celebrity among the police for her involvement in solving several high-profile murders.

"Ma!" Harry called, waving to someone on the porch.

A woman turned, and Sarah could see it was Minnie. She waved back when she saw Sarah was with him and came forward to meet her. Sarah was almost to the porch steps when one of the men in the group stepped in front of Minnie and stopped at the head of the steps to look down at Sarah. He didn't look at all happy to see her, either.

"Malloy!" she said in surprise.

"Mrs. Brandt," he replied grimly. "What brings you out on a fine day like this?"

She heard the sarcasm in his voice, but she doubted anyone else would notice. "Mrs. Lee sent for me," she replied with a rebellious smile. "What brings *you* out?"

"Oh, Mrs. Brandt," Minnie cried, brushing Malloy aside to take his place at the top of the steps. "We found Angel, and somebody's killed her!"

Sarah instantly turned her attention to Minnie. "I'm so sorry! I could hardly believe it when Harry told me," Sarah said, hurrying up the steps and past Malloy to comfort her.

Minnie had the blank look of someone in shock. Plainly, she hadn't really registered the full horror of her loss yet. "I sent Harry for you so you could get your friend here, but the officer knew who we wanted, soon as we said your name. He sent for Mr. Malloy right off."

Sarah hazarded a glance at Malloy. His eyes had narrowed dangerously, so she decided to stop looking at him. "I'm so glad," she said sincerely. "What happened to poor Angel?"

Minnie shuddered slightly at the mention of her daughter's name, and her eyes grew round with the blank stare of one who has been thoroughly beaten. "She was married, Mrs. Brandt. She married that boy she'd been sneaking out with." Minnie laid a hand over her heart, as if to still it. "I was that relieved, I was. I was thinking such horrible things that could've happened to her, and here she was, really eloped."

"Harry told me that your husband found her."

"Oh, yes, just the other day. Took him a while, but once

we knew the boy's name, it was only a matter of time. Charlie found him, and there she was with him. They lived in this building," she said, gesturing vaguely at the tenement behind her. "With his people."

"You must have been so happy to find her safe," Sarah said.

Minnie nodded, but her eyes filled with tears. "She wasn't safe at all, though, was she? Somebody up and killed her!"

Sarah could see the reality of it finally sinking in as her blank stare dissolved into naked pain. "Maybe you should have Harry take you home," Sarah suggested gently.

"I ain't leaving my girl!" Minnie protested tearfully. "They don't care nothing about her here. How do I know what they'll do with her if I leave?"

Sarah glanced at Malloy again, this time with a silent question.

"The coroner will be here soon, Mrs. Lee," he said gruffly. "He'll take the body away."

Minnie made an agonized sound, and Sarah instinctively clutched at her arm. "Can someone get her a chair?"

Numerous chairs were stacked on the porch, and Malloy grabbed the nearest one and brought it to her. Sarah eased Minnie down into it. Then she looked around at the others gathered on the porch. She saw no familiar faces and noted that they were all hanging back, as if they wanted no part of Minnie's grief. Minnie had no friends in this bunch.

"Is your husband here?" Sarah asked Minnie.

She shook her head. "He don't know yet. He was at the laundry when they came to get me, and I didn't . . . I couldn't hardly believe it myself when I heard. I had to make sure it was true before I sent for him."

Sarah glanced around again and easily found Minnie's son standing off by himself in the yard. His bright yellow shirt made him easily visible. "Harry, could you go fetch your father now, please?" Sarah asked the boy.

"Ma?" he asked uncertainly.

"Yes, go get him," Minnie agreed wearily. "No use putting it off anymore."

Harry took off again. Sarah patted Minnie on the shoulder and wondered what else she could do to offer comfort.

"Can I have a word with you, Mrs. Brandt?" Malloy asked with exaggerated courtesy. She knew how furious he was with her, and she couldn't really blame him. Hadn't she promised him she wouldn't get involved in any more murders?

"Of course, Mr. Malloy," she replied just as politely.

He took her elbow in a grip that wasn't as gentle as it probably looked to the bystanders and led her over to the end of the porch, where they could speak in private.

"I guess this is your missing Chinese girl," he said.

"Yes, it is, unfortunately," she said. "I'd told the mother that I knew a police detective who could help her locate her daughter."

"So when her mother starts talking about getting her friend Mrs. Brandt to help, the beat cop figures he should send for me."

Sarah smiled apologetically. "If I'd known they'd already sent for you, I wouldn't have come down here," she told him honestly. "I'm not going to get involved, Malloy. I only wanted to make sure you were assigned to the case."

"Good. You can go back home now."

"Can't you at least tell me what happened to poor Angel before I go?"

He sighed in resignation. "You know as much as I do. The girl ran off with this O'Neal fellow, and they got married. Her father, the Chinaman, he found out where she was living, but she wouldn't go home with him. Wanted to stay with her husband, which isn't too surprising. A little while ago, somebody finds her out here in the yard, dead. Looks like she was strangled, but the coroner will tell us for sure."

"Where did they find her?" Sarah asked, looking around. "If she was killed out here in broad daylight, someone surely saw something," she added, looking up at all the windows that faced the yard.

"I don't know exactly where they found her because her husband carried her inside, or at least that's what he claims," he said, not bothering to hide his frustration. "She was inside the flat where the whole family lives, all covered up with a blanket, when the beat cop got here. They all claim they don't know anything about it and didn't hear or see anything at all."

Plainly, he didn't believe this for an instant, but it would take some time and hard work to unravel the mystery. She knew that only too well from her past experiences working with him in murder investigations.

"I could ask a few questions—"

"No!" he snapped. "You aren't going to ask anybody anything. You're going to leave right now. You're going to forget you ever heard of these people."

Sarah couldn't possibly forget any of this, but she nodded obediently. "I can't leave Mrs. Lee alone, though. I'll just wait until her husband comes to take her home. Then I'll go."

He wasn't pleased, but he knew better than to insist. She'd just dig her heels in and refuse. "Don't talk to anybody else, though. I don't need your help with this case, Sarah, and I don't want you involved in any more murders."

"All right," she said as meekly as she could manage.

He blinked in surprise and then leaned in to look at her

more closely, his eyes narrowed suspiciously. "Do you really mean that?"

"Of course I do!" she said indignantly.

He didn't look convinced, but he nodded. "Until the husband gets here, and then you leave," he reminded her. "I've got to talk to these people in the yard before they get bored and disappear, see if they know anything useful."

"Go right ahead. Don't worry about me, Malloy. I'll be fine."

She thought she heard him grumbling something under his breath when he turned away, and she bit back a smile. She really was going to keep her word not to get involved. But of course, if she accidentally learned anything important, she'd certainly let him know.

FRANK WISHED HE HAD THE AUTHORITY TO ORDER Sarah Brandt away. He didn't think *anybody* had that kind of authority, though. She'd do what she always did, which was whatever she wanted, regardless of what anybody else thought or what was in her own best interest or even what was safe.

With a weary sigh, he went down the porch steps and into the yard where the crowd of neighbors still stood. He figured they were waiting to see the body being carried out. That meant he had a few minutes to ask them some questions. "Did any of you see what happened to the girl?"

Many heads shook, and a few voices muttered denials.

"I was the one found her," a voice said. Frank looked down at a middle-aged woman with a lined face and hollow eyes. She clutched a moth-eaten shawl around her emaciated body. Her unnaturally pale face and bluish lips indicated that her frailty was caused by disease, not by starvation.

"Can you show me exactly where she was and what you saw?" he asked as gently as he could. He judged that she'd respond better to kindness than to bullying, and he was right. She didn't look happy about it, but she walked over to where the alley ended at the yard.

"She was right there," she said, pointing to a spot on the ground right beside the building.

"How was she laying?"

The woman considered for a moment. "On her side. Her hands up like this." She pulled her arms into her chest so her hands were beneath her chin. "Her head was toward the alley, and her feet toward the yard."

"Were her clothes disturbed at all?"

"You mean did somebody try to interfere with her?" the woman asked scornfully. "Didn't look like it. Her skirt was down, and everything fastened up tight, like it should be. Nothing seemed wrong with her at all until I saw her eyes was staring at nothing. Then I let out a howl to wake the dead."

"What happened then?"

"People started looking out the windows, and then they come running to see what was wrong."

"Who moved her?"

"The O'Neal boy. Somebody said she was his wife, though she didn't look old enough to me. Looked like a child, she did."

"She *was* a child," Frank said. "How did he act when he saw her?"

"Like his heart was gonna break. He starts to crying and carrying on. Then he picks her up—she wasn't any bigger than a flea—and takes her into the building."

"Mary, what're you doing?" a man's voice called angrily.

They looked up to see an unshaven lout in his longjohn

top and threadbare trousers, his suspenders hanging around
his hips. He was striding toward them, his bloodshot eyes
furious.

"I'm telling him what I saw," the woman replied tartly.

"You know better than to get mixed up with the police.
He'll have you in the Tombs for killing the girl yourself!"

Frank gave him a look that stopped him in his tracks.
His face turned scarlet, but he didn't back off. Frank turned
back to the woman. "Did you hear anything earlier? Or see
anybody around?"

"I didn't hear nothing. I live upstairs. I just come down to
empty the slop jar and saw her foot where it was sticking out
past the end of the porch. I thought maybe she fell or took a
fit or something, so I went over to see was she all right."

"Thank you for your help," he said, more politely than he
ordinarily would have because her husband was watching.
He wanted to shame the man for falsely accusing him.

The woman shrugged. "Can I go now?"

Frank got her name and the number of her flat and wrote
it in his notebook before letting her go. Then he looked
around carefully, trying to judge which windows might have
afforded a view of the girl's last moments. The spot was oddly
sheltered. The porch roof extended far enough to shield the
area where she'd lain from most of the vantage points in the
yard. Only a few windows in one building would have had a
clear view. What were the chances someone had been looking
out one of those windows at the right time? And if they had,
what were the chances they'd be willing to talk to the police?

A FTER HER CONVERSATION WITH MALLOY, SARAH WENT
back to where Minnie was sitting. The poor woman looked

shattered, although she had yet to shed a tear. That would come later, when she was alone, without distractions, and with nothing to think about except her awful loss.

"Did you have a chance to see Angel after your husband found her?" she asked Minnie.

Minnie nodded. "Charlie was that mad at her when she wouldn't come home with him. He was ready to wash his hands of her, he said, so I decided I'd see if I could change her mind. I didn't really think I could, but even if she'd just say she was sorry for scaring us like that . . . Charlie didn't want to see her again, he said. The Chinese can be real stubborn, or at least Charlie can. I didn't know whether to believe him or not when he said he didn't want anything to do with her, but the only hope was for Angel to apologize to him."

"So you went to see her?" Sarah prodded when she fell silent.

"I didn't know what to expect. About her husband, I mean. What kind of a man steals a girl away from her family like that? He did marry her legal and all, but I just didn't know."

"Angel loved him," Sarah reminded her. "He must have some good qualities."

Minnie made a disgusted face. "He's handsome. That's all the Irish boys have to recommend them. Besides that, they're just lazy drunkards. Why do you think I married a Chinaman?"

Sarah had no answer for that. "What did she say when you saw her?"

"That she would never leave her husband. *Her husband!*" she scoffed. "She wasn't nothing but a baby. What did she know about being married?"

"She was a new bride," she reminded Minnie sympathetically. "She was still in that first blush of happiness."

"She didn't look all that happy, though," Minnie recalled with a troubled frown. "And how could she be? They was sleeping on the floor in his family's flat with seven other people! Didn't have no privacy at all. Wasn't much of a honeymoon, that's for certain. I don't even know if he treated her good. She wouldn't say a word against him, but I could see she was miserable. I know when my girl's happy and when she's not."

"Did she say anything about the rest of the family? About how they felt about having her there?" Sarah asked.

Minnie twisted her hands in her lap as she remembered. "They didn't like her being Chinese. She didn't say so, but I could tell. The way they looked at her. The way they looked at *me* for being married to one. I've seen it often enough, believe me. Didn't matter that she was beautiful and smarter than all of them put together. They hated her and thought she was trash," she added, her voice thick with suppressed anger.

Sarah wished she had some comfort to offer or at least that she could assure Minnie that she'd been mistaken. Unfortunately, she felt sure Minnie was correct in her assumptions about Angel's in-laws. She didn't have the heart to ask Minnie any more questions, so she stood silently beside her as they waited.

She watched Malloy dealing with one of the lazy, drunken Irishmen that Minnie held is such low esteem. Then the men from the coroner's office made their way down the alley and found Malloy.

"Who's that?" Minnie asked, straightening in alarm.

"They've come to take Angel," Sarah said.

Minnie jumped to her feet. "What will happen to her?"

Sarah heard the edge of hysteria in her voice. She didn't think it would be wise to explain the autopsy process to a grieving mother. "The coroner will examine her to determine how she died," she hedged. "When he's finished, you'll be able to have a funeral and bury her."

Minnie watched intently as the men entered the building, carrying a stretcher. "You're sure they'll give her back to us?" Minnie asked as they waited.

"Oh, yes," Sarah said, and then she thought of something else. "Unless . . ."

"Unless what?" Minnie pressed her.

"Nothing," Sarah hastily assured her. "I mean, I don't imagine the O'Neals could afford the cost of a funeral. They'll probably be glad to let you handle everything."

"I don't care if they are or not. They'll never get their hands on her again," Minnie vowed fiercely. She began to pace while the coroner's men took care of their business.

After what seemed an age, they came out again. They'd wrapped Angel's body in a sheet so no part of her was visible, but still Minnie gasped in horror when the stretcher emerged. The tears at last appeared, pooling in her eyes and spilling down her cheeks as she stared transfixed at her daughter's body being carried away.

A tall young man emerged from the building, following closely behind the sad little procession. His face was a mask of desolation, and Sarah felt certain he must be Quinn O'Neal, Angel's husband. He stopped to wait as the coroner's men maneuvered down the porch steps, being careful not to drop their tragic burden. Then a disturbance in the yard caught his attention and everyone looked over to see Charlie Lee and his son Harry enter the yard from the alley.

O'Neal's expression changed instantly from grief to rage, and like a madman, he shoved the coroner's men aside, nearly causing them to drop Angel's body as he bolted down the porch stairs.

"Murderer!" he cried as he launched himself at Charlie Lee.

5

FRANK HAD SEEN THE CHINAMAN COMING DOWN THE alley and figured it was the girl's father. In his experience, the Chinese usually weren't much trouble. They respected—or feared—the police and tended to stay on the right side of the law whenever possible. Even when you raided their gambling houses, they were orderly and polite. He kept an eye on him anyway, though, which is why he didn't see the attack coming.

O'Neal bolted down the porch steps and barreled straight into the Chinaman, bellowing "Murderer!" at the top of his lungs. The two slammed to the ground before Frank could even react. Muttering a curse, he hurried over to where O'Neal was trying to pummel his smaller opponent. The Chinaman had thrown his arms over his head and was successfully warding off the blows when Frank arrived.

Frank took hold of O'Neal's collar and heaved, jerking the young man up and back and sending him sprawling on the packed earth of the yard. Before he could catch his breath, Frank planted a foot squarely in the middle of his chest to hold him down. "That's enough of that," he informed O'Neal, who was sputtering in outrage.

"But he killed Angel!" the boy protested.

"You saw him do it, I guess," Frank said mildly.

O'Neal's eyes grew wide as his feeble brain processed the question and recognized an opportunity. "Yeah, I did!" he claimed triumphantly. "I saw him kill her!"

A woman nearby gasped, probably Mrs. Lee, but Frank took no notice. "You did, did you?" he asked in feigned amazement. "Let me get this straight. You saw him choke your wife to death, and you just stood by and let him, and then you watched him walk away and went back inside to wait for somebody else to find her body."

"I . . ." O'Neal began but stopped when he realized he couldn't admit to such a preposterous claim. "Well, no, I didn't actually *see* it, but he killed her all right. Who else could've done it?"

Frank glanced over at the Chinaman. He was on his feet again, and his son was brushing the dirt off his well-made suit. The beat cops who had been hanging around the yard had rushed over right behind Frank. They would've helped a white man to his feet, but they stood back from this fellow, merely waiting to see if they would be called upon to act.

Mrs. Lee had reached her husband by now and was asking him if he was all right. He replied by pushing her away impatiently. "Is my daughter dead?" he asked Frank.

"I'm afraid so," he replied.

If Lee felt any grief, he did not betray it. "Then he the one who kill her," he said, pointing at O'Neal.

The boy would've jumped up and had at him again, but Frank put his weight on his leg and held him pinned down as he struggled like a bug on its back. "Calm down or I'll have to lock you up," Frank warned.

"I didn't hurt Angel," O'Neal insisted. "I never would! Ask anybody!"

The coroner's men had been waiting for things to settle down, still holding Angel's body on the stretcher between them. They must have decided Frank had matters under control, because they started moving again, carrying their burden toward the alley that led to the street.

"Where they take her?" Lee demanded, pointing.

"They're taking her to the coroner," Mrs. Lee explained. "He has to decide how she died."

For the first time, Frank saw a flicker of emotion on Lee's face. He would be too proud to let these strangers see his pain, but he couldn't mask it entirely. He might have been mad at the girl for running off, but he still loved her. That was good to know.

Everyone fell silent as the men carried the stretcher away. When they were gone, Frank said to the Lees, "You folks might as well go on home now. There's nothing you can do here."

"But you're gonna find out who killed my girl, aren't you?" Mrs. Lee asked anxiously. "You're not gonna let her killer get away!" Her voice held that hysterical edge that he'd heard so many times before from bereaved family members eager for justice. Or maybe just revenge.

Before Frank could promise to do what he could, which

really was all he could say, Sarah said, "Of course he won't," with far more certainty than she had any right to feel.

Frank gave her a murderous look, which she ignored. "Mrs. Brandt," he said through gritted teeth, "why don't you see that the family gets home?"

He saw the understanding reluctantly reflected in her eyes, which meant he didn't have to remind her of her promise to stay out of this investigation in front of all these people.

"There's nothing more you can do here," she said to Mrs. Lee. "I'm sure Mr. Malloy will let you know if he needs anything from you."

To Frank's surprise, this earned him a black look from the Chinaman. He probably wouldn't get anything from Lee no matter how much he needed it. Without waiting for another invitation, Lee turned and walked away with as much dignity as a man who'd just been lying flat on his back in the dirt could muster. His son followed, but Mrs. Lee hesitated. She turned back to Frank one more time.

"Please find out who killed my girl, Mr. Malloy. She didn't do nothing to deserve this, and whoever killed her should pay."

Frank didn't know how to answer without making a promise he might not be able to keep. This time when Sarah rescued him, he almost didn't mind. "Come on, Minnie, and give Mr. Malloy a chance to do his job."

Reluctantly, Mrs. Lee let Sarah lead her away. When they were gone, Frank turned to where the crowd of neighbors still stood, watching with avid interest. "All right, everybody, clear out now. There's nothing more to see." He gestured to the beat cops, who took the hint and began to encourage people to be on their way with some gentle nudges from their locust clubs.

"Can I get up now?"

Frank looked down to where O'Neal still lay beneath the weight of his foot. "If you promise to behave yourself," he said and released the young man.

O'Neal scrambled to his feet and began to dust himself off. "You should've let me finish what I started," he told Frank. "I would've got him to confess to what he done."

Frank had learned long ago never to waste time arguing with stupidity. "Let's go back inside. I need to ask you some questions."

His young face twisted in dismay. "I really don't know who killed her."

"Then I'll ask you something else," Frank promised. "Let's go."

Malloy pushed the boy ahead of him back to the porch and up the steps and into the dim interior of the tenement. The family lived several floors up. The rents declined with each flight of stairs, and the O'Neals lived pretty cheaply.

The whole building smelled of cooked cabbage and garbage, and refuse lined the hallways and the stairwells. The O'Neal flat was pretty much what Frank had expected. He'd seen hundreds just like it. The furniture was old and worn, scarred from use. No pictures hung on the walls, no carpets covered the floors. Each family member would own no more than two sets of clothes and few items of comfort. They'd live from day to day, never sure if they'd have enough from that day's earnings to ensure that no one in the family went to bed hungry. Morning would bring a brand-new struggle with the same goal, a cycle repeated endlessly and not always successfully.

The rest of the O'Neal family had apparently remained downstairs. Frank pointed to one of the rickety, mismatched chairs gathered around the kitchen table. "Sit," he told O'Neal. He did.

Frank pulled up a chair opposite him. "So tell me, how'd you come to marry a Chinese girl?"

O'Neal bristled instantly. "She ain't Chinese!"

"That was her father down in the yard, wasn't it?" Frank challenged.

"She was born in America," he said stubbornly. "She's American."

He noticed O'Neal spoke of her as if she were still alive. "All right, how did you come to marry her then?"

He ran a hand through his hair. It was the color of dry leaves, and Frank noticed his eyes had filled with tears. "We just did."

Frank considered giving the boy a smack to induce him to improve his responses, but he decided to try kindness first. If he could get the boy to break down, he'd blubber everything he knew. "She's pretty young," Frank said. "How did you meet her?"

"She . . . at the market. Gansevoort. She used to go there with her friends."

"What were you doing there?"

"I get work there when I can," he said sadly. "I help unload wagons for anybody who'll pay me."

"Did you pick her because she was Chinese?"

"I didn't know she was when I met her!" he exclaimed indignantly. "I just thought she was pretty, that's all. I couldn't tell . . . I never saw a half-Chinese girl before. She and her friends, they just looked . . . different."

"All right, you saw her at the market. Then what happened?"

"I talked to them a little, being friendly. She was pretty, like I said. She . . . she told me later that they looked for me the next time they went. So I talked to her some more when I saw her again. After that, she'd tell me when they were coming back, and I'd make sure I was there."

"You started meeting her other places, I guess."

"Yeah, after the weather got cold. I . . . Sometimes I work at the pawn shop down the street, cleaning up, things like that. The owner, he thought it was funny I liked a Chinese girl. He let me take her in the back."

Frank doubted the man did so out of the goodness of his heart, but he let that go for now. "So you'd take her in the back and have your way with her."

"No!" he almost shouted. "It wasn't like that! She was a nice girl. I just . . . We didn't do nothing like that."

"So she wasn't in a family way when you got married?"

"No! I told you, she was a nice girl. She let me kiss her and . . . and other things, but we never did nothing wrong."

The coroner would tell him if there was a baby or not. "If she wasn't in a family way, why did you run off and get married?"

"She . . . Her father wanted her to marry some old Chinese man," he explained, leaning forward in his chair. "She was scared to death. She didn't want that, and neither did I. I told her to refuse, but she said her father would make her do it anyway. He didn't care if they lived in America. He still did things like they did in China, she said."

"So you decided to be a hero and rescue her," Frank guessed.

"You should've seen her! She was crying and carrying on like she was gonna die. I couldn't let them do that to her. I told her we could get married, and then she'd never have to worry about it no more."

"Who married you?"

"My priest. She's Catholic, too, so he didn't fuss too much. We had to say she was . . . that there was a baby, but it was a lie, like I said. I didn't like to lie to a priest, but he wouldn't've done it without her parents' approval otherwise."

Frank figured that was probably true. "How'd you plan to keep a wife with what you earn cleaning out stores and unloading wagons?"

He had the grace to flush. "I didn't think about that. I just figured we'd manage like everybody else does."

Frank knew how everybody else "managed." It was no way to live, especially for a girl who'd been raised in comfort and never wanted for anything. "So then you brought her here. What did your family think of her?"

"They all liked her," he said quickly. He was a poor liar.

"I guess they weren't too happy that you brought home a Chinese girl," Frank said.

"I told you—"

"I know, she's *not* Chinese. Your family thought she was, though, didn't they? They probably didn't want her here, eating their food and taking up space, especially because she wasn't earning any money. Did they want you to turn her out to earn a few dollars on the street?"

O'Neal's face flushed scarlet. "You can't talk about her like that!"

"I wasn't talking about her," Frank pointed out. "I was talking about your family. A pretty girl like Angel could earn a lot on her back. Is that what they told you?"

"I'd never do that to her!"

Frank noticed he didn't deny that his family had suggested

it, though. He glanced appraisingly around the modest flat. "Who lives here with you?"

"My mother," he said defensively. "My two brothers and my sister, and my brother Donald's wife and their baby."

Frank glanced around again, this time in disapproval. "Not much room for so many people."

"That's none of your business!"

Frank shrugged. "It is if it made somebody mad enough to kill Angel," he pointed out.

"Nobody was mad. I told you, they all liked her. Her and Keely was thick as thieves, always going off together someplace and talking."

"Who's Keely?"

"My sister. I'm telling you, they all treated her like she was one of us."

"I'm glad to hear it. Tell me, where was everybody today?"

O'Neal sat up straight in his chair. Obviously, he recognized this as an important question. "I don't know. I don't keep track of them."

"Then how do you know one of them didn't kill Angel?"

"Because I do!"

"Well, I don't, so tell me where they all were today."

He ran a hand over his face. "Ma was here. She was watching the baby while Iris went to deliver the vests they made."

Women in the tenements frequently did piecework at home to earn extra money. Jobs for females were scarce, and women with children couldn't leave home to take them, anyway.

"Who's Iris?"

"My brother Donald's wife."

"Where were your brothers?"

"Out. I don't know where. They go looking for work most days."

Or for cheap beer, Frank thought. "Why weren't you with them?"

"I worked yesterday," O'Neal defended himself. "Angel was upset today, so I stayed with her."

"Why was she upset?"

He bristled at the question, defensive again. "She gets scared when she's here without me."

"Who's she scared of?"

"Nobody!" he snapped, then caught himself. "I mean, she gets homesick. She's still just a kid, and she misses her family."

They heard a commotion in the hallway, and then the door opened. A woman came in carrying a grubby toddler in a threadbare gown on her hip. Frank figured she was probably in her forties, although she looked older. Life had worn her out, and everything about her looked faded—her hair, her eyes, her skin, her dress. She stopped in her tracks when she saw Frank sitting at her kitchen table, and he watched the various emotions play across her face. She feared him because he was with the police and could only bring trouble to her family, but she also hated him for having such power.

"What's he doing here?" she asked the boy.

"Asking me questions about Angel," he told her.

"Wasting his time," she sniffed, shifting the baby she carried to her other hip. He stared at Frank with vacant eyes. His nose was running. "You want to know who killed her, you should be asking her family. They was the ones who was mad."

"What were they mad about?" Frank asked.

"Because she married my boy," Mrs. O'Neal said in a

tone that said she thought Frank stupid for not having figured that out himself. "You ask me, they shoulda been happy a white boy would have her. Not many would."

"How about you, Mrs. O'Neal?" Frank asked casually. "Were you happy your boy married her?"

She gave him a hateful look. "He's too young to be getting a wife. Can't even keep himself, and here he is, bringing home this girl we never even saw before."

"And a Chinese girl at that," Frank remarked. "That must've been a shock."

"I'll tell you it was!" Mrs. O'Neal said, warming to the subject. "I didn't even know he knew any Chinese, much less one he wanted to marry." She glared at Quinn, who dropped his gaze. "I hope you're happy now," she scolded. "I told you that girl'd be nothing but trouble! Always thought she was too good for us and crying all the time."

"You son said she was homesick," Frank said.

"Homesick? I guess she was. Nothing we had was good enough for her, and do you think she'd turn her hand to help out? Not a bit of it! Expected us to wait on her, she did."

"That's not true," the boy protested. "She'd help when you told her what to do!"

His mother made a rude noise. "You mean when I *taught* her what to do! I don't know how that girl got to be as old as she was. Didn't hardly know how to feed herself when she come here."

"Ma!"

"It's the God's truth. Lazy and worthless, like the rest of them Chinamen."

"Where were you when Angel was killed, Mrs. O'Neal?" Frank asked mildly.

She looked at him in surprise, as if she'd forgotten he was

there for a moment. Then her face turned an unbecoming shade of purple. "I was right here, taking care of Baby."

"Anybody else with you?"

"No, why should there be?" she asked belligerently, although he could see the fear in her eyes. She knew Frank could arrest her or anyone in her family and charge them with murder and make it stick.

"No reason," Frank said. "I was just wondering where Quinn was."

"Oh, he was here, too," she said too quickly. "I forgot about that."

"No, I wasn't," the boy said.

"Shut up!" his mother warned him. "Of course you was. You was here with me when they come to tell us she was dead in the yard."

So neither of them had an alibi, Frank noted. "When was the last time you saw Angel?"

The two exchanged a look, but Frank couldn't read their expressions. "I don't remember," Mrs. O'Neal claimed.

"I took her downstairs to buy her something to eat around noontime," Quinn said. "From a street vendor."

"What did you do after that?"

Quinn looked a little sheepish. "We sort of . . . We had a little argument. I went for a walk to cool off."

Frank looked at Mrs. O'Neal. "Did she come back up here?"

Mrs. O'Neal didn't look happy. "I guess she did, for a while. Next thing I know, she's gone again, though."

"What time was it?"

"How should I know?" Mrs. O'Neal asked. "I was working."

"Did she go off with Keely?" Frank asked, remembering what Quinn had said about the two girls.

The question seemed to startle Mrs. O'Neal. "No, she . . . Keely wasn't . . . Angel went off by herself."

"Why did she go outside again?" Frank asked.

The two of them exchanged another look. The boy had realized he needed to get his story straight with his mother's or else keep his mouth shut. He chose silence.

"Who knows?" she said. "She was a strange girl, always going off by herself. Hiding," she decided, "so nobody'd ask her to do anything."

"That ain't true!" the boy claimed, but his mother silenced him with a sharp look, and this time he took the hint.

The door to the flat still stood open, and a younger woman came in, looking bewildered. She was dressed for the street in a ratty hat and cape. Her hair was untidy, as if she'd just stuck a few pins in it this morning without bothering with a comb or brush. "They said Angel's dead," she said before she noticed Frank. When she saw him, she made a small sound of distressed surprise.

"She got herself killed," Mrs. O'Neal said. "Outside in the yard. Where've you been, and where's the goods?"

"They didn't have any work for us," she replied angrily.

"What do you mean, no work?" Mrs. O'Neal demanded in alarm.

"They said they'd have some tomorrow. The cloth didn't come in yet."

"I knew I should've gone myself," Mrs. O'Neal moaned. "You can't believe them. They gave the work to somebody who'll do it cheaper."

"But they said they didn't have any cloth!" she protested.

"You stupid bitch!" Mrs. O'Neal cried, raising her free hand to strike her, but the girl dodged out of the way.

Quinn jumped to his feet to intervene, grabbing his mother's arm and yelling, "Ma!"

"You must be Iris," Frank said, surprising all of them.

Iris looked at him with renewed terror. "That's right." She kept glancing over at Mrs. O'Neal and back again to Frank, as if trying to judge which was the bigger threat.

"What did you think of Angel?"

"Why does that matter now?" she asked in dismay.

"I don't know that it does, but tell me anyway."

She gave the matter a few seconds of consideration. "She was all right, I guess," she allowed. "Didn't have much to say for herself. You'd hardly even know she was here except . . ." She caught herself, glancing over at Mrs. O'Neal again.

"Except what?" Frank prodded.

He watched as Iris weighed her options. Refuse to answer and risk his wrath or answer and risk Mrs. O'Neal's. After a few seconds, a slow, cunning smile creased her plain face. "Except when Quinn was trying to poke her. Then she'd scream like a banshee. Didn't like it much, I guess," she added with a sneer at her brother-in-law.

Quinn cursed and lunged to his feet. He would've come across the table at her if Frank hadn't clapped a hand on his shoulder and shoved him back down in the chair. "Now, now, nothing to get riled up about," he cautioned.

Quinn called her a few choice names, but she just grinned back at him.

"Mrs. O'Neal," Frank said, "where were your other children today?"

"I already told you," Quinn reminded him indignantly,

but Frank silenced him with a pinch to a particular spot on his shoulder that he knew would cause excruciating pain. It did, and Quinn's howl made the women flinch.

When he was quiet again, Frank said, "Your other children, Mrs. O'Neal?"

She swallowed. "I don't know," she claimed. "The boys, they usually go out in the morning looking for work. Nobody's offering steady work, so they got to do whatever they can find."

"When did they leave this morning?"

"I don't know. Early."

"What about your daughter?"

"She's, uh . . . she's in school."

"She's young then," Frank guessed.

"Fifteen," she admitted reluctantly.

Same age as Angel, Frank remembered. Few girls in this neighborhood were still in school at fifteen, though. She'd be helping out with the piecework unless she was lucky enough to get a job at a factory. What was her mother hiding?

Frank turned to the younger woman. "When did you see Angel last?"

Iris frowned. "I don't know. I didn't pay attention. She was here when we all woke up this morning. After that, I don't remember."

"Where were you?"

"When do you mean?"

Frank realized he didn't know exactly when Angel had died, so he said, "Tell me everything you did today."

She glanced at her mother-in-law, but Mrs. O'Neal offered nothing. "We all got up, like I said. I ate a roll for breakfast, then tied up all the vests to take to the Sweater," she said, using a slang term for the man who provided the raw materials for their piecework. "Then I took them over to Broome Street and delivered them."

"At least tell me you got paid!" Mrs. O'Neal interrupted. Iris refused to meet her eye.

"Holy Mary," Mrs. O'Neal lamented. "You let them have the goods and didn't get any money at all!"

"I got some!" Iris defended herself. "He said they weren't as good as usual, though, so he gave me a dollar less."

"Stupid cow!" Mrs. O'Neal screeched. The child in her arms puckered up his face and began to cry, and so did his mother.

Frank sighed. "I'll be back later to talk to the rest of the family," he shouted above the din and made his way to the door.

The two women were screaming at each other, so no one really noticed his departure.

Once outside, Frank consulted his notebook, where he'd jotted down Mrs. Lee's address earlier, before Sarah had arrived and things got out of hand. With a sigh, he headed over to Chinatown.

He found the building a block off Mott Street. Mott was the heart of Chinatown, where all the businesses that catered to the Celestials—as the Chinese were called—were located. Real estate there was too valuable for living space. Gambling houses and opium dens mingled with dry goods stores and laundries, all of them doing a brisk business and making their owners rich. The building where the Lee family lived contrasted sharply with the one he'd just left. It was new and well kept, the hallways and stairwells neatly swept. Chinatown as a whole was almost eerily clean, even the streets, as if it didn't really belong to the rest of the city. Mrs. Lee answered his knock.

Her expression lightened the instant she recognized Frank. "Did you find out anything yet?"

"No, I'm sorry, I haven't," he said. "I need to ask you and your family some questions, though. Do you mind if I come in?"

"No, not at all," she said, stepping aside so he could enter. "We'll do anything we can to help."

Frank doubted that she spoke for her husband with that promise, but he let it pass. He looked around the Lee flat as he had done at the O'Neals', and what he saw here couldn't have been more different. The furniture was fairly new and of high quality. They had carpets on the floor, draperies on the windows, and wallpaper on the walls. Paintings hung on long wires from the picture molding, and the bric-a-brac that was so fashionable was present in abundance, cluttering tabletops all around the room.

"Please, sit down," Mrs. Lee said, indicating the over-stuffed sofa.

Frank took the offered seat gratefully, and also accepted a cup of coffee. Minnie Lee was an interesting lady, Frank decided after watching her for a few minutes as she served him. She must have been a typical Irish girl once, big boned and hearty. Not blessed with beauty, she would have been hard pressed to find a hardworking white man to marry her. Men with something to offer had their pick, and they invariably picked the pretty ones. The rest of the men, the worthless ones, would use whatever charm they possessed to find a woman who'd be willing to slave for them and bear their children and keep them in beer money by doing piecework eighteen hours a day in a suffocating tenement flat. That was the life Mrs. O'Neal had chosen. Minnie Lee had taken a different path.

Choosing to marry outside her race had probably cost her some friends and maybe earned her the disapproval of her family, if she had any to disapprove. In exchange, she lived in a nice house and wore good clothes and never had to worry about her children starving.

"What do you want to ask me, Mr. Malloy?" she asked when Frank had his coffee and she was seated on the sofa opposite him.

"I need to know a little more about Angel," he began as gently as he could. "So I'll know who might have wanted to harm her."

He watched the pain shudder through her, but she raised her chin in silent defiance against it. Only her red-rimmed eyes betrayed the anguish she'd endured today. "I'll tell you what I can. I thought I knew her better than anyone, but I never would've guessed she'd run off like she did."

"What do you know about Quinn O'Neal?"

"Not much. I'd never heard of him until a week or so ago. Mrs. Brandt got the idea to question Angel's friends," she reminded him. "We'd already talked to them, and they said they didn't know where she was, but Mrs. Brandt made them admit the truth."

Frank nodded politely, not betraying his inner rage. If Sarah was an expert detective, he had no one but himself to blame, so the rage was at himself. At least he could take comfort in knowing she wasn't going to be involved in this case anymore.

"What did they tell you exactly?"

She took a deep breath, as if fortifying herself to dredge up the painful memories. "They said she'd been sneaking out to meet this boy . . . Well, I suppose he's a man, isn't he? Anyway, she'd tell me she was going to visit her friends— they live upstairs—and then she'd climb down the fire escape and go to him. I don't know how long she'd been seeing him, but it was several months, I guess."

"Why do you think Angel ran off with him when she did?"

He saw the slight tightening of her lips and knew she was going to lie. "Children do foolish things when they think they're in love. Angel was innocent and didn't know any better. We never warned her about men like this O'Neal. Why should we? She never should've even met him."

"He said they ran away because you were going to force Angel to marry an old Chinese man," Frank said.

Her whole body stiffened and the color drained from her cheeks. She hated him for this, for making her remember that she might have driven her child away. For a second he thought she might even deny it. Lots of mothers would have. "We only wanted the best for Angel," she said, her voice as thin as paper. "Mr. Wong isn't old at all, not even forty. He's also very successful. He would have made a good husband. Better than that good-for-nothing O'Neal!"

Frank thought that was probably true. "How did Wong react when he found out the girl had run away with another man?"

She swallowed. "He was . . . upset, of course. He . . . You can't blame him."

"No," Frank agreed. "If I was him, I'd be pretty mad."

"I . . . I didn't talk to him myself," she hedged. "You'll have to ask Mr. Lee."

"What about the people in the neighborhood? I guess Angel made this Mr. Wong a laughingstock, didn't she?"

She stared back at him, her silence telling him far more than words. Wong would have been totally humiliated, and probably mad enough to strangle the girl. He'd have to talk to Wong. And to Charlie Lee, too.

"I understand that Mr. Lee went to Angel and asked her to come home with him," Frank said.

She blinked at the change of subject. "Yes, he did, as soon as we found out where she was living. He was that mad at her, but we couldn't leave her in that awful place with those people. What would become of her?"

Frank nodded his understanding. "Why do you think she refused to go with him?"

"I don't know!" she cried, her composure cracking a bit as she realized Angel might still be alive if she had. "She said she loved her husband and all that foolishness, like young girls do when they don't know any better. She said she'd never go home again."

"I guess that made your husband even madder."

She looked at him for a long moment, judging his meaning. She didn't like it one bit. "He would never hurt her, Mr. Malloy. He never raised a hand to her in her whole life!"

"He was going to marry her off against her will to somebody she didn't like," he reminded her.

"That would've been better than what she got, now wouldn't it?" she countered.

Before Frank could reply, they heard footsteps outside and then the front door banged open. Charlie Lee came through it, half carrying, half dragging a Chinese man with him.

"He was in opium den," Lee said in disgust, apparently to his wife.

He threw the fellow onto the floor, and when he rolled over onto his back with a groan, Frank got a good look at him. It was Charlie's son, Harry Lee.

6

THE BOY SEEMED UNAWARE OF WHAT WAS HAPPENING around him. He stared at nothing, his face set in a slight smile, as his mother howled in renewed anguish, knelt beside him, and tried to rouse him. Frank was amazed at the transformation in Harry. When he'd come to the scene of his sister's death, he'd been dressed as a white man and could have passed unnoticed anywhere in the city. Now he wore a blue silk blouse and baggy black pants with embroidered, thick-soled slippers and white socks. Like a uniform identified a soldier, these clothes identified a Chinaman.

Charlie Lee finally noticed Frank, who had risen to his feet. "Why you here?" he demanded.

Mrs. Lee looked up from her vain attempt to slap Harry back to consciousness. "He came to ask some questions about Angel," she said. "He's trying to find out who killed her."

"Does not matter," Lee informed him. "She still dead. I no pay!"

"I'm not looking for a reward," Frank told him testily. He didn't have to take abuse from a Chinaman, of all people. "I just want to find out who killed your daughter."

"Why?" he challenged. "No punish for man who kill Chinee girl."

Frank had to admit he had a point. "I'll make sure her killer is punished," he tried.

His promise earned him a disgusted glare. Charlie Lee straightened his well-made suit jacket and turned back to his wife and son.

"He's barely breathing," Mrs. Lee said in alarm. "He wasn't gone very long. How could he have smoked enough to make him unconscious?"

Frank vaguely registered Mrs. Lee's unusual knowledge of opium's effects.

"He eat, not smoke," his father reported in disgust.

"He ate too much, then," she cried. "He's poisoned himself! What can we do?"

Lee muttered something in Chinese and bolted from the room, presumably to get some help.

"Noooo!" Mrs. Lee was wailing in despair as Frank stood by, helpless.

He'd seen plenty of people die from taking too many drugs, but he'd never been called upon to save one. In most cases, the poor wretches were better off dead anyway. This case was different, though. Harry Lee shouldn't die, not on the same day his sister was murdered. For one single second, he found himself wishing . . .

"What's going on?" a familiar voice demanded from the doorway.

Charlie Lee had left the door hanging open, and Frank was somehow not at all surprised to see Sarah Brandt coming through it. His reluctant wish had come true.

"Harry's eaten opium," his mother informed her. "I can't wake him up!"

Sarah looked down at the boy and instantly realized he was dangerously ill. His skin was bluish, and when she touched his cheek, she found it clammy. His breath was shallow and slow. "I'll need to get my bag," she said.

"Where is it?" a familiar voice asked.

She looked up in surprise. "Malloy! What are you doing here?"

"Investigating a murder," he said in that tone she knew too well. "The question is, what are *you* doing here when you were supposed to go home."

"I walked Mrs. Lee home, and then stopped in to see the other Mrs. Lee, my patient, the one who had the baby," she explained defensively. "We heard all the commotion so I came up to . . . Well, it doesn't matter now. My bag is downstairs in the other Mrs. Lee's flat. Will you get it for me?"

His look told her he'd have more to say to her later, but he moved quickly to do her bidding.

Sarah turned back to the boy. "Help me get him on his feet. We have to try to keep him awake. Do you have any coffee made?"

The next hour was a blur as Sarah found the emetic in her medical bag and forced it down Harry's throat. To her great relief, they were able to get him to vomit up a good bit of the opium he'd eaten. Then they poured coffee down his throat, and between the three of them, they walked him around the room to keep him as awake as possible as the effects of the drug wore off.

Mr. Lee returned to the flat at some point with a small Chinese man. The two of them shouted at each other in Chinese, gesturing wildly, and then Mr. Lee told his wife what to do. Sarah surmised that he was from the establishment where Harry had obtained his opium. He'd brought along some herbs, but since they were to induce vomiting, Sarah informed him they weren't needed. The man eventually confirmed that Sarah was already doing everything that needed to be done, and then he left.

When he was gone, Mrs. Lee turned on her husband. "What was Harry doing in that place? He knows better!"

"Ask Harry," was her husband's bitter suggestion. Then he took Sarah's place supporting his son as they continued to walk him around the room.

The sun had long set by the time Harry was lucid enough to convince Sarah the danger had passed. Sitting slumped in a chair while his attendants glared at him wearily, he frowned up at them in confusion. "Am I in hell?"

His mother cuffed him across the head. "Is that any way to talk?" she demanded. "You *would* be in hell if it wasn't for Mrs. Brandt here, who saved your life, you ungrateful brat!"

Harry stared at Sarah for a long moment, as if searching his memory in vain to identify her.

"What were you thinking!" his mother asked, her voice cracking with grief now that the crisis had passed. "You could've killed yourself! It's not bad enough I lost your sister today!"

His young face crumpled as the memory came rushing back. "Angel," he murmured, and then he smiled bitterly. "She's dead," he remembered. "She's the lucky one."

His mother gasped in horror, and his father made a strangled sound in his throat. Sarah gasped herself, but she quickly said, "He's still not himself. It's the drug." She didn't know if that was true or not, but she had to soften his outrageous statement somehow.

Minnie looked at her, desperate to believe her. "Yes, of course it is," she agreed. "The drug. He don't know what he's saying, Charlie."

Mr. Lee simply stared at his son, his expression unreadable.

"We should be going, Mrs. Brandt," Malloy said. "You've done all you can here."

Sarah knew he was right. More things would be said, and she and Malloy shouldn't be here to hear them. She gave Minnie some final instructions for Harry's care, and then she allowed Malloy to bundle her off into the night.

When they reached the street, she gratefully inhaled the cool evening air, glad to have escaped the suffocating atmosphere of the Lees' flat. Every bone in her body ached from helping to haul Harry around his parents' flat, and she wasn't sure she'd make it home if she had to walk.

"Do you think we can find a cab?" she asked.

"I'll find one," he said with amazing confidence, taking her arm and heading for the nearest corner.

Sure enough, he did find one, and his sigh of relief echoed hers as they settled into it for the long ride to Bank Street.

"How did you know what to do for the boy?" he asked when the cab had lurched into motion.

"I was a nurse before I was a midwife, Malloy," she reminded him wryly. "I know how to do a lot of things besides deliver babies."

He made a disgusted noise but refrained from expressing his disapproval. He knew it wouldn't make any difference.

"Do you have any idea who killed Angel yet?" she asked after a moment.

"No. She managed to irritate a lot of people, though, so I'll have a lot of suspects to choose from."

"Who did she irritate? Besides her parents, I mean."

"The man her father wanted her to marry, for one. I guess he's pretty mad that people are laughing at him. Then there's the whole O'Neal family. They thought she was sneaky and lazy and above herself."

"She wasn't!" Sarah protested.

"Maybe not, but that's what they thought."

"She was just homesick and frightened!" Sarah insisted. "And who wouldn't be in that situation?"

"Yeah, it must've been a shock to go from that place where she lived to the O'Neals'," he agreed. "The women do piecework all day, and they'd expect her to help, to earn her keep. I guess she and her new husband didn't have any privacy for their honeymoon, either," he added meaningfully.

"Oh, dear." Sarah knew there were no secrets in a tenement flat. How awful to find herself sleeping with a man who wanted to enjoy his new wife while all his relatives were only a few feet away, witnessing everything. Not at all the romantic adventure she must have envisioned. "No wonder she was unhappy."

"Why didn't she go home with her parents, then?" he asked.

Sarah considered, trying to remember how it felt to be fifteen. "Pride, maybe. She didn't want to admit she'd made a mistake. Or maybe she was afraid of what they'd do to her."

"Punish her, you mean?"

"That, or maybe she thought they'd still marry her off to

the old man. Would she have thought that would be worse than what she had to endure at the O'Neals'?"

"Maybe. Young girls can be really stupid," he said.

"Young boys, too," she reminded him. "Why do you suppose Harry ate too much opium?"

"He probably didn't know it was too much," he said.

"But why take any at all? Do you suppose he's a regular user?"

"His parents didn't think so," he reminded her, "and I expect somebody would tell an important man like Lee if his son was a hophead."

"So on the day his sister is found dead, he goes to an opium den for the first time and swallows enough opium to kill him," Sarah mused. "Was he that upset over her death?"

"I don't know," Malloy said, "but I'll find out."

"Maybe he killed her," Sarah said. "Maybe he couldn't stand the guilt, so he decided to kill himself."

"*Sarah,*" Malloy said sharply, the warning thick in his voice.

She couldn't see his face in the shadowed interior of the cab, but she knew what his expression would be. She'd seen it a hundred times. "I'm not going to get involved," she insisted. "I promised!"

"Yeah, and then you show up at the Lees' flat when their boy is sick after you swore you were going straight home."

"I don't think I said *straight* home," she argued. "I was only going to check on Cora and the baby first. There's no harm in that. I didn't know the boy was going to take opium!"

He didn't reply. He didn't say a word. She wanted to punch him.

"It's a good thing I was there, in any case," she pointed out. "He might have died."

"The Chinaman that Lee brought knew what to do, too," he reminded her.

Sarah sighed. She knew he was right. She really shouldn't be involving herself in murder investigations. She'd put herself in danger more than once in the past. Things had been different when she only had herself to think of, but now she had a child. Catherine needed her. "I'm going home now," she reminded him. "And I'm not going to do another thing in regard to Angel's murder. I'm just going to wait for you to show up on my doorstep one morning to tell me that you've solved the case. Is that what you want to hear?"

"Yes," he sighed. "But I'd also like for you to mean it."

Sarah arrived home in time to put Catherine to bed. The child clung to her and didn't seem to want to let go when Sarah kissed her good night. She remembered how upset both Catherine and Maeve had been when they heard about Angel's death earlier that day.

"Were you frightened when you heard about the girl who died?" Sarah asked.

Catherine nodded uncertainly, as if she didn't want to admit it but wanted Sarah to know, too.

"I'm sorry you had to hear about her, but you don't have to be scared. Nothing like that can happen to you and Maeve. You're safe here."

Catherine's soft brown eyes were wide and solemn. She shook her head and pointed at Sarah, jabbing her finger into Sarah's chest several times to make her understand her real fear.

"Me?" Sarah asked in surprise. "You're afraid something will happen to me?"

Catherine nodded vigorously at that.

Tears sprang to Sarah's eyes, and she hugged the child tightly to her breast. How she wished she could promise that nothing would ever happen to her, that she would be there for Catherine forever. No one could make such a promise, though, as well she knew. She'd seen too many people die tragically and well before their time—Tom and her sister Maggie and poor Angel and all those whose other deaths she'd helped Malloy investigate.

Still, she could promise one thing. "I'll be careful, sweetheart," she whispered into Catherine's soft hair. "I want to watch you grow up into a beautiful young woman."

And if that meant she wouldn't help Malloy with any more cases, then it was a small price to pay.

When Sarah finally released her, Catherine reached up with one small finger and wiped a tear from Sarah's cheek. Sarah smiled reassuringly. "I love you," she said.

Catherine wouldn't let go of Sarah's hand, so she sat beside her until the child was, at long last, fast asleep. Then she made her way downstairs to find Maeve sitting at the kitchen table waiting for her.

"That girl," she asked when Sarah took a seat at the table opposite her. "How did she die?"

"Someone strangled her," Sarah said. She wouldn't have been so blunt with any other girl Maeve's age, but she knew Maeve wouldn't want her to sugarcoat the truth. She'd already seen far more of the ugly side of life than Sarah ever would.

"Do they know who did it?"

Sarah shook her head. "Not yet. It seems a lot of people were . . . unhappy with her."

"Was it a man? That made her run off, I mean."

"Oh, yes, you were right about that. She eloped."

"He *married* her?" Maeve marveled.

"I know, I was surprised, too," Sarah admitted. "They were in love. She'd been sneaking out to meet him for months."

"He didn't have to marry her, though," Maeve said. "Even if she was going to live with him. But he did. That's really something."

Plainly, Maeve still had some romantic notions left, in spite of her hard life.

"Her mother said she didn't seem very happy, though," Sarah said. "Both her parents tried to convince her to come back home with them."

"Why would she want to do that if she was married?"

Like most girls her age, Maeve thought marriage would be the solution to every problem and the guarantee of a happy life. "Her father was rich," Sarah explained, exaggerating for Maeve's sake. To her, anyone who lived as the Lee family did would be rich beyond her wildest dreams. "Her new husband wasn't."

"But she was in love," Maeve argued. "And she was married!"

"Before you decide to run off and get married," Sarah warned, "you should be sure that you'll be better off than you are now."

"But—"

"Just being married won't make you happy, Maeve. It also won't guarantee that you'll be fed and clothed and have a decent place to live. When you choose a husband, make sure he's got more to recommend him than a handsome face."

Maeve thought this over for a moment. Then she said, "Your family was rich, and your husband wasn't."

Oh, dear, how to get out of that one? Sarah thought, but

she smiled. "My husband wasn't as rich as my family, but he wasn't poor, either. He supported me, and he bought me this house. We never went hungry or had to worry about paying the rent."

"The dead girl, she would've had to worry about that, I guess."

"Her new husband didn't have a regular job. They were living in a tenement with his family. I think there were six or seven people living there with them. They didn't even have a room to themselves."

"Oh," Maeve said. Sarah had never asked, but she imagined that Maeve had lived much like that before she'd been put out to make her own way in the world.

"Angel must have had a hard time adjusting to her new life, but she still wouldn't leave her husband and go back home with her parents."

"She was in love," Maeve said confidently.

"Or too proud to admit she'd made a terrible mistake," Sarah suggested.

"Did he kill her . . . her husband, I mean?"

"I don't know, but he seemed very sad that she was dead," Sarah said.

"I hope he didn't," Maeve said fervently. "For him to have killed her, the one she loved and gave up everything for, that would be too awful, wouldn't it?"

"Yes," Sarah agreed. "It would, indeed."

FRANK MADE AN EARLY VISIT TO THE O'NEALS THE NEXT morning. He wanted to catch the rest of them at home and find out what they had to say for themselves. He knew he wouldn't get far questioning them with their mother there, and he didn't want them to hear what answers the others gave, so he'd brought along a couple of beat cops and a Black Maria in which to cart the boys away.

He had to pound on the door several times before somebody finally roused and came to open it. He could hear lots of cursing and complaining in the background, and then the baby started to howl.

"What do you want?" It was Iris, the surviving daughter-in-law, who peered out blearily. "It's the middle of the night!"

Frank didn't bother to reply. He pushed the door open, forcing her to stumble backward. Her plain face registered surprise in the instant before she backed into the mound of someone sleeping on the floor and fell over him, earning a stream of renewed curses.

"What's this now?" Mrs. O'Neal demanded, emerging from a back room in a filthy wrapper, with her hair sticking up six ways from Sunday.

"Just wanted to have a word with your other sons," Frank explained cheerfully. He gave the nearest pile of rags a less-than-gentle nudge with his foot, jarring loose another stream of profanity. "Get this one on his feet, boys," he instructed the men he'd brought with him.

They obliged, and by the time they'd gotten the first O'Neal up, the two others had come stumbling over to see what the trouble was.

"Which ones do you want?" one of the officers asked.

"All of them," Frank said.

"What are you doing?" Mrs. O'Neal screeched, slapping ineffectually at the officers, who were starting to march her sons out into the hall. Luckily, they slept in most of their clothes, so the cops wouldn't need to wait for them to dress. "Where're you taking them?"

"Down to Police Headquarters," Frank explained.

"Iris, get my coat!" yelled one of them. Iris scrambled to do his bidding, and to gather up other assorted articles of clothing the two other men deemed necessary for a trip to Police Headquarters.

"You can't lock them up!" Mrs. O'Neal protested. "They didn't do nothing!"

"Then I won't lock them up," Frank said agreeably.

"If all you want is to ask questions, do it here!" she pleaded.

Frank ignored her. "Where's your daughter?" he asked instead.

She sobered instantly. "What do you want with her?"

"I've got some questions for her, too. Is she here?"

"She's already gone off to school," the old woman lied. It was way too early for that.

"I'll be back for her, then," Frank said, earning an evil scowl.

By now the O'Neal brothers were halfway down the first flight of stairs, being hurried along by the officers and their locust clubs. Frank followed, as Mrs. O'Neal hurled her invectives after him.

Down at Headquarters, Frank had the brothers put in separate interrogation rooms. The building was relatively quiet at this hour. The drunks brought in the night before were sleeping it off in the holding cells in the basement, along with any real criminals who had been caught. Most of the mischief perpetrated in the city had ended with the rising of the sun, though, and anyone who had escaped the long arm of the law that night was now tucked away for a few hours of rest before beginning the relentless breaking of the law again at sunset.

Frank took some time to eat a bite of breakfast, purchased from a street vendor outside. This also gave the O'Neal boys time to think about their helpless position and the possibility that Frank might charge one of them with Angel Lee's murder, even if he wasn't guilty. It wouldn't be the first time an innocent man had been charged. Innocent men even got executed sometimes. Mistakes happened, especially when the police didn't particularly care if the right person got punished. Lucky for the O'Neal boys, Frank did care. He wasn't going to tell them that, though. A little fear would make them more cooperative.

"Which one are you?" Frank asked as he sat down at the table opposite the scowling man. The interrogation rooms were small and dirty and very grim. Furnished with a battered table and some rickety chairs and decorated with a few splatters of dried blood on the walls, they were intended to put the suspect in the proper frame of mind to be interrogated.

"Donald," the man said belligerently. "Donald O'Neal." He looked a lot like Quinn, only older and fleshier. He'd spent those extra years of life drinking more than was good for him, Frank guessed. He was still handsome, though, the way worthless men who'd learned to get by on their charm often were. His mother would've spoiled him.

"You the oldest?"

"That's right."

"Is Iris your wife?"

"What if she is?"

Frank glanced over at the officer he'd brought along to keep order and gave him a silent signal. He strolled over and gave Donald O'Neal a smack on the head.

"Hey!"

"Mind your manners, Donald," Frank warned him. "If you answer my questions, you'll be home before you know it."

He didn't look as if he believed Frank, but he said, "Yeah, Iris is my wife."

"How long you been married?"

He shrugged one shoulder. "A year or so, I guess."

"What do you do for a living, Donald?"

Donald took offense at that. "What the hell does that—" he started, but caught himself when the officer took a step forward with his locust club raised. "I get work when I can," he quickly corrected himself.

"Doing what?"

Donald swallowed, glancing at the officer again. "Whatever I can find. I ain't particular."

"What were you doing yesterday?"

"Yesterday?" He frowned.

"Yeah, yesterday. You can't have forgotten already, Donald," Frank chided. "What 'not particular' work did you do yesterday?"

"I . . . uh . . . I didn't get any work yesterday," he admitted reluctantly.

"What did you do all day then?"

Donald licked his lips, as if he were thinking how good a beer might taste just now. "I . . . uh, I spent most of the day at a bar."

"What bar was that?"

"Well, not a bar exactly. It . . . it's in the basement of the building next to ours."

"A stale beer dive?" Frank inquired, naming the lowest type of drinking establishment in the city.

"No, nothing like that!" Donald exclaimed. He wasn't much, but he had a little pride. He didn't want to be identified as someone destitute enough to drink the stale beer thrown out by the reputable bars, doctored with chemicals to induce an artificial head, and sold for pennies in the filthy cellar rooms of abandoned buildings. "This fellow, he runs a place in his flat."

"I guess you can play some games of chance there, too," Frank said.

"Just a friendly game," Donald assured him hastily. "I can't afford high stakes."

"Were you there all day?"

"I got there around noon. I did look for work that morning," he defended himself. "Didn't find any, though, so I went there."

"How long did you stay?"

He tried to remember. "I don't know. Late. Past supper anyway. When I got home, Ma told me about Angel. Hell of a thing."

"What did you think of her?"

The question surprised him. "Angel? I didn't think nothing of her."

"Come on, Donald," Frank coaxed. "She was a pretty little thing. You must've thought about her a little."

"She was a damn Chinaman," he reminded Frank with disgust.

Frank raised his eyebrows. "I guess you weren't too happy your brother married her, then."

"You're right about that. I could see why he'd want her, I guess. She was pretty, like you said, but he never had to marry her to get what he wanted! That was a damn fool thing to do, and I told him, too. She wasn't even knocked up!"

"Is that why you married Iris?" Frank asked mildly.

Donald gave him a look that would've curdled milk, and

his face reddened dangerously, but he didn't reply. Always the gentleman, Frank thought with some disgust of his own.

"What did the rest of the family think about Angel?"

"Same as me. Nobody could figure why he married her. Then he brings her home, and she won't work. Doesn't even know how to. All she does is sit and cry all day and all night. Especially at night."

"Why was she crying?"

"Damned if I know! Homesick, maybe. She was scared of everything, too. Got all hysterical when she saw a rat in the alley, like she'd never seen one before! Thought she was better'n us, too. She didn't say much, but you could tell the way she'd stick her nose up in the air about everything."

"Who do you think killed her?"

He obviously hadn't expected to be asked that question, and he gave it a few moments' thought. "If I had to guess, I'd say her family. They was real mad that she run off with Quinn. Tried to get her to go back home, but she wouldn't. Her ma, she just cried, but her old man . . ." Donald shook his head.

"What about her father?"

"Them Chinamen, you can't never tell what they're thinking, but with him . . . Well, you could see he was mad enough to do murder when she wouldn't go with him. If it was me, I would've told him to take her, but Quinn, he's got more pride than brains. He told the Chinaman that if he wanted to take her, he'd have to fight all three of us. He never asked me and Rooney if we was willing to fight, but I guess the Chinaman didn't want to take a chance."

Frank studied Donald O'Neal for a few seconds. Then he asked, "Do you have friends at that bar where you say you were yesterday?"

"Yeah, of course I do!" he replied, affronted.

"They'll confirm that you were there, I suppose?"

He wasn't quite so sure of that. "I can't promise what they'll say, but I was there, I swear to God. They should remember."

One day was like another to a drunk, as Frank had learned in his years on the force. "We'll find out if they do."

Frank got up and started for the door.

"Can I go home now?" Donald asked hopefully.

Frank pretended to consider the request. "I think we'll wait until we've had a chance to talk to your friends at the bar."

"What for?" he demanded in outrage. "I never killed Angel! Why would I?"

But Frank was already in the hallway. The officer locked the door behind them, muffling the sounds of his shouted protests. Next Frank chose the second brother, Rooney.

Rooney was asleep, his head resting on his folded arms on the table top. Frank kicked the chair out from under him, sending him sprawling on the floor. His howl of outrage died in his throat when he looked up and saw Frank and the officer standing over him.

"Why'd you do that for?" he whined, picking himself up and rubbing his elbow gingerly.

"Have a seat, Rooney," Frank offered, pointing to the overturned chair.

He righted it and sat down as instructed, still watching Frank warily, like a dog who had been kicked too many times. Frank sat down opposite him at the table and studied him for a long minute.

He was also older than Quinn. Frank's experience told him that the second son often took the brunt of abuse in the family.

The oldest child was prized, and the youngest spoiled, but the middle child enjoyed no privileged attentions.

"So tell me, Rooney, what did you think about your brother bringing home a Chinese girl?"

He frowned, as if he thought Frank was trying to trick him with such an easy question. "I didn't care one way or the other," he said after a few seconds, "and I didn't kill her, if that's what you're thinking."

"Is that so?" Frank asked, feigning interest. "Who do you think did, then?"

"I don't *think* nothing about it. I *know*. I know exactly who killed her."

7

SARAH WOKE UP EARLY THE NEXT MORNING, SO SHE WAS up and dressed when Mrs. Ellsworth arrived. The older woman had been to the market early that morning and had a lovely piece of beef she was going to show the girls how to roast in a pot so that it was melt-in-your-mouth tender.

"I certainly hope I'm here to enjoy it this evening," Sarah said, admiring the cut of meat.

"If you aren't, we'll save you some, won't we?" Mrs. Ellsworth asked the girls.

Catherine nodded fervently, and Maeve just grinned.

"You girls go off and play for a while and let Mrs. Brandt and me visit a bit," Mrs. Ellsworth said. "We don't have to start cooking the roast just yet."

When they were alone, Sarah poured them each some coffee, and they sat down at the kitchen table.

"I guess you're wondering about the girl who was killed," Sarah said.

"I am, of course. Maeve told me about it when I stopped by to check on the girls yesterday. She was upset. I'd never seen her so emotional about any of the murders you've investigated."

"The girl was her age," Sarah said. "In fact, I'd discussed Angel—her name was Angel—with Maeve several weeks ago. She'd run away from home, and Maeve is the one who suggested she might have run off with a man and that I should question her friends more closely because they'd surely know the real story."

Mrs. Ellsworth's eyebrows rose. "She suggested that *you* question them?" she asked skeptically.

Sarah mentally pinched herself. "No," she admitted sheepishly. "She suggested *someone* question them. She was right, too. Angel had eloped with a man she'd been seeing secretly."

"That's it then," Mrs. Ellsworth said. "When this Angel was killed, Maeve felt a kind of kinship with her."

"It may have been a little more than that. Maeve was asking me questions about her last night. Maeve seems to think that when a girl gets married, all her problems are over, and she lives happily ever after."

"What would make her think that?" Mrs. Ellsworth scoffed.

"I have no idea," Sarah replied with some amusement. "She must have seen unhappy marriages in her lifetime. Still, you know how romantic girls can be. They think Prince Charming is going to make their lives perfect."

"I hope you explained the truth to her."

"I tried, but it's impossible to know if I succeeded or not.

I hope I at least made her think a bit. But she's still upset about Angel's death. Catherine is, too."

"Oh, dear!"

"Yes, she's afraid something will happen to me, though."

Mrs. Ellsworth stared at her solemnly across the table for a long moment.

"Now don't you start," Sarah chided her. "It's bad enough that Malloy is always angry with me."

"Mr. Malloy is right," Mrs. Ellsworth said. "Solving murders isn't a job for a nice lady like yourself."

"Even if it means the murder doesn't get solved?"

Mrs. Ellsworth shook her head. "Nothing is worth your life, Mrs. Brandt."

Sarah felt a chill go down her spine, and she shivered involuntarily.

"Someone is walking over your grave," Mrs. Ellsworth informed her.

"As long as I'm not in it, I don't mind," Sarah informed her right back in a poor attempt at humor.

Mrs. Ellsworth refused to smile. "This is serious," she said. "You've got a family now, a child who depends on you."

"I know. I'm not going to take any foolish chances, even if Malloy would let me."

Mrs. Ellsworth sipped her coffee thoughtfully. Then she said, "Do you have a handkerchief?"

Sarah blinked in surprise at the sudden change of topic. "Of course," she said, reaching into her pocket and pulling one out. No lady would be caught without a handkerchief any more than she would go outside naked. "It's clean," she added, thinking Mrs. Ellsworth wanted to use it.

Instead, she took it and tied a knot in one corner. "There," she said, handing it back. "That will protect you."

Sarah stared at the knotted fabric. "Protect me from what?"

"Yourself, I'd say," Mrs. Ellsworth said tartly. "I don't expect for a minute that you'll be able to keep from helping Mr. Malloy with his murder investigations, but a knot in your handkerchief will ward off evil."

Sarah stared at her in dismay. She should have known. Mrs. Ellsworth's superstitious nature was legendary. "Oh."

"Don't look at me like that. It doesn't matter if you believe it or not, it still works. Put the handkerchief in your pocket and keep it with you all the time."

Sarah managed not to smile. "All right." Obediently, she put it back in her pocket.

"Now tell me all about that poor girl and how she died."

Sarah did so, sparing no detail since she didn't have to worry about Mrs. Ellsworth's sensibilities.

"Who do you think killed her?" the old woman asked when Sarah was finished.

"At this point, I don't have any idea. I'm sure people will naturally assume it was her father, since they hate the Chinese so much."

"Killing your child, that's a horrible thing," Mrs. Ellsworth observed. "I don't know much about the Chinese, though. Maybe they don't care for their children the way we do."

"I think he loved her the same way white people love their children," Sarah said, aware that she was defending a man who was at least indirectly responsible for his daughter's death. If he hadn't insisted on marrying her off to his friend, she might not have run away with Quinn O'Neal. Or at least she might not have run away with him when she did.

"Why would someone want to kill her at all, though?"

Mrs. Ellsworth asked. "Seems to me she should have been the one doing the killing. I can think of a few people who'd made her unhappy enough to deserve it."

Sarah could, too. "I know. It doesn't make any sense."

"Then let's think about it a bit. What are the reasons a person kills another person?"

Sarah considered. "Greed."

Mrs. Ellsworth shook her head. "I doubt the girl had anything valuable."

"Love or some twisted version of it."

"And jealousy," Mrs. Ellsworth added. "That naturally follows love."

"Oh, my, there's the man Angel was supposed to marry."

"Chinese, was he?" Mrs. Ellsworth asked. "Don't know if he'd be jealous, but his pride would be hurt for certain. No man wants to be thrown over for another, especially when he thinks the other man isn't half as good as he is."

"No question, Mr. Wong would be bitter to learn his rival was a shiftless bum," Sarah agreed.

"That settles it, then," Mrs. Ellsworth said slyly. "No man likes to be made a fool in front of everybody he knows. He did it for sure."

"Well," Sarah said with a grin. "We should send for Mr. Malloy and tell him we've figured it out: Mr. Wong killed Angel."

"IT WAS THAT WONG WHAT DONE IT," ROONEY INFORMED Frank with an air of certainty that might have been impressive if it wasn't so self-serving.

"How do you know that?" Frank asked with interest.

"Easy. She made him a laughingstock. Rich man like that, getting throwed over by some girl for a fellow like Quinn? He'd be plenty mad."

"You know that for a fact?" Frank asked curiously.

Rooney leaned back in his chair, a cocky grin on his face. "Sure."

Frank gave the officer a meaningful glance, and he strolled over and gave Rooney a slap across the head.

"Hey!" he cried in outrage, rubbing his head. "What was that for?"

"Let's talk about something else," Frank said. "Something you know about, for instance. Like where you were yesterday."

"Yesterday? You mean when Angel was killed?"

Frank nodded.

He frowned and considered the question for a moment. "I was working."

"Doing what?"

"I . . . uh, I was down on the docks, loading ships."

"Who were you working for?"

His gaze was all over the place, up to the ceiling, on the wall behind Frank, on the table, on his hands. Everywhere but on Frank. "I don't remember," he finally decided.

"Too bad." Frank turned to the officer. "Take him downstairs and lock him up."

"Wait!" Rooney cried.

"For what? You're lying through your teeth, and only guilty people lie." He shoved his chair back and started to rise.

"I'm not guilty! I'm just . . . I can't tell you what I was doing yesterday!"

He looked genuinely frightened, but Frank didn't particularly care. Rooney should be more frightened of him than of whomever he'd been with yesterday. Frank stood up. "Take him downstairs."

"Wait! Don't leave! I can't tell you! They'll kill me." He really did look frightened, and he'd know Frank wasn't going to kill him. The police might beat him up, but they had no reason to really kill him. Frank couldn't match the threat, so he'd have to provide protection.

"If you're innocent, I won't need to tell anyone what you were doing when Angel died," he tried.

He swallowed. "I really was loading boxes."

"Stealing them, you mean."

"I was just hired to do the work," he insisted. "I don't know who was paying or nothing. They offer you work, and you take it. You don't ask questions. They pay real good so you don't. You take boxes out of one warehouse and put them into another one."

"In broad daylight?" Frank scoffed.

"Nobody pays attention in broad daylight," Rooney said. "They figure nobody'd do something illegal in front of God and everybody."

Frank would have to give this some further thought later, when he had more time. "How long did you work?"

"Until we was finished. I didn't pay no attention to what time it was."

"What did you do then?"

"We was all hungry, so we went to get something to eat."

"Where?"

"I don't know," Rooney said desperately. "I didn't pay no attention. Someplace close to the warehouse. A bar. I might could show you."

"We'll worry about that later. What time did you get home?"

"Late. Everybody was asleep. Ma woke up when I come in and told me what happened to Angel."

"What did you think of Angel?" Frank asked.

Rooney frowned. He didn't like the question. "What do you mean?"

"I mean your brother brought a girl home to live with you. What did you think of her?"

"I didn't think nothing of her," he tried.

"That's hard to believe," Frank marveled. "A pretty young girl comes to live in the flat with you. She's sleeping there every night with your brother, probably in the same room. You can hear him poking her. Donald's got a woman in his bed, too. Must be hard for you, laying there every night, listening to that, then seeing her every day."

Rooney was squirming. "Didn't bother me," he lied.

"I think it did," Frank said. "I think it made you mad. Who was Quinn to have a wife when you didn't? Maybe you even thought he should share her with you."

"I never!" he cried, trying for outrage but falling a bit short.

"Yes, you did, Rooney. You thought he wouldn't care because she was Chinese and not worth much. You told Quinn to give you a turn with his girl, didn't you? What did Quinn think about that?"

"Nothing! I never asked him no such thing!"

"Maybe Quinn said yes, but I'm going to guess that he didn't want to share. That made you even madder, so when you caught Angel outside, all alone, you decided to take a turn anyway."

"No! I wouldn't do that!"

"But Angel didn't want to go along, did she? She put up a fight. You didn't mean to do it, Rooney, but she made you so mad that you put your hands around her throat and—"

"*No!*" Rooney came up out of his seat and would have launched himself across the table at Frank, but the officer gave him a whack with his locust club. He fell back into his chair with a howl, clutching his injured shoulder.

"Or maybe you got what you wanted from her," Frank continued as if nothing had happened. "Then you were afraid she'd tell Quinn, so you had to make sure she didn't, and that's why you choked her. Is that why, Rooney?"

"I never choked her! I never did nothing to her," he insisted, still rubbing his shoulder.

"You tried, though, didn't you?" Frank asked. "You wouldn't be a man if you didn't try."

But Rooney wasn't going to admit to anything. He just glared at Frank.

Frank sighed and pushed himself to his feet. "Let's see what Quinn has to say about all this."

"I didn't never touch her!" Rooney was shouting as the officer closed the door behind them. "You tell him that!"

Quinn was awake, but he looked pretty bad, like a man whose wife had just been murdered. He probably hadn't slept much last night. "Why'd you bring us in?" he demanded. "We didn't do nothing!"

"Your brother was involved in a warehouse robbery yesterday," Frank said. "I don't call that nothing."

"Who, Rooney?" Quinn made a rude noise. "He wasn't involved in nothing. He just does what he's told."

Frank figured that was probably true. "Did you tell him he could have a turn with Angel?"

"What? Who told you that?" Frank noticed his face had turned red.

"I heard he liked her," Frank said. "Couldn't blame him, I guess. You liked her yourself."

"But I didn't . . . She was my *wife*!"

"And Rooney is your brother. Share and share alike. Blood is thicker than water. Don't tell me he didn't ask."

Quinn's glare told him he was right.

"And what did you tell him when he asked?" Frank inquired.

"I told him to go to hell!"

"He didn't, though, did he? He kept bothering you about it. Did he bother her about it, too?"

Quinn's expression was murderous. "I told him to leave her alone."

"Was that why Angel kept disappearing?" Frank wondered. "Maybe she was hiding from your brother."

"She wasn't hiding from nobody," he said stubbornly.

Frank leaned back in his chair and studied the boy for a moment. "What did you and Angel have a fight about yesterday?"

"What?" he asked stupidly.

"You told me yesterday that you and Angel had a fight when you took her downstairs to get her something to eat from a street vendor. What did you fight about?"

The color rose in his face again. "Nothing. It wasn't nothing."

"People don't fight about nothing," Frank said, folding his hands over his stomach. "I'm in no hurry, and Officer Kelly over there is probably getting bored. I could tell him to give you a couple whacks with his locust club to keep him busy. After that, I'm thinking you'll be more willing to answer my questions."

"I'm answering!" he claimed a little desperately.

"What did you argue about?"

Quinn rubbed the back of his hand across his mouth. "It was nothing, really," he began, but when Officer Kelly took a step forward, he hurried on. "It was just . . . I knew she didn't like doing it up in the flat, with everybody around. She was ashamed, she said, for them to know what we was doing. I told her it was all right, since we was married and all, but she . . ."

"I think I understand," Frank said. "So what did you fight about?"

"I told her I found a place, down in the cellar, where we could be alone. We could go down there and do it whenever we wanted, and nobody'd see or hear us."

"And she didn't like that idea?" Frank asked curiously.

Quinn rubbed his hand across his mouth again. "I wanted to go right then, but she said . . . she said there's rats down there, and it's dirty. She didn't want to go."

"Did you make her go anyway?"

"I tried, but . . . she ran away. Went back inside to the flat, I guess."

"What did you do?"

"I was pretty mad. I went off by myself, walking, trying to figure out what to do."

"What to do about what?" Frank asked.

Quinn shrugged. "About everything. What good is it, being married, if your wife won't let you do anything?"

"No good at all," Frank agreed. "Is that why you killed her then?"

Quinn started. "I didn't kill her!"

"Nobody could blame you," Frank said agreeably. "Pretty girl like that, sleeping with you every night but not letting you do anything. You must've been going crazy. Then you find a nice place where you can do it without your whole family watching, and she won't go. Maybe she made fun of you. Maybe she said she was going to go back home to her parents. Maybe she said she hated you."

"No, it wasn't like that!"

"What was it like?"

"I . . . She just started crying and ran away."

"And you went after her and caught her in the alley and put your hands around her throat and—"

"No! I didn't! I didn't touch her! I didn't kill her!"

Frank smiled. "Then you don't have anything to worry about, do you?" He rose from the chair and left the room, with Officer Kelly right behind him.

"What do you think?" Kelly asked when they were in the hall.

Frank sighed. "I think this is going to be a long investigation."

THE POT ROAST WAS SIMMERING, SURROUNDED BY POTAtoes and carrots, filling the house with a mouthwatering aroma. Maeve and Catherine had gone upstairs to play, and Mrs. Ellsworth had returned to her home. She'd promised to return later to claim a portion of the meal for herself and her son Nelson.

Sarah had just finished tidying up the kitchen when she heard someone ringing her doorbell. Her heart sank. She'd been looking forward to enjoying the meal with the girls, but now it appeared she was being summoned to a delivery. When she opened the door, however, she saw Minnie Lee standing on her doorstep.

"Mrs. Lee, please come in," she said, standing aside. "Nothing wrong with Cora or the baby, I hope."

"Oh, no, they're both fine," Minnie said distractedly. She came in but stopped dead when she saw Maeve and Catherine staring at her from the bottom of the stairs.

"Mrs. Lee, this is my daughter Catherine and her nursemaid Maeve," Sarah said.

"Are you leaving?" Maeve asked, trying not to let her disappointment show.

"No," Sarah said. "Mrs. Lee has come for a visit." Then she glanced at Minnie and realized she wasn't entirely certain of that. "Or did you need me to go with you?"

"Oh, no," Minnie assured her. "I just . . . I needed somebody to talk to, and I can't bother Cora. She's already so upset over Angel, and she needs to keep up her strength for the baby."

"Are you Angel's mother?" Maeve asked, surprising her.

"Why, yes," Minnie said. "Did you know her?"

Maeve shook her head. "But I'm sorry that she died."

Minnie's eyes filled, and her face twisted in pain. "Thank you, child," she said hoarsely.

"Please come into the kitchen," Sarah urged. "I'll make you some tea, and we can talk. Girls, you go on back upstairs now so we can talk in private."

Mrs. Lee left her wrap and her hat hanging in the hallway and followed Sarah through her office to the back of the house.

"Something smells good," Minnie said with forced cheerfulness as she took the offered seat at the table.

"My neighbor is an excellent cook. Luckily for me, she has decided to teach Maeve and Catherine, and we all get to enjoy the results. Would you like a piece of her pie?"

Minnie shook her head. "No, thank you. I can't seem to eat anything since . . ."

Her voice broke again, and Sarah pretended not to notice. She put the kettle on and got out the teapot and canister and measured out the tea. After a moment's thought, she also cut two pieces of the latest pie Mrs. Ellsworth had insisted they take and set one down in front of Minnie.

"Try," Sarah said when she would have protested. Then she sat down at the table opposite Minnie. "What did you want to talk about?"

Minnie sighed in despair. "I guess I don't really know. What I really want is for somebody to tell me it was all a big mistake and Angel is still alive. I know that won't happen, but it doesn't stop me from wanting it."

"That's a perfectly normal reaction," Sarah said. "How are Harry and your husband doing?"

The color rose in Minnie's wan cheeks at the mention of her son. "Harry's pretty ashamed over the business with the opium. I don't know what got into him. He swears he never used it before, and he says he didn't intend to use too much. He just . . . He's upset over Angel, of course."

"Were they close?"

Minnie shrugged one shoulder. "They fought, like brother and sister will do. Harry complained about her, but let anybody else say something to her, and he was on 'em like a tiger."

"I guess Angel looked up to her big brother, too."

"Oh, yes." Minnie's eyes shone at the memory. "When they was little, she'd follow him everywhere. He didn't want his kid sister tagging along when he was with his friends, of course. That caused more than one tear to be shed, I'll tell you."

Sarah waited, giving Minnie a chance to savor her memories and work up the courage to talk about the present.

Finally, she cleared her throat. "Do you know what . . . ? What will they be able to find out when they . . . examine her?" she asked.

Sarah could hear the pain in her voice. She hoped Minnie had no idea what an autopsy entailed. No one wanted to think of someone doing those things to a loved one, especially a sweet young girl like Angel. Sarah wasn't about to explain it, either.

"They'll be able to tell exactly how she died," Sarah said. "And they'll be able to tell if she had other injuries."

"You mean if he beat her or something?"

"Yes." She wouldn't mention rape unless Minnie thought of it herself. "They can sometimes tell approximately when the person died. That can sometimes help in determining who couldn't have done it because they were someplace else at the time."

"And who was nearby and could have," Minnie guessed.

"That's right. They also look for signs that Angel fought back. If she has blood under her fingernails, for example, that means she probably scratched him. The killer would have scratch marks on him, too."

The water was boiling, so Sarah got up and poured the water into the pot. She brought the tea tray to the table, so the tea could steep for a while before she poured it, and sat down again.

"That would make it easy," Minnie said. "If she marked the killer, I mean."

"It would certainly help. Of course it also helps if someone saw the killer with her or at least saw something suspicious. That doesn't always happen, though."

"If no one saw anything, how will they ever find out who did it?" Minnie asked.

Sarah smiled reassuringly. "Mr. Malloy is very good at his job. If anyone can find Angel's killer, he can."

For a long moment, Minnie sat staring blankly at the table top. "You know, it's funny. If you'd asked me, I would've thought it was Harry who would come to grief," she mused.

"Boys do tend to be more reckless than girls," Sarah agreed.

Minnie didn't seem to have heard her. "When you do things in your life, you never think . . ." She looked up, and her eyes were full of despair. "I picked Charlie to marry, but they didn't have any say in it. Harry and Angel, they had to live with what I gave them."

"You gave them a good life," Sarah reminded her.

Minnie's face twisted in pain. "That's what I thought. They never was hungry or cold, not once in their lives. Not like I was, coming up, I can tell you. I could've married a white man, but not one who could take care of me and mine like Charlie did."

Sarah thought she was probably right about that. Most women like Minnie and Cora lived like the O'Neals, if they were *lucky*. The less fortunate fared far worse.

"I never cared what people said behind my back," Minnie was saying, her voice rising as she made her case. "Or to my face even. Why should I? It was all my own doing. So I never cared, but Angel—"

Her voice broke, and Sarah instinctively reached over and clasped her hand in silent comfort.

Minnie turned her hand and squeezed Sarah's tightly, almost desperately. "Angel never seemed to care, either," she said in a terrible whisper. "She never did, but if she'd been white, would she still be alive?"

* * *

Frank left the O'Neal boys to cool their heels and went to visit the coroner. Doc Haynes was in his office. His desk was piled high with papers both modern and ancient, some probably concerning bodies that had long since turned to dust. The smell of death hung in the air, permeating everything in the building. Frank steeled himself against it and cleared the only other chair in the room and sat on it.

"You'll be wondering about the Chinese girl, I guess," Doc said.

"I would," Frank agreed. "What can you tell me?"

Doc shifted a few sheets of paper and found the one he was looking for. "I didn't cut her open yet, but I don't expect I'll find anything much I don't already know. She was manually strangled. Didn't put up much of a fight, nothing under her fingernails, so it was quick and a surprise. Didn't have any other marks on her that I could see. If whoever did it hit her right before she died, she wouldn't have had time to bruise, but I'll find it when I do the *post-mortem*."

"Was she raped?"

Doc frowned. "Kind of hard to tell."

"What do you mean?"

"Well, you said she'd been married just a couple weeks."

"That's right."

"She had some irritation down there, but that's pretty much the case with new brides. Young couples can't get enough of it and all that."

Frank nodded, remembering. The memories were bittersweet, as always when he thought of his lost Kathleen. "So do you think she was or not?"

"I'd say not. No semen was present. Her clothes were all intact, too."

"The family carried her inside after they found her," Frank reminded him. "Maybe they cleaned her up."

"That's possible. You can ask them, of course, but I'm thinking she wasn't assaulted. Whoever did this probably just put his hands around her throat in a fit of passion and broke the hyoid bone before he had a chance to think better of what he was doing. She was surprised and only had a few seconds to resist before she was unconscious."

"The hyoid," Frank mused. "That's the bone in the throat?"

"Yeah," Doc said, pointing to a spot on his own neck. "If it's broken, we know it was strangulation. Like I said, I haven't cut her open, but you can see the marks on her throat right where it should be, so I'm pretty sure that's what I'll find."

"Would the killer have to be strong to break it?"

"If you're asking if a woman could do it, the answer is yes. Most women who do housework would have the strength."

This wasn't good news. With no sexual assault, almost anyone could have killed Angel. "Can you give me an idea of how long she'd been dead?"

"I'd say not more than an hour or two before they found her. Maybe less. Rigor mortis hadn't started yet, and she couldn't have laid there long without somebody seeing her."

Frank sighed. Not much to go on. "Anything else?"

Doc shook his head. "Pretty little thing. Hardly more than a child. How old was she again?"

"Fifteen, according to her mother."

"What was she doing married?" he asked in disgust.

"Young love," Frank said sarcastically. "She eloped."

Doc shook his head. "Didn't have much of a happily-ever-after did she?"

8

"Don't do this to yourself," Sarah told Minnie gently. "You aren't thinking clearly. If you hadn't married Charlie, you never would have had Angel," she pointed out. "None of this is your fault."

Minnie wanted to believe her, but her guilt just wouldn't let her. "I should've known she was seeing that boy."

"How could you? Angel was doing her very best to keep it a secret," Sarah reminded her. "And her friends were helping her."

"I could've talked to Charlie, though," she said, staring past Sarah as if she were arguing with someone unseen.

"Why didn't you?"

Minnie straightened abruptly. "What?"

"You said you could have spoken to your husband. Did you mean about Angel marrying Mr. Wong?"

The color rose in Minnie's face. "No, I didn't mean that," she said too quickly. "I'd never . . . I couldn't . . . Angel was his child."

Sarah wasn't sure what she meant by that, and before she could reply, Minnie rose.

"I have to go. I . . . I didn't mean to stay so long. You must be busy."

"You didn't even have any tea," Sarah protested. "At least have a cup before you leave."

"I have to go," Minnie insisted, hurrying out of the kitchen without waiting to see if Sarah would follow.

Sarah caught up with her in the front hall. She was putting on her hat. "I'm glad you stopped by," Sarah said. "I hope I was able to help a little."

"You did," Minnie said without meeting her eye. "I'm sorry I . . . I mean, thank you for . . . for your time," she added lamely.

Sarah had only managed to say, "You're welcome," before Minnie was out the front door. Sarah watched her rushing down the street as if she was afraid Sarah was going to chase her and stop her.

What had made her leave so suddenly? Sarah tried to remember what they'd been talking about when Minnie had bolted, but nothing struck her as particularly disturbing. Perhaps Minnie had simply remembered something she needed to do immediately. That was a logical explanation, but Sarah wasn't convinced. Part of her wanted desperately to find out, to investigate and see if Minnie's distress had anything to do with Angel's death. Then she would put whatever she learned together with what she already knew and decide if any of it would help identify whoever had killed Angel.

She wasn't going to do that, though. She was going to stay right where she was and forget all about Angel Lee's murder. She was going to be a mother to her child and let Frank Malloy do his job without her help. He'd done it for many years before he met her, and he didn't need her help now.

But even as she closed the front door, she was thinking of other ways that she could help. Ways that wouldn't put her in danger. She could think of at least one.

FRANK STOOD IN THE BACK ALLEY BEHIND THE O'NEALS' tenement and stared down at the spot where Angel's body had been found. All he saw was a bare patch of ground just like all the rest of the ground around it. Nothing to indicate a young girl has lost her life there, and certainly nothing to tell him who had killed her.

From what Doc Haynes had told him, this was around the time she'd died yesterday. Except for an occasional visitor to the privies, the yard was remarkably quiet this time of day. The weather wasn't warm enough yet to encourage people to gather on the porches or fire escapes. Whatever chores the women did—laundry, emptying chamber pots—had been accomplished much earlier. Those residents lucky enough to have jobs were gone, and the rest would be doing piecework indoors, like the O'Neal women, or warming a barstool, like the O'Neal men.

As hard as it was to believe, Angel's death might really have passed unobserved. Frank had to make sure, though. Witnesses in neighborhoods like this one seldom volunteered information to the police. Their lives were hard enough without getting involved in a murder. They might also have good reason to want to avoid interaction with the police. With a weary sigh, Frank climbed up the back porch steps and entered the nearest building in search of an eyewitness who'd actually tell him something useful.

The sun had set by the time Frank made it to the top floor of the second tenement that overlooked the murder scene. Most of his knocks had gone unanswered. Either the flats were empty or the tenants were hiding. They'd all know who he was. They'd have seen him yesterday or else they simply recognized him as a policeman by his bearing. Even though he dressed in a dark suit, like half the men in the city, people always knew who he was. He'd long ago given up trying to figure out what gave him away. Usually, it worked to his advantage anyway.

Those who did answer the door to him claimed to have seen and heard nothing. He'd worked his way up to the fifth floor and down the hallway, knocking only on the doors of flats that faced the yard below, where Angel had died. To his surprise, one of the last doors opened before he'd even knocked on it. An elderly woman stood there, glaring at him. Her body seemed to have shrunk inside her clothing, and stray wisps of white hair stood up in tufts over her pink scalp. Her wrinkled face was almost completely devoid of color, as if she'd already died but was just too stubborn to admit it and lie down.

"About time you got here," she informed him.

Frank blinked in surprise. "I'm Detective Sergeant Malloy," he said, thinking maybe she'd confused him with someone else.

"I don't care what your name is," she snapped. "Come in. I got something to tell you."

Frank did as he was told. The flat was like a thousand

others. Furnished with castoffs and wooden crates, the place was neat more from a lack of belongings than any attempt at orderliness.

"You want to know who killed that girl, don't you?" she asked. Without waiting for a reply, she turned and hobbled over to a window that overlooked the yard below. "I seen it all from here." She pointed a gnarled finger at the dirty glass before plopping down into an ancient rocking chair that was positioned so she could peer out without even turning her head.

"This is where I sit," she said, leaning forward until her nose almost touched the glass of the window. "I seen her down there."

Frank felt the first spark of hope he'd experienced since finding out Angel was dead. He leaned forward, too, and determined that the window provided an excellent view of the scene of the girl's murder. Still, they were five stories up. He looked at the old woman again. She was watching him with her rheumy eyes. How much could she really have seen?

"You think I'm blind, don't you?" she said. "Well, I ain't. Can't see to sew no more or do nothing close, but far away, everything's clear as day."

"Tell me where the girl's body was, then," Frank challenged her.

She made a rude noise. "Right there," she said, pointing, although she might have been pointing at anything. "Beside the porch, on this side, where the alley comes out."

That much was true. Somebody could've told her that, of course. "Did you see who killed her?"

"I seen her with somebody, and then I saw she was laying

there and not moving. Didn't see her actually get killed. Had to use the chamber pot, you know."

Frank didn't know, of course. "Tell me exactly what you did see, then."

"They said the girl was Chinese. That true?" she asked instead.

"Half-Chinese," Frank corrected her. "Her mother is Irish."

The old woman pulled a face. "Ain't right, mixing races like that. What's this world coming to?"

Frank imagined his mother would have the same opinion. "Couldn't you tell she was Chinese?" he asked to test her.

She gave him another glare. "Not from up here. Can't see faces plain. Neither can you," she added with a toothless grin.

That was true, of course. "How do you know you saw the dead girl then?"

"Because the girl I saw was the one laying down there dead, is why. I could tell by her clothes. Her hair, too. Pitch black it was. Guess that's from the Chinese blood."

"All right," Frank said patiently. "Just tell me—"

"I seen her down there before," she continued, ignoring him. "I could tell it was her from the way she walked and from her dark hair. Never saw her before a couple weeks ago. New here. They said she married one of the boys from across the way."

"Who keeps you so well informed?"

"My family," she said, then cackled at Frank's surprise.

"You think I live up here all by myself? I got a son, and he's got a boy and two girls. They all got jobs. At least, most of the time. The girls, they work in a factory, and the boy and my son are draymen. There's always work for a man can drive a wagon."

"So they deliver the news to you up here?"

"The girls do," she said. "My son and the boy, they don't know nothing that goes on. The girls tell me what's what."

"And they told you about the Chinese girl, I guess."

"Lord, yes! Ain't every day we get a Chinese moving into the neighborhood. The girls said her eyes was funny look-ing, slanted like the Chinese even though she's half-white. That true?"

Frank tried not to sigh. "Just tell me what you saw yes-terday."

The old woman huffed, insulted, but she cooperated. "I seen her come out on the back porch. She was sitting out there for a while. I thought that was funny because it's too cold for sitting out, but she'd do that. She'd sit out there for the longest time."

"You'd seen her there before?"

"Almost every day."

"At the same time?"

"No, different times. Sometimes she'd stay out a long time, and sometimes she'd go back inside pretty quick. Maybe it was too cold for her."

"She ever talk to anybody?"

"Not that I saw. People must've thought she was strange, her being Chinese and all. Nobody ever talked to her. Walked by like she wasn't there. Sometimes they'd hurry, you know? Like they was afraid she'd do something to them."

"Did somebody talk to her yesterday?"

"Oh, yeah. I saw it real plain. This fellow, he comes down

the alley." She pointed again. "She don't look up at first. I guess she must've heard him coming, but she don't look around. Why should she? Nobody takes an interest in her, so why should she take an interest in them?"

"But she says something to him?"

"He must've said something first. She sort of jumps like she's surprised, and then she comes down off the porch to meet him." She looked out the window, staring down as if she were seeing it all over again.

She must have known him, Frank thought. That would help a lot. "How long did they talk?"

"I don't know. Not long. They started off civil enough, I reckon, but then they started in to fighting."

"They were hitting each other?" Frank asked in surprise.

"No," she said, waving away the very idea with one bony hand. "Arguing, I should've said. Having words."

"How do you know if you couldn't hear what they were saying?"

"I could tell. They started moving their hands around, like people do when they're mad." She illustrated, curling her knobby fingers into fists and shaking them in an unconvincing imitation of anger.

Still, Frank felt his excitement rising. She might actually be telling the truth! "Then what happened?"

"This went on for a couple minutes, and then he puts his arms around her."

This didn't make sense. "You mean he *hugged* her?"

The old woman pursed her lips as she remembered. "I thought that's what he was doing. He had his back to me, and when he does that, I can't see her no more. He's in the way now, with her in front of him. I *thought* he was hugging her."

"Now you're not so sure?"

The old woman looked up at him apologetically. "When they told me she was dead, I started having my doubts."

Frank gritted his teeth. "What happened after he started hugging her?"

"I didn't see."

"What do you mean, you didn't see?" Frank asked sharply.

She winced but didn't back down. "I had to piss! The girls don't like it when I don't make it to the pot, so I had to leave. I thought they was making up!" she defended herself. "How was I to know he'd kill her?"

She couldn't have, of course. Frank swallowed down his frustration. If he frightened her, he wouldn't get any more information out of her. "What did you see when you got back to the window?"

"I saw her laying there on the ground. The boy was gone, and she was on the ground. I thought that was real odd at first, but I never thought she was dead. Not for a while, at least. I thought maybe she fainted or something. But when she didn't move, not even a little bit, I started thinking maybe she was dead."

"Why didn't you do something?"

"Like what?" she asked in surprise.

"Like get some help. Tell somebody what you saw."

She looked at him like he was crazy. "How was I supposed to do that? I ain't been out of this flat in two years or more. Can't walk down the stairs, and if I could, I'd never get up them again. Next time I'm outside will be when they take me away to the cemetery."

Frank swallowed down hard again, holding his temper with difficulty. "Do you know what time it was when all this happened?"

She glanced meaningfully around the room. People like her didn't own clocks, she was telling him silently.

"Maybe you heard a clock strike outside," he tried. The city was filled with tower clocks that chimed the hours to let people like her know the time.

She shrugged one shoulder. "Maybe it struck three a little after I noticed her just laying there. I can't be sure, though. The time just goes for me. Every day is pretty much like another, and every hour is, too."

Frank was certain this was true. Once again he swallowed down his frustration. "I don't suppose you'd recognize the man who killed her."

She glanced out the window, silently reminding Frank of how far down it was to where they'd been standing. "I can tell you one thing, though. He was a Chinaman."

Frank doubted very much she could be certain of this. "If you couldn't tell *she* was Chinese from up here, how could you tell *he* was?"

"His clothes," she said with obvious satisfaction. "He was wearing them baggy clothes they all wear."

"Are you sure?" Frank asked in amazement, trying not to let himself hope it would be this easy.

"Of course I'm sure, and that ain't all," she added, her sunken eyes glittering with glee.

"All right," Frank said, willing to play along. "What else is there?"

"His hair," she informed him smugly. "He had one of them long, black pigtails hanging down his back."

Frank managed not to grin. He guessed he could let the O'Neal brothers go home now.

* * *

Sarah found the church easily. Through her work at the Prodigal Son Mission, she'd learned about other Christian charity groups in the city. She knew that at least two dozen churches were operating Sunday schools for the Chinese, to teach them the error of their heathen ways, and many of those churches also offered evening classes where volunteers helped the immigrants learn English.

"Are you here to volunteer?" an elderly lady asked Sarah when she stepped inside. The woman had been sitting at a table with a young Chinese man, apparently tutoring him, as others were doing with other Chinese men at the tables scattered around the large room in the church basement.

"I . . . I'm interested in finding out more about your classes," Sarah said. It wasn't a complete lie. "Is there someone I could speak with?"

"Oh, yes," the lady assured her. "Mrs. Adkins. She's the one who started the school. Wait here, and I'll get her."

Sarah gave her name and watched the woman scurry toward the back of the room.

While she waited, Sarah had an opportunity to observe the lessons in progress. Most of the students were younger men, some of them still in their teens. The oldest ones were probably no older than thirty. All of them were paying the strictest attention to their tutors, whether they were receiving individual attention or were part of a small group. Learning English was apparently serious business to them.

The tutors were far more diverse, however. Women outnumbered the men, two to one. The men were middle-aged or older, dressed in suits and boiled white shirts. The women varied much more greatly in age. The lady who had helped her appeared to be the oldest. Some of the others were obviously wealthy matrons, ranging in age from twenties to fifties, their tastefully fashionable gowns betraying their financial status. A few were younger, probably not yet married, and a couple appeared to be hardly out of the schoolroom themselves.

Mrs. Adkins was coming toward her from the back of the room, the elderly lady in her wake. She was about Sarah's age, a handsome woman who had discreetly not worn any jewelry to adorn her simple outfit. Sarah's experience told her that her dress had been custom made, however. Discreet or not, Mrs. Adkins was among the privileged few.

As she came closer, Sarah realized Mrs. Adkins was looking at her rather intently, and for an instant, Sarah's guilty conscience pricked her. How could this woman know she was here under false pretenses? But then something else pricked her, a vague sense of recognition.

"Sarah?" Mrs. Adkins asked when she reached her. "Sarah Decker?"

Sarah needed another moment to study the other woman's face. Then she remembered. "Corinne Fink!"

Both women laughed with the delight of finding an old friend unexpectedly after many years. Corinne gave Sarah her hand, and Sarah pressed it warmly.

"What brings you here?" Corinne asked.

"I wanted to learn more about the work you're doing," Sarah said, feeling not the slightest twinge of guilt because this was perfectly true. "Could you spare a few minutes for me?"

"Of course!" She looked around. "Thank you, Mrs. Ott," she said to the elderly lady. "As you can see, Mrs. Brandt and I know each other quite well." She turned back to Sarah. "There's a small room right over here where we can talk."

"I hope I'm not taking you away from your students," Sarah said.

"Not at all. I have plenty of able assistants."

Corinne led her into an adjacent room and closed the door so they wouldn't disturb the students. The room was furnished with a table and several chairs, and they seated themselves across from each other.

"I should have remembered your married name," Sarah said. "I was at your wedding."

"And I *heard* about yours," Corinne said with amusement. "You ran away with a poor, young doctor, I believe. Quite the scandal."

"My parents have never forgiven me," Sarah confirmed.

"Do you have any children?" Corinne asked.

Sarah managed a smile. "Tom and I never had any, and he died four years ago."

"I'm so sorry! I didn't know."

Sarah didn't want to linger over that news. "Do *you* have children?" she countered.

Corinne brightened at once. "Yes, four. Three boys and a girl."

"That's wonderful! I've recently fostered a little girl from a mission down on Mulberry Street. I was doing volunteer work there, and I fell in love with her."

Corinne nodded. "It's easy to do. I even find myself falling in love with my students here."

Sarah couldn't hide her surprise.

"Oh, not romantically, of course," Corinne hastened to explain. "The young men are so sincere, though, and so eager to learn. They want to better themselves, and they'll do whatever they must."

"How did you become involved in this work?" Sarah asked.

Corinne smiled knowingly. "You're wondering how a woman with a husband and four children has time to do anything else. That's what everyone wants to know. But *you* should know how it really is. The servants take care of everything in the house, and the children are in school most of the day. I can only go to so many teas before I die of boredom. I wanted to do something important."

Sarah nodded. She understood completely. "But why this?"

"A missionary visited our church. He'd been in China for twenty years, and he spoke so passionately about the Chinese people. He introduced a young man who had come to America and studied medicine so he could return to his people and help them better themselves. We wanted to help, too, so the church opened a Sunday school for the Chinese here in the city. We quickly realized their greatest need was to learn English, though, so we started this school, too."

"And you're in charge?" Sarah asked in amazement.

"I'm one of many of the people who support it," Corinne corrected her.

"What does your family think about your work?"

"They aren't as enthusiastic as I am, I'm afraid, but they can't criticize too much, since I'm working through the church. If they knew the truth, though, I don't think they'd approve at all."

"What do you mean, *the truth*?" Sarah asked in surprise.

Corinne shook her head sadly. "They believe we're helping convert the Chinese so that when they return to China, they will win other converts there as well."

"You don't think they're really sincere about converting to Christianity?"

"Oh, some of them are very sincere. It's not that. It . . . it's the part about them returning to China. Most of them have no intention of returning at all."

"Do people really think they'll all go back someday?" Sarah asked in amazement.

"As strange as it may seem, I believe they do," Corinne confirmed. "Even though the Chinese have been coming to this country for decades, the government still doesn't allow Chinese females to immigrate. After all these years, there are still only a handful of them in this country. That's because the government believes that if the Chinese can't bring their women over, they will be forced to return home."

"And instead they've married American women," Sarah said.

"Don't let anyone here hear you say that," Corinne chided, only half in jest.

"But surely everyone knows already."

"Knowing about it and seeing it in your own church are two very different things," Corinne said. "At our school, we have to be very careful that none of our female teachers gives the slightest appearance of interest in the Chinese men. If there was to be any romantic attraction, the scandal would probably compel us to close the school."

"But surely—" Sarah began.

Corinne interrupted her. "I know what you're thinking, that no respectable white woman would be attracted to a Chinese man, but that's not the case at all. I said that I loved my students, and that's because they are so sensitive and caring. I've rarely met such true gentlemen, and they treat females with the utmost respect. Girls who are accustomed to the rough manners of even the most well-bred white boys are quite taken with the Chinese manners."

"So I've heard," Sarah said.

"What do you mean?" Corinne asked in surprise.

"Did you know that I'm a midwife?"

"A midwife? Sarah, however did you manage that?"

"When I rebelled, I did a very good job of it," Sarah said wryly. "I recently delivered a baby down in Chinatown, and I've gotten to know several women who married Chinese men."

"Then you understand," Corinne said with relief. "We had a case here . . . It was nipped in the bud, but it was almost the end of our school. The daughter of one of our teachers had been coming along to help her mother. She developed an attachment to one of the young men. I don't know how serious it was, but her parents sent her off on a European tour the instant they discovered it. If word had gotten out . . . Well, as I said, it could have been tragic."

"And yet the women I know are very happy with their choice of husband."

"Perhaps they are, but the Chinese still suffer terrible persecution. Some of our students have been accosted and even beaten for daring to enter this neighborhood. It happens all over the city. Tormenting a Chinaman is considered great sport by far too many."

"Yet they still come."

"I told you, they're determined to better themselves."

Sarah thought about Charlie and George Lee and the lives they'd built for themselves and their families. She knew Corinne was right.

"Tell me, Sarah," Corinne asked after a moment. "What brought you down here this evening?"

"I wanted to learn more about the Chinese."

"Because of the women you met?"

"No," Sarah admitted sadly. "You see, a young girl was murdered a few days ago."

"How awful! And you knew her?"

"Yes, she's the daughter of a Chinese man and his Irish wife. She'd run off with a white man, someone her family didn't even know about and would never have approved of."

"And he killed her?"

"We don't know who killed her yet. Her father had wanted her to marry an older Chinese man, and that's why she ran away. I've been trying to figure out who might have killed her. I thought if I understood the Chinese better, that would help."

"I think I understand the Chinese very well," Corinne said. "And I can promise you one thing: the person who killed that girl was not Chinese."

Frank found Mrs. Lee at home the next morning. She needed a moment to recognize him, and when she did, her face lit with hope.

He quashed it instantly. "I don't have any news," he said quickly. "I have to ask you a few more questions."

The hope faded from her face, but she kept her composure. "Come in," she said, stepping aside so he could enter. "But I don't know what else I can tell you."

"How's your son doing?" he asked as he took a seat on the chair she indicated.

"Better," she said without much enthusiasm. "He's ashamed for what he did, scaring us like that. He didn't mean to hurt himself. He said . . ." She drew a deep breath to ward off the tears. "He said he just wanted to forget what happened to Angel."

"That's easy to understand," Frank said.

She nodded, pulled a handkerchief from her sleeve, and dabbed at her eyes. She was dressed in black, mourning her daughter. In spite of her grief, Frank noted, she was still well turned out. Her dress looked fairly new and fit her as if it had been made for her. It probably had. He noticed again the high quality of the furnishings in the room. Not as fancy as Sarah's family, of course. Sarah's parents were Old Money and had nothing but the very best. The Lees had it pretty good, though. Nothing old or worn. Nothing cheap or shabby. Frank felt a pang of envy. Charlie Lee had done well for himself.

"What did you want to ask me about?" she asked, breaking into his thoughts.

"I wanted to ask you about Angel's friends," he began. "In particular, the Chinese boys."

"The boys?" she echoed in surprise. "Why just the boys?"

Frank made up a lie on the spot. "We think she must've been strangled by a male. A female wouldn't have had the strength."

"Why would you think it was a *Chinese* boy, though?" she asked indignantly. "Ain't it more likely to be that boy she married or one of his brothers?"

"I questioned them, too," Frank said. "Seems like they were all someplace else when she died, and I want to make sure we aren't missing anybody."

She stared at him for a long moment, then shuddered slightly and dabbed at her eyes again. "This is so hard."

"I'm sorry, Mrs. Lee," he said quite truthfully. Her pain was difficult to witness. "Maybe I could ask your son instead. He'd know which boys Angel knew. Is he around?"

She looked up in surprise. "I . . . Yes, he is. He's been in

his room since . . . Well, since he came to himself again, after the opium."

"Could I see him?"

She silently debated his request. She didn't know whether
to trust him or not, and Frank couldn't blame her.

"I'm only going to ask him a few questions," he promised. "It won't take long."

She considered another minute or two and then said, "I'll
get him."

"I can go to him," Frank said. "It might be better if we
had some privacy anyway. He may not want you to hear
what he tells me."

This time her tears were too quick for her, and they over-
flowed before she remembered the handkerchief. "Angel
was a good girl," she insisted, scrubbing at her cheeks with
the delicate scrap of linen.

"I know she was," Frank said. "Quinn O'Neal said he
never touched her until they were married." He hadn't said
that exactly, but it was what Mrs. Lee needed to hear.

She made a small, tortured sound and looked away.
"I'll take you back to Harry's room," she said, rising to
her feet.

Frank followed her down the hallway, and he admired
the pictures hanging on the walls and the carpet that muf-
fled their footsteps. Frank had never realized there was so
much money to be made in laundries.

Mrs. Lee didn't knock. She just opened the door to her son's
room. Looking over her shoulder, Frank could see the boy lying on a narrow bed that was pushed up against the wall. He
lay on his side, his face turned toward that wall, his knees
drawn up as if to protect himself from a blow.

"Harry," his mother said. "Detective Sergeant Malloy is here. He needs to ask you some questions about Angel."

Harry didn't move, and after a few seconds, Frank felt the awful sense of dread stealing over him. If Harry was dead, too, how would his mother ever bear it?

9

SARAH SAT ACROSS HER KITCHEN TABLE FROM MRS. Ellsworth. They'd been drinking coffee and sampling some donuts Mrs. Ellsworth had fried up that morning. The older woman had listened intently as Sarah told her about her visit to the church last night.

"Why is your friend so sure that it wasn't a Chinese who killed that girl?" she asked.

"Because the Chinese are so meek."

"Meek?" Mrs. Ellsworth echoed with a frown. "What does she mean by that?"

"I think she meant it in the Biblical sense, as in turning the other cheek instead of fighting back. They're tormented terribly, but in general, they don't fight back."

"Is that because they're meek or because they're afraid?" Mrs. Ellsworth asked skeptically.

"I'm sure being afraid has a lot to do with it," Sarah said. "They're almost always outnumbered, so if they tried to fight back, they'd certainly be killed. It's not just about being afraid of someone stronger, though. Even children torment them."

"Street Arabs, you mean?" Mrs. Ellsworth asked, referring to the homeless children who lived wild in the streets.

"I'm not sure it's only them, although I'd hate to think children from respectable homes would harass the Chinese. They throw rocks through their windows and otherwise vandalize their property, and the police won't do a thing about it. And if the Chinese victim tries to retaliate, the neighbors attack *him*."

"I'm no champion of the Chinese, like your friend Mrs. Adkins, but that isn't right. If they aren't hurting anyone, why won't people leave them alone?"

"For the same reason bullies will always find a victim, I suppose."

"So your friend thinks the Chinese are too meek—or afraid—to have murdered this girl."

"She also thinks they aren't a violent people. She said they rarely even fight among themselves. They treat each other with respect."

"I'm sure they all behave themselves when they're at the church, but there must be at least a few bad apples in the bunch," Mrs. Ellsworth argued. "Nobody's that perfect."

"I thought so, too. That's something Mr. Malloy will know about. But Corinne insisted the Chinese are all devoted family men. There's also the practical matter of not wanting to do anything that would attract the attention of the police."

"There's nothing to say the killer was a member of the

girl's family, is there? He could have been another Chinese, but someone not related to her. How about the man the girl was supposed to marry? I thought we'd already decided he was the most likely suspect," Mrs. Ellsworth reminded her.

"I haven't met him, so I don't know enough to say one way or the other," Sarah replied. "Although it would be quite satisfactory if he were the killer, since we don't know him and therefore don't care about him."

"Exactly," Mrs. Ellsworth agreed.

Sarah was getting up to pour them more coffee when she heard her front doorbell ring. This time she really was being called to a delivery. She packed her medical bag and set out.

FRANK STARED AT HARRY'S STILL FORM, REFUSING TO believe he could be dead. Then slowly, ever so slowly, as if every movement pained him, Harry straightened his legs and turned his head to see who had disturbed him.

His eyes—those strangely round eyes—stared hard at Frank, taking his measure. Finally, he said, "You were here the other day."

"When you took the opium," Frank confirmed. "Yeah, I was here. I helped save your life."

A spasm of emotion flickered over his face. Frank hadn't expected gratitude, but he hadn't expected resentment, either. Harry looked as if he very much minded Frank's interference.

"Thank you, Mrs. Lee," Frank said. "You can leave me and Harry alone now."

"Alone?" Harry echoed, struggling to sit up. "Why do we need to be alone?"

"I want to ask you about your sister's friends," Frank

said, easing past Mrs. Lee into the room and gently closing the door in her face. "I thought you might be more honest if your mother wasn't listening."

"I never knew Angel was seeing that white fellow," he insisted. "She never said a word about him to me."

"She wouldn't have wanted you to know," Frank said reasonably. "You might've warned her away or told your parents. She thought she was in love."

"Maybe she did, but *he* didn't love *her*," Harry insisted.

"You sure about that?"

"How could he? She was Chinese."

Frank raised his eyebrows. "You don't think a white boy could love a Chinese girl?"

"They hate us," he said bitterly. "The whites all hate us. If he wanted Angel, it was because he wanted to use her and throw her away. I tried to tell her that, after we found her with him. Ma did, too, but she wouldn't listen."

Frank walked the short distance to the bed and sat down on the foot of it. Harry quickly drew his legs up, pulling his knees to his chest, and scooted back until his shoulders touched the headboard. He was either being polite to make more room, or he was repulsed and didn't want Frank touching him. Frank took a moment to look around.

The furniture in here was also good quality, and the room was much neater than he had expected a boy's to be. A shelf on one wall held several bowls of sand with long thin sticks stuck into them and a few small bowls that appeared to hold dried-up bits of food. A picture of a saint with slanted eyes hung on the wall above it, along with some Chinese lettering on a piece of rice paper. It looked strangely like an altar, although Frank had never seen a Chinese altar and couldn't imagine why anyone would have one in the bedroom.

He looked over at Harry again, noticing for the first time his odd choice of clothing. "Nice suit you're wearing," he remarked.

Harry self-consciously fingered the fabric of his ratty shirt. "Sackcloth," he said.

It did look like a sack, or rather, like he'd made it out of sacks. The rough brown fabric couldn't possibly be comfortable. "Doesn't it itch?"

"It's supposed to itch. It's for mourning," Harry explained with a hint of impatience.

"Your mother isn't wearing it."

"*Chinese* mourning," he clarified tersely. "Only the parents and grandparents are supposed to wear it, but I thought . . ." He cleared his throat. "I'm doing it for Angel."

"Do you usually dress like a Chinese?"

His expression hardened. "Most of the time."

"What about the rest of the time?"

"When I don't want to attract attention, I dress like an American."

Frank knew what kind of attention he might want to avoid. The Chinese were always a temptation to any drunk who wanted to cause trouble. "Your father always wears American clothes," Frank remembered. Charlie Lee wore a business suit, but like Frank, he still couldn't hide what he was. If Frank's attitude gave him away, Lee's complexion and features betrayed him, no matter how he might dress.

His son was different, though. His features weren't noticeably Chinese. If he dressed like an American . . .

"My father does what he has to," Harry said.

"Why does he have to dress like an American?"

"To do business."

Frank nodded his understanding. Business was business,

and Charlie Lee was a practical man. He'd even cut his hair in the American style. "You don't have a pigtail, though," Frank noted.

The boy's hand shot up to touch the back of his neck where it would have hung. "My mother . . . she made me cut it off."

"When was that?" Frank asked curiously.

"A couple years ago."

That meant Harry wasn't a suspect. Frank was glad. He wouldn't have wanted Mrs. Lee to lose both her children.

"I thought you wanted to ask me questions about Angel," he reminded Frank irritably.

"Tell me about the boys Angel knew."

"If I'd known she was sneaking around, I would've stopped her. She wouldn't have married that bastard, and she'd be alive now," he said angrily.

"I know she didn't tell you about Quinn O'Neal, but what about the Chinese boys she knew?"

"What about them?"

"Who are they? How did she know them? Did any of them pay particular attention to her?"

Harry frowned. He looked a lot like his mother when he frowned. "What difference does that make?"

"It makes a lot of difference if one of them wanted her for himself and couldn't stand the thought of her being with O'Neal."

"Nobody was in love with her," Harry said confidently.

"You're sure about that?" Frank challenged. "You said yourself, you didn't know about O'Neal."

"The boys she knows . . . knew," he corrected himself painfully. "The Chinese, they're all babies. They would never . . . That's a stupid idea."

Frank didn't like being called stupid, but he was willing to consider the possibility. "But if a Chinese man killed her, who could it have been?"

Harry stared at him, his dark eyes shocked at first as he absorbed the implication. Frank could almost see his mind working as he thought it through, and once again his hand shot up to the back of his neck. "A Chinese man," he repeated, obviously remembering Frank's question about the pigtail. "He had a queue."

"If that's what you call a pigtail, then yeah, he did."

"Someone saw him, and he had a queue," Harry decided. Clever boy. Frank had to admire his powers of deduction.

"And if someone did see him, who could it have been?" Frank asked.

He waited as Harry considered. Finally, the boy nodded his head, satisfied he'd figured it out. "There's only one Chinese man with a queue who'd care if Angel got married to somebody else."

"And who would that be?" Frank asked.

Harry's expression hardened. "The man my father was going to marry her off to—John Wong."

MRS. LEE HELPFULLY TOLD FRANK THAT JOHN WONG owned several businesses in the city. In addition to some restaurants, he ran boardinghouses for single Chinese men. Mr. Wong wasn't present at any of these legitimate businesses on this fine morning, as Frank discovered the hard way, but Frank learned Wong also ran an establishment that Mrs. Lee hadn't known about and that no one else would explain exactly. This was because it was a combination opium den and gambling parlor.

The Chinese didn't play normal games of chance like dice and poker. They had their own, and their favorite was fan-tan. No one seemed to know why it was called that. Certainly, there were no fans involved. Near as Frank could figure, the players sat around a low table and bet on something to do with how many coins would be left over from a big pile when the cashier had removed most of them. The important thing for him to know was that sometimes the players thought they got cheated and started a fight. That was about the only time the police got involved with a disturbance by the Chinese. Amazingly enough, even that didn't happen very often. They were a quiet bunch. If a few rowdies didn't insist on beating one up every now and then, nobody would even know they were around.

After checking all of Wong's other businesses and not finding him at any of them, Frank finally barged into the mystery business, causing quite a stir because, of course, everyone recognized him as a policeman. Most scattered instantly, leaving the hall deserted except for a couple of fellows enjoying their opium dreams, and a big, unhappy man who was probably the manager.

"What you want? We pay money to Tom Lee. We no get trouble," he insisted, convinced Frank was there to raid the place. Tom Lee, no relation to Charlie, was the Chinaman who handled the bribes from his countrymen to ensure the police wouldn't bother them.

"I'm looking for John Wong. Is he here?"

"No here. No here," he said, waving his hands excitedly. "Never here. Go away."

Frank looked around at the fan-tan table with its pile of coins. "I could arrest you for gambling," he remarked, then glanced over at the dozing customers. "Or I could arrest you for selling opium. I could even say I found a bunch of un-deraged white girls in here that you'd kidnapped."

"No girl, no girl!" the man shrieked frantically. "You see, no girl."

"I don't actually have to find one to say that I did," Frank pointed out. "But if you'd tell me where to find Mr. Wong, I'll just forget about whatever I saw here and be on my way."

The man was frightened. The question was, did he fear Frank more than he feared John Wong?

"You no say I tell you," he negotiated.

"No, I won't say anything about how I found him," Frank promised.

The fellow gave Frank an address and escorted him out the door.

To Frank's surprise, the address proved to be a well-kept house on a side street near Mott. If the Lee family lived well, John Wong was doing even better. Frank rang the doorbell and waited. After a while, a young Chinese man answered. He wore the silk blouse and baggy pants that were almost a uniform for the Chinese in the city. He had wrapped his queue around his head, probably so bullies wouldn't be tempted to pull it.

"What do you want?" he asked with a worried frown. Once again, Frank had been correctly identified.

"I want to see Mr. Wong."

"He not here."

"Where is he?" Frank asked mildly. No sense in getting riled up until it was necessary.

"I not know. He gone. Not come back."

"Isn't this his house?" Frank asked in feigned confusion.

The young man nodded. "Yes, yes, his house. He not here now."

"When will he be back?"

The fellow's dark eyes flitted nervously about. "Tomorrow," he finally decided. "Come back tomorrow."

Frank shook his head. "I'm here now. I'll wait for him."

Catching the fellow by surprise, he pushed the door open, forcing him backward, and stepped inside. The front hallway ended in a stairway to the second floor, and doorways on either side led to spacious rooms. Carpets on the floor and lace curtains in the windows, Frank noticed enviously in the moment before the young fellow started shouting something in Chinese. Frank didn't have to understand the language to know he was shouting a warning to John Wong.

He heard a disturbance upstairs, the sound of feet hitting the floor and people scrambling to either escape or hide. Frank pushed past the young man, who was trying to block his way, and started up the stairs, taking them two at a time. He could hear someone in one of the rooms shouting what sounded like, "Kee-ree, kee-ree!" Then a door opened, and a Chinese man appeared. He was wrapping a silk robe around his naked body and looking harried. He stopped dead when he saw Frank.

"What do you want?" he demanded with an authority that indicated he owned the place.

"John Wong?" Frank asked.

"I have done nothing wrong," he informed Frank haughtily.

"Then you won't mind answering a few questions."

"Question about what?"

"About Angel Lee."

Wong's expression hardened. "I know nothing about her. She is married—to a white man. Why do you come to me about her?"

"I'm trying to find out who killed her."

Wong's eyes narrowed suspiciously. "Kill? What you mean, kill?"

"I mean she's dead," Frank said, wondering if it could be possible that Wong didn't know.

"Angel is dead?"

Frank tried to read his expression, but the man was too used to concealing his true feelings. "Yes, she was murdered. Do you mind if I ask you a few questions?"

Wong shook his head. "I know nothing about this."

The fellow who had answered the door had crept up the stairs behind Frank, and now he asked Wong something in Chinese. He responded tersely, and the young man scampered down the stairs again.

"You are from the police?" Wong asked Frank.

"That's right. I'm trying to find Angel's killer, and I need some information from you."

"I do not know who killed her," he insisted.

"You might know something that will help me find out who did, though."

Wong didn't want to cooperate. He wanted to throw Frank down the stairs. Frank could see it in his eyes, but then he glanced at the door through which he'd come, and instantly, his attitude changed.

"You will let me dress myself," he said, gesturing toward the silk robe, which was all he wore over his slender frame. "Then I will speak with you . . . Downstairs," he added.

Then he called out something in Chinese to the young man, who was waiting at the foot of the stairs. The young man hurried back up to escort Frank. Frank didn't want to leave Wong. He might try to escape down the back stairs or something, but Frank figured he wouldn't be very cooperative if Frank tried to force the issue. Better to let Wong think he was in charge of the interview. He let the boy lead him down to the front parlor.

Frank had a few minutes to think about what had just happened while he waited for Wong to put on some clothes. Plainly, the fellow who answered the door knew Wong was busy, and Wong certainly hadn't wanted to be disturbed. The fact that he'd been naked, in his bedroom, in the middle of the day, told Frank a woman was involved. He didn't particularly care if Wong had a woman up there, although Wong might expect him to, especially if she was white, and she undoubtedly was.

The newspapers liked to print stories about young white girls being kidnapped by the Chinese and forced to smoke opium so they'd become helpless sex slaves. The stories enflamed the prejudices against the Chinese, but they had very little basis in fact, at least from Frank's experience. He'd never found a white girl in an opium den who wasn't there of her own free will, and there seemed to be plenty of white women perfectly willing to go with Chinese men, making kidnapping totally unnecessary.

Like Mrs. Lee, for instance. And the woman upstairs was probably another.

Frank made himself comfortable in Wong's lavishly furnished parlor, but he didn't have to wait long. Wong appeared in just a few minutes, dressed in a silk blouse and baggy pants, but his "uniform" was made of much higher quality material than that worn by the ordinary Chinese laborers in the street. It had also been tailored carefully to fit. Wong had donned richly embroidered slippers, and smoothed his hair and wound his queue neatly around his head. He was a handsome man, for being Chinese, and well built. Frank guessed he must be around forty.

"I am very sorry about Angel," he said when he had taken a seat in a chair near Frank's. "Her father is old friend."

"Is that why he wanted you to marry her?"

Wong didn't like the question, but he wasn't going to say so. "Charlie Lee want me take care of his daughter."

"It must've hurt your pride when she ran away."

He chose his words carefully. "She very young. Does not know what is best."

Frank noted that he still used the present tense. He wasn't used to her being dead yet. "You think she would've been happier married to you?" Frank asked skeptically.

"Yes," he said without hesitation. Frank let his surprise show, so Wong continued, "Look around. Do you not think so?"

He did, but he couldn't agree. "Angel was young, like you said. She must've had lots of young fellows chasing after her."

"Chasing?" Wong echoed with a frown.

"Courting," Frank clarified.

Wong shook his head emphatically. "Her father not permit."

"Are you saying none of the Chinese boys she knew wanted her for themselves?"

"They cannot support wife," Wong explained patiently. "They never look on her."

Frank was impressed with Wong's ability to speak English. He had an accent, of course, but Frank wasn't having any trouble at all understanding him. The only thing that bothered him was the way Wong couldn't seem to pronounce "l" clearly. He'd noticed that most Chinese had the same difficulty. They pronounced it like an "r" instead.

"Where were you the day before yesterday?" Frank asked suddenly.

Wong didn't like this question, either. "I tell you, I not kill Angel."

"Then you must have been doing something else," Frank replied reasonably. "What was it?"

Wong frowned as he considered. "I here."

"Here, at home, all day?" Frank asked.

Wong nodded.

"Was anybody with you?"

Frank noticed Wong's gaze flicker upward, as if he was thinking about the woman upstairs. Had she been keeping him busy for *three days*?

"I alone," Wong lied. "Except for Ah Woh, my nephew. He tell you I am here."

"I'm sure he will." Ah Woh would undoubtedly swear to anything John Wong wanted.

A loud thump on the ceiling startled them both, and Wong looked up again. The woman wasn't being very discreet. What had Wong called her? Kee-ree.

Suddenly, Frank knew exactly who was upstairs. He was on his feet and out the door in an instant, Wong's surprised cry of protest echoing behind him. Once again he took the stairs two at a time, with Wong close behind him.

"Kee-ree!" Wong shouted in warning, but she misunderstood.

She thought he was summoning her. She opened the bedroom door and looked out. "Johnny?" she replied, and started when she saw Frank barreling down on her. She tried to shut the door, but Frank caught it and pushed it open again.

She went stumbling backward, catching herself on the bedpost. She wore a beautiful red silk robe and apparently nothing else. She was a tall girl and buxom. The robe probably belonged to Wong, and it fit her fine, her curves filling the soft fabric invitingly.

"Keely," Frank said, pronouncing it correctly. "Keely O'Neal." Behind him, Wong made a furious sound, but he quieted at a look from Frank.

Keely gaped at him in surprise. "Who are you, and what do you want?"

"Detective Sergeant Frank Malloy," he informed her. "And maybe I'm looking for you. Have you been kidnapped?" Certain things were starting to make sense now, like why Mrs. O'Neal had been lying about her daughter's whereabouts. She must have known Keely was here.

Keely looked genuinely puzzled. "Kidnapped? Who would kidnap me?"

Frank looked around. An elaborately carved, four-poster, walnut bed dominated the room. The bedclothes were rumpled, the spread half on the floor. He glanced meaningfully at Wong, then back at the girl. "Oh, maybe a rich Chinese man who wanted a concubine."

"What's a concubine?" she asked, curling a strand of her long, dark hair around one finger. It hung nearly to her waist and needed a good brushing.

"From the looks of things, you are," he replied.

"I ain't no whore, if that's what you're talking about," she informed him indignantly, pulling her robe more tightly around her. "Johnny, tell him. We're getting married!"

"Are you old enough to get married?" Frank asked before Wong could confirm or deny.

"I'm eighteen," she lied.

"No, you're not," Frank said. "How long have you been here?"

"I don't know," she said defiantly. "A couple days."

He knew she'd been gone from home at least since Angel died. He looked at Wong for confirmation.

Wong's face was a dull red, but whether from anger or embarrassment, Frank couldn't tell. "Four day," he said through gritted teeth.

Frank didn't bother to hide his amazement. "You've been up here with her for *four days*?"

"All except for when you went down to talk to Mr. Lee," Keely reminded him quickly. "He was with me the rest of the time."

Frank couldn't speak for a moment. *Four days!* Miss Keely O'Neal must be much more interesting and not nearly so innocent as he would've suspected. "When did you talk to Lee?" he asked Wong finally.

"Three day," Wong said, now obviously furious.

Before Angel was killed, Frank noted. "And what were you doing *two* days ago?" he asked Wong for the second time.

Wong just glared back at him, and after a few seconds, Keely laughed wickedly. Frank turned to her.

"He was up here with me all day," she told him with obvious delight. "What do you *think* he was doing?"

"The whole time between noon and early evening?" Frank asked to clarify.

"Oh, yes." Keely grinned provocatively and looked at Wong. "That was the day I dressed up, remember?"

Wong remembered, but it wasn't something he wanted

Frank to know about. "Angel is dead," Wong told her bluntly.

Keely's grin vanished. "I heard him telling you that somebody killed her. Was that when she was killed? In the afternoon, two days ago?"

"That's right," Frank said.

"Well, we was both right here the whole time. You can ask Ah Woh."

Naturally, Wong's nephew and his mistress would both swear he was here when Angel was murdered. Neither was a very reliable witness.

"You don't seem too upset to hear about Angel," Frank said to her. "I thought you were friends."

"We wasn't never *friends*," Keely said with distaste. "She would just cry to me about how miserable she was because nobody else would listen to her."

"Kee-ree," Wong said sharply. "Put on clothes."

Keely seemed startled to realize she'd been holding a conversation with a strange man wearing nothing but a flimsy robe.

"Don't bother," Frank said, turning away. "I'm finished." He strode out of the bedroom. Wong followed him, closing the door behind him. Frank turned to face him in the hallway.

"She was not kidnap," Wong said with the faintest hint of apprehension. He knew Frank could ruin him with an accusation like that. Outraged whites would destroy his home and his businesses and probably string him up in the bargain.

"Who brought her here?"

"No one. She come herself," Wong said. "She say . . ."

"What did she say?" Frank pressed.

He had to force himself to speak the words. "She say Angel tell her about me. Angel say I make good husband."

"And you believed her?" Frank asked in amazement.

"No," Wong admitted.

Now that made sense. "But you let her stay anyway," he guessed.

Wong didn't need to answer. Only a fool would have turned her away, and Wong was no fool.

"What did you and Charlie Lee talk about the other day?" Frank asked.

Wong stiffened slightly in silent resistance. "Business."

"His business or yours?"

"Business," he repeated stubbornly. He thought it was none of Frank's concern what they had discussed. Maybe it wasn't, but Frank would find out eventually anyway.

"Do you have any idea who might have wanted to kill Angel Lee?" Frank tried.

Wong gave the question a few moments' thought. "She not obey father. She is punished."

"You think her father killed her?" Frank asked, surprised that Wong would make the accusation.

"I do not know," Wong said. "But I did not."

Frank wasn't sure about that, but he decided to take his leave for now. He started down the stairs, and Wong followed. Either he was playing the good host and seeing him out, or he just wanted to make sure Frank left.

When they reached the front door, Ah Woh was there to open it. Frank gave him one of his fiercest glares. "Where was your uncle two days ago?"

The fellow's eyes widened with terror, and the color drained from his face, but he looked to Wong for guidance.

"Tell him," Wong said.

"Here," the boy fairly squeaked, pointing upstairs. "He sleep, all afternoon."

No surprise there. Frank started out the door, then stopped and turned back to Wong. "You really going to marry her?"

Wong stared back, revealing nothing.

10

Sarah was playing with Catherine upstairs when she heard someone ringing her front doorbell. Catherine's disappointment mirrored her own. She'd just gotten back from her last delivery a short while ago. Maeve went down to answer the door, and Sarah waited with Catherine for the inevitable summons.

"Mrs. Brandt," Maeve called up after a few minutes, "Mr. Malloy is here!"

Catherine's face lit with happiness, and she was halfway down the stairs before Sarah even got to her feet. By the time she reached the front hallway, Malloy was holding the child in his arms and asking her questions. She responded by nodding or shaking her head, but Malloy didn't mind that she wasn't speaking.

"Malloy," Sarah said in greeting. She didn't bother to

hide her delight at seeing him. Why his presence always brought her so much pleasure, she didn't bother to question. He was, simply, the most interesting person she knew, and the one who made her feel most alive. For a long time, she'd tried to pretend that was because he had involved her in his investigations, but she now knew that wasn't the real reason. The real reason was because when she was with him, she felt like a woman.

"Mrs. Brandt," he replied, looking just as pleased to see her as she was to see him.

"Mr. Malloy, we've got some chocolate cake," Maeve said. "Would you like some?"

He pretended to consider. "Did you make it or did Mrs. Ellsworth?"

Maeve grinned slyly. "We did, but she helped us, so it's very good."

"All right then," he said, making the girls laugh with delight. "I'd love to taste it."

The girls escorted him back to the kitchen with Sarah following along behind, watching fondly as he teased them and made them giggle. Children could never be fooled by a person's character, and the fact that the girls adored Malloy told her everything she would ever need to know about him.

Half an hour later, when Malloy had sampled the cake and declared it delicious, he asked Maeve to take Catherine back upstairs so he and Mrs. Brandt could talk for a bit.

When they were alone, Sarah refilled their coffee cups and took a seat opposite him. "Do you have news for me?"

"I haven't found Angel's killer yet, if that's what you mean, but I figured I better give you a report pretty soon or

I'd find you waiting for me down at Headquarters some morning, demanding an explanation."

Sarah smiled. The last place Sarah would choose to track down Malloy would be Police Headquarters. She'd once been locked in an interrogation room for several hours for trying that. "I've been thinking about it a lot," she confessed. "It's been very difficult not being involved."

"I figured it was," he said, and she saw the sympathy in his dark eyes.

"Don't keep me in suspense any longer," she said. "What have you found out?"

"I found out Angel wasn't very happy with her new life," he began.

"That's what her mother said, but she still couldn't convince Angel to leave Quinn and come back home."

"Why do you think she wouldn't go?" he asked.

Sarah shook her head. "Pride, probably. No girl wants to admit she made a terrible mistake and go crawling back to her parents."

"Could she have been afraid of going back? Maybe that they'd punish her?"

"I don't know what Angel thought, of course, but I think her parents would have been so happy to get her home that they wouldn't have dreamed of punishing her."

"What about the arranged marriage? Would they still have forced her to marry Wong?"

"She was already married," Sarah reminded him. "They would've had to get an annulment or something."

"Unless the Chinese don't care about that. Maybe they'd just give her to Wong and marry them in some Chinese ceremony."

"I can't imagine Minnie Lee would allow that, since Angel was married in the church."

"Maybe she didn't have any say. Charlie Lee went to see John Wong two days before Angel died."

"Why?"

"I don't know yet."

"But you think it had something to do with Angel's death," she guessed.

He shrugged. "I found a witness who saw Angel with a Chinese man right before she died."

"Oh my! Did this witness see Angel get killed?"

"No, but I'm pretty sure the man she saw was the murderer."

"Oh, dear," Sarah said in dismay.

"What?"

"It's just . . . I went to see an old friend of mine the other day. She runs a Chinese Sunday school and also gives English classes to the Chinese."

"I thought you weren't going to get involved in this case," he reminded her with a disapproving frown.

"I haven't!" she claimed, then added, "At least not very much," when he raised his eyebrows skeptically. "I was curious, though. I thought if I learned more about the Chinese people, I might be able to help a little."

He didn't seem impressed by her reasoning. "What did your friend tell you?"

"She has great respect for the Chinese," Sarah reported. "And she doesn't believe a Chinese man would have killed Angel."

"I suppose she has a really good reason for thinking that," he said in disgust.

"She thinks they're too . . . gentle."

Malloy sighed. "Even gentle people commit murder, and I haven't noticed the Chinese being particularly *gentle*."

"I'm just telling you what she said," Sarah reminded him.

"And I'm just telling you what the witness said. She saw a Chinese man."

"Did he see the man's face?"

"The witness is a she, and no, she didn't. She only saw the clothes."

"Do you think it was John Wong?"

"I did until I went to see him."

"Did he have an alibi?"

"He has a mistress."

"A mistress?" Sarah echoed in surprise.

"Yes, and you'll never guess who she is—Keely O'Neal, Quinn's sister."

Sarah needed a minute to take that in. "His sister is Wong's mistress? How on earth did that happen?"

"From what Wong told me, Keely showed up on his doorstep four days ago and offered herself to him."

"But how would she even know . . . ? Oh! I guess Angel must have told her about Wong, that her parents had wanted her to marry him."

"According to Wong, Keely claimed that Angel had recommended him as a possible husband."

"That sounds very strange."

"I thought so, too. Even Wong didn't believe it. But Keely and Angel are the same age, and Quinn said they spent a lot of time together, off by themselves, talking. They probably did talk about Wong, but what could Angel have said to make Keely run off to find him?"

Sarah considered, trying to put herself in the girls' places and imagining what might have happened. "Angel hated Wong," Sarah recalled, remembering the day Angel had burst into Cora Lee's flat to beg her to save her from the unwanted marriage. "She wouldn't have sent Keely to him, so she must have *inadvertently* convinced Keely she'd do well with him."

"How could she do that?"

"Let's see, what would a girl like Keely want in a husband?" Sarah mused, and then she realized she didn't have to imagine at all. "Let's ask Maeve."

Sarah summoned Maeve and quickly explained the situation to her. "What could Angel have said about Mr. Wong that would make Keely want to marry him?"

"That girl Angel, her family was rich," Maeve said after some thought. "She had pretty clothes and a nice place to live. She was never cold or hungry, and she didn't have to work. She never had to be afraid of anything."

Sarah understood instantly. "Keely would think that sounded like heaven."

"Sure she would," Maeve confirmed. "And that Mr. Wong, he's even richer than Angel's father. Keely probably thought that if Angel didn't want him, she'd take him so she could have a life like Angel did."

"So she finds Mr. Wong and presents herself," Sarah said in amazement. "Is she smart enough to have figured out a plan like that?" she asked Malloy.

"Oh, yes," Malloy confirmed. "Keely O'Neal could probably run Tammany Hall," he added, naming the Democratic Party Headquarters where crooked politicians controlled much of what happened in the city.

"Do you think this Keely killed Angel?" Maeve asked.

"No, a witness saw a Chinese man kill her," Sarah said. "Mr. Malloy thought it might have been Mr. Wong."

Maeve frowned. "Why would he kill her if he had this Keely to take her place?"

"He might have been mad at her for running away," Sarah explained. "Angel insulted him by eloping with the Irish boy so she wouldn't have to marry him."

"Maybe," Maeve said, "but killing somebody . . . Seems like he'd need a better reason."

"You'd be surprised at the reasons people kill other people," Malloy told her grimly. "Thanks, Maeve. You've been a big help."

When Maeve was gone, Sarah said, "What other Chinese men could have done it?"

"The only ones that were close to her and might have had a reason are her father and brother."

"I hate to think one of them did it," Sarah said. "Besides, her brother hardly even looks Chinese."

"The witness was looking out a fifth-floor window," Malloy said. "Remember, all she could see for sure were the clothes."

"Well, Harry does dress like a Chinese sometimes."

"Most of the time, according to him," Malloy said. "Lucky for him, he doesn't have a pigtail."

"Did the witness see a pigtail?"

"Yes."

Sarah tried to picture Harry Wong dressed in his Chinese clothes. "Are you sure Harry doesn't have a pigtail?"

"Yes. Remember, he didn't have one that day when he was drugged and we were walking him around? That was only hours after Angel died. He told me this morning that his mother made him cut it a couple years ago."

That didn't sound right. Sarah would have sworn . . .

"He dresses like a white man when he wants to pass

unnoticed," Malloy was saying. "He couldn't do that if his hair was long."

"I guess you're right," Sarah said. When he had come to her house to tell her his sister was dead, he'd been wearing Chinese clothes. She must have just assumed he had a pigtail, too. "So if it wasn't Harry . . ."

"That leaves Charlie Lee and John Wong," Malloy said.

"Maybe it was a stranger," Sarah argued.

"According to the witness, when Angel saw the man, she got up off the porch and went out into the yard to meet him. She knew him and wasn't afraid of him."

"Maybe she had a Chinese boyfriend we don't know about."

"Then nobody else knew about him, either. Harry swears none of the Chinese boys would have bothered with her, and Wong confirmed that. They knew she was out of their reach."

"But would she have gone out into the yard to meet John Wong like that? She didn't like him and would probably have been afraid of him."

Malloy sighed wearily. "You're probably right, but that only leaves her father, and I hope to God it wasn't him."

FRANK DECIDED TO CONFRONT CHARLIE LEE AT HIS business instead of at home. He didn't want to upset Mrs. Lee any more than he had to. If Charlie had an alibi, then she wouldn't ever have to know he'd been a suspect.

Lee owned several laundries, but Frank easily found the one where he had his office. The large building fairly hummed with activity, as a small army of men worked diligently sorting, scrubbing, rinsing, ironing, and folding. The place carried the familiar smells of laundry day in the tenement yard, multiplied a thousand times.

After a brief wait, one of the men escorted Frank into Charlie Lee's inner office at the rear of the building. The room was as Spartan as his home was luxurious. Lee didn't believe in wasting any money here, apparently. A cheap desk and chair, a filing cabinet, and a straight-backed chair for visitors were the only furnishings. No pictures on the walls, no carpet on the floor.

Lee didn't bother with a greeting and didn't offer to shake hands. "Do you know who kill my daughter?"

"Not yet," Frank said. "I need to ask you a few questions." He took the empty visitor's chair without being invited.

This clearly annoyed Lee, but he knew better than to antagonize a policeman. "I tell you, I know nothing."

"What did you talk to John Wong about the day before Angel was killed?"

He stared back at Frank in surprise. "How you know this?"

"He told me. What did you talk about?"

"Did he not tell you?"

"I want to hear your version."

Lee was as angry about revealing the topic of this discussion as Wong had been. "I tell him Angel be home soon," he said as if the words were being pulled from him.

"I thought she'd refused to go home with you."

"She would come," Lee said confidently, although Frank thought he wasn't as confident as he pretended.

"You mean, you'd force her to leave her husband and come home with you."

"No force," Lee insisted. "She not happy. She come home soon."

"And then what? You'd marry her off to Wong?"

Lee didn't like having to defend his decision. "We make agreement," he said stubbornly.

Frank pretended to consider this. "Let me get this straight. You made a deal to sell your daughter to Wong, who's old enough to be her father, even though she told you she didn't want to marry him."

"I not sell Angel!" he protested indignantly.

"Don't lie to me!" Frank snarled, leaning in to intimidate him. "How much did he pay you?"

"He pay bride-price!" Lee snarled right back.

Frank wasn't sure he'd heard him correctly. "What?"

"A man pay father of girl for right to marry."

"So you did sell her!"

"Not sell," Lee insisted. *"Give."*

"So you were going to give your daughter to an old man."

"Wong not old!"

"Too old for Angel!"

"No! He rich. He take care of her. She be safe!"

"Safe? Safe from what?"

"Safe from . . ." He seemed to be struggling to find the right words. "From *America*!"

"What are you talking about?" Frank demanded in confusion.

"She Chinese girl. White no like. Make trouble. All the time, trouble. Wong, he keep safe. No trouble." Tears welled in Lee's eyes. "My Angel, I want keep her safe. All her life, safe. Wong, he do that."

Frank stared at him dumbfounded. "Are you saying you wanted Angel to marry Wong because he could protect her from . . . from people who hate the Chinese?"

"He give her house, food, clothes. He take care. Not like American boy. She starve with American boy!"

Frank thought he was probably right about that. But no matter why Lee had wanted her to marry his friend, he would still be angry when she defied him. Wong had said Lee might be angry enough to kill Angel. "You must've been pretty mad when she wouldn't go home with you," he tried.

"She foolish girl. She not want to say she make mistake. But she come home soon. I know this."

"And so you promised Wong that she would still marry him."

"Yes."

"And then you went to see Angel, and she refused to come home."

"No, not see her. I wait. She not happy. She be more unhappy tomorrow. I wait."

"When was the last time you saw Angel?"

"Five day, six day, maybe."

"Where were you the afternoon Angel died?"

"You think I kill Angel?" he asked angrily.

"I just asked where you were when she died," Frank said.

Lee's glare was murderous. "Here. I work here."

"And all your workers saw you, I guess." And they'd swear to it whether they had or not.

"I here. They see me," he insisted. "I not kill Angel."

Lee, he noticed, wore his queue wrapped around his head. When he had a hat on, as he would when he was outside and wearing his American suit of clothes, he could pass almost unnoticed on the street, unless someone looked directly into his face. *That's* what had been bothering Frank.

"Do you ever wear Chinese clothes?" Frank asked abruptly.

Lee's expression hardened. "No."

"Why not?"

He hesitated, as if revealing this secret to Frank caused him actual pain. "American no respect Chinese."

Of course. That made perfect sense. It also meant that

John Wong was the only suspect left who could have killed Angel.

WHILE SARAH AND THE GIRLS WERE ENJOYING THE STEW that Mrs. Ellsworth had shared with them this evening, Sarah couldn't stop her mind from wandering back to the conversation she'd had with Malloy earlier. Something was wrong with their reasoning, but she couldn't figure out what it was.

"Is something bothering you, Mrs. Brandt?" Maeve asked a little later, when she was helping Sarah clear the table.

"Catherine, why don't you go upstairs and play while Maeve and I do the dishes?" Sarah said, not wanting the child to hear any more about Angel Lee's murder. When she was gone, Sarah said, "I can't stop thinking about what Mr. Malloy told me this afternoon."

"You still don't think that Mr. Wong killed Angel, do you?"

Sarah smiled at her perception. "No, and I don't want to think it was her father, either."

"I didn't know you thought her father might've done it," Maeve said, slipping the last plate into the soapy water.

"I don't, or at least I hope he didn't, but he's one of the few Chinese men who could have had a reason." Sarah took a towel from the rack and began to dry the dishes as Maeve finished washing them.

"Is it certain that a Chinese man killed her?"

"Mr. Malloy found a witness who saw a Chinese man with Angel in the yard right before she died, so yes, that part is fairly certain."

"Did the witness see the man's face?"

"No, she was in one of the tenements, on the fifth floor, looking out the window."

"Can't see much from up there, can you?"

"She could see the man was wearing the kind of clothes a Chinese man wears, and that he had a pigtail."

"Then it could've been just about any Chinese man."

"No, it was someone Angel knew. When she saw the person, she went out into the yard to meet him. She wouldn't have done that if she didn't know the person well."

"Even still, she must've known other Chinese men besides Mr. Wong."

"None who would have gone to see her there, apparently. Except her father and brother, of course."

"Her brother was the one who came here to get you the day she died, wasn't he?"

"That's right."

"Why doesn't Mr. Malloy think her brother could've done it? My brothers used to whale on me something awful. Maybe he was just whaling on her and didn't really mean to kill her."

Sarah almost dropped the plate she'd been drying. This was the first time Maeve had ever mentioned her family or the life she'd had before she'd come to the Mission. Sarah's heart twisted in her chest at this hint of how awful that life had been, but she dared not reveal the slightest reaction. She didn't want Maeve to think she'd shocked her, or she'd never reveal another thing.

"No," Sarah said evenly. "Her brother couldn't have done it. The man who killed her had one of those pigtails the Chinese men wear, but her brother doesn't have one."

"He doesn't?" she asked in surprise.

"No, his hair is cut short."

"That's funny. I thought . . ."

"What did you think?" Sarah asked when she hesitated, re-alizing Maeve had had the same reaction as she over whether Harry Lee had a pigtail or not.

"I guess I thought he did."

"I did, too, but then Mr. Malloy reminded me that we'd spent a lot of time with Harry the evening Angel died, when he took the overdose of opium. His hair was definitely short."

"You'd know, then. Maybe I thought he had one because he was wearing those clothes and all. Whenever you see a Chinese man, seems like he's got a pigtail hanging down his back."

"That must have been it," Sarah agreed.

Maeve handed her the last glass to dry just as someone knocked on the back door. Sarah opened it to see Mrs. Ellsworth standing on the back stoop, holding something with a towel draped over it.

"I baked some pies today, and I thought you might want one," she said cheerfully, coming in without waiting for an invitation.

She stopped when she was only a few steps into the room, however, and looked closely at Sarah and Maeve. "Such seri-ous faces! What on earth were you two talking about?" she exclaimed.

"We were talking about who might have killed that poor Chinese girl," Sarah said.

"And about whether her brother has a pigtail or not," Maeve added sheepishly. It did sound a little silly when one tried to explain.

"A pigtail?" Mrs. Ellsworth echoed doubtfully.

"Yes, the long, single pigtails that Chinese men have," Sarah said.

"Oh, yes, I know what you're talking about," Mrs. Ellsworth said brightly. "Like that boy had, the one who came for you the other day."

FRANK WAS SITTING ON THE SOFA, HOLDING HIS SON Brian in his lap while the boy showed him the signs he'd learned that day, and Frank's mother translated. "Pretty soon he's going to know more words than I do," Frank remarked to her.

"Won't take much," she replied tartly.

Before he could think of a suitable response, someone knocked on their door.

"Who could that be at this hour?" his mother grumbled, getting up to answer.

Brian hadn't heard the knock, of course, but he stopped his signing to watch her expectantly. When he saw she was going to the door, his little body tensed with anticipation, and his blue eyes sparkled. A visitor was always exciting, and when he saw who it was, he scrambled down from Frank's lap and ran to the door, babbling incoherent sounds of delight. His grandmother wasn't nearly so happy.

"Good evening, Mrs. Malloy," Sarah Brandt said. "How are you?"

"I'm alive," Mrs. Malloy said sourly. "How are you, Miss Catherine?" she asked the child accompanying Sarah with much more enthusiasm.

Frank got to his feet as Brian fairly dragged Catherine into the room. Sarah came more slowly, having to sidle around Mrs. Malloy, who hadn't moved quite enough to allow her easy entrance.

"Good evening, Mr. Malloy," Sarah said with an impish gleam in her eye.

"Nice to see you, Mrs. Brandt," he said. "What brings you out?" He knew it had something to do with Angel Lee's murder. Nothing less would have brought her here where she knew she wasn't welcome.

"I needed to discuss something with you," she said with a strained smile.

Frank looked at the children. Brian had taken Catherine over to the corner where he kept his toys, and they were already engrossed in examining his wooden train.

"Ma, would you keep an eye on them while I get Mrs. Brandt a cup of coffee?"

"Thank you," Sarah said, directing it to his mother, who ignored her.

She knew the way to the kitchen, and Frank followed her. "I really don't need anything," she said, taking a seat at the table before he could pull out a chair for her. "Have you arrested anyone for Angel's murder yet?"

"No," he said, sitting down opposite her at the table. "What's wrong?"

"Maeve asked me about the case tonight while we were doing the dishes. I was telling her how the witness said the killer had a pigtail, and Maeve thought that Harry Lee had one. Remember I thought he had one, too? Maeve thought she'd seen one the day he came to tell me Angel had been murdered."

"But he doesn't have one," Frank reminded her.

"I know! I remembered seeing him the day Cora Lee's

baby was born, and I didn't think he had one then. And the day Angel died, when his father brought him home from the opium den, he also didn't have one. But earlier that day, when he came to get me, he did have one, Malloy. I thought I remembered seeing it, and so did Maeve, but Mrs. Ellsworth is positive she saw it!"

"Mrs. Ellsworth? Was she there when he came?"

"No, but you know that nothing happens on Bank Street that she doesn't know about. She *just happened* to be looking out her window when I came out of the house with Harry."

Frank couldn't help his grin. Mrs. Ellsworth was famous for *just happening* to notice things. They knew better than to complain, though. Her nosiness had once saved Sarah's life. "And she got a good look at Harry?"

"Just his back, she said, but she distinctly remembers that he had a pigtail."

"That's impossible," Frank said as kindly as he could.

"I know, but I saw it, too! When she was so certain, I finally remembered that I'd noticed it when we were walking up the stairs to the train station that day. He was in front of me, and people were staring at him. I guess I didn't think about it being out of the ordinary because I was so upset about Angel."

Frank frowned. He'd never known her to be fanciful. "But he didn't have it later that day, when his father brought him home," he reminded her.

"I know, and he didn't have it when I met him at Cora's, either. When I saw him that first time, I thought how he didn't look at all Chinese except for his clothes. I'm sure his hair was short then."

Frank ran a hand over his face. "All right. We agree he

didn't have it before Angel was killed, and he didn't have it the evening after she was killed," he said patiently. "How could he have one earlier that day?"

"I can't be positive, of course, but I think we may have figured it out. That was the only time I saw him wearing a hat."

"A hat? I thought we were talking about a pigtail."

"He was wearing one of those round hats the Chinese men wear. It looks like a dome."

"I know the kind you mean," he said.

"I think the pigtail must have been attached to it."

He wasn't sure he'd heard her right. "Attached to it?"

"Yes. I remembered that you told me Harry said his mother had made him cut his pigtail off a year ago."

"Two years," Frank corrected her.

"Two years, then. But what if he'd kept it? What if he felt he needed a pigtail in order to really look Chinese? You said yourself he almost always wears Chinese clothing."

"That's what *he* said," Frank allowed.

"Then he could have attached the pigtail to the hat. When he was out, he would be wearing the hat, and no one would notice it wasn't his real hair."

"Why didn't he have it when his father brought him home from the opium den, then?"

"I don't know, but he wasn't wearing a hat at all then. Maybe it fell off along the way, or maybe he left it behind. All I know is that he had a pigtail and a hat earlier that day."

Frank considered the ramifications of what she was telling him. "You know what this means, don't you?"

"Yes, it means Harry might have killed his sister. I don't think he did it on purpose, though," she quickly added. "I think he must have gone there to convince her to come home. She probably refused and argued with him. Whatever happened, he got mad and put his hands around her throat. He didn't mean to kill her. He probably was frustrated and angry. You know how brothers and sisters fight."

"The coroner did say she died real quick. There's a small bone in your neck, and if somebody squeezes it just right . . ." He let his explanation trail off when he saw the expression on Sarah's face. He cleared his throat. "But whether he meant to kill her or not, Angel is dead. That means Harry is guilty of murder."

"I know. That's why I hurried over here tonight. I wanted you to find out from me before you figured it out yourself and arrested Harry."

"You don't want me to arrest him?" Frank asked in amazement.

"We still don't know for sure that he did it," she reminded him. "We only know he might have. I wanted to be sure you knew that Harry could be a suspect, so you didn't arrest an innocent person. And to ask you . . ."

"Ask me what?" he prompted her with a feeling of foreboding.

"To ask that if you do find out Harry killed his sister, you pretend you couldn't solve the case and let him go."

11

FRANK HAD NEVER THOUGHT HE'D SEE THE DAY WHEN Sarah Brandt wanted to let a killer go free. He could almost understand it in this case, though. The Lee family hadn't done anything to deserve losing a daughter in the first place. It wouldn't be fair to find out their son was responsible, at least to Sarah's way of thinking. The problem was, in order to find out if Harry did kill his sister, he'd have to question him. If Harry *wasn't* guilty, that meant someone else was, someone Sarah didn't mind if he arrested, someone who needed punishment very badly. Frank wasn't going to let *that* person get off just because *Harry* might be guilty. But if he found out Harry was guilty, then he'd have to decide what to do about it. Sarah might want to let him go, assuming he'd killed Angel in the heat of passion, but Frank wasn't so sure.

So Frank was back at the Lees' flat the next morning. Mrs. Lee opened the door. This time she tried to control her hope, and Frank helped by instantly saying, "I need to ask Harry a few more questions."

She invited him inside. "He's still in his room. Can't get him to come out for anything, and he's still wearing that awful sackcloth suit. Even Charlie told him he was being silly. Angel never would've wanted that."

Frank thought Harry's excess of grief for his sister was more than suspicious. "Whatever happened to his hat?" Frank asked as if it didn't matter. "The one that has the queue on it?"

"I ain't seen it," she said with a hint of disgust, instantly confirming Sarah's theory. Frank had to cough to cover his reaction. Luckily, she was too distracted to notice. "I'd be just as happy if it was lost for good. He used to have a queue clear down to his waist. Grew it for years. I finally told him he had to cut it off. His father said the same thing. He didn't want Harry to look like a *coolie*, he said."

Knowing how Charlie had wanted to protect his daughter from the indignities of being Chinese, Frank shouldn't have been surprised that Charlie also wanted his son to rise above his Chinese heritage. "But Harry still dresses like a Chinese," Frank said.

Mrs. Lee's expression changed. She looked away and walked over to a chair. She started rearranging the lace doily that lay over the back, even though it had looked perfectly straight to Frank. "Yes, he . . . I guess he likes it," she said stiffly. Then, "I'll tell him you're here to see him." She hurried out, leaving Frank to wonder what he had said to disturb her.

A few moments later, she was back, with Harry following

at her heels. He looked like he'd been on a three-day drunk. His hair—his short hair—was uncombed, and his eyes were red-rimmed and sunken.

"What do you want?" he asked listlessly. If he'd killed his sister, he didn't seem too concerned about being questioned by the police.

"I want you to come down to Police Headquarters with me," Frank said.

"What for?" Mrs. Lee asked in alarm before Harry could even react.

"I've got some questions—"

"You can ask them right here, then," she insisted, a shrill edge to her voice.

"I'm going to take him down to Headquarters, Mrs. Lee," Frank said firmly, taking the boy by the arm. His eyes were wide with confusion. He didn't know why he should be afraid, but his mother certainly was.

She grabbed his other arm. "No! You can't take him! He didn't do nothing!"

"He's not under arrest," Frank assured her, although she'd know that didn't make any difference. Frank could beat him up and do a lot of damage without ever arresting him.

"*No!*" she screamed, pulling on the boy and trying to wrest him from Frank's grip.

The door burst open, and Officer Donatelli, who had been waiting outside, charged into the room. Frank had worked with the large Italian before, and he knew he could trust him. Frank nodded at Mrs. Lee, and Donatelli wrapped his arms around her and plucked her away as if she were a little child. She was screeching now and flailing her arms and legs, but Donatelli held her easily, lifting her feet off the ground so she couldn't make any progress.

"Ma!" Harry cried frantically, but Frank was already wrestling him out the door. "He's hurting her!" he shouted.

"No, he's not," Frank said. "He's just holding her until we're gone."

"What are you going to do with me?" he asked, his mother's hysterics finally having convinced him of his danger.

"I told you," Frank said, catching the boy when he stumbled slightly on the steps. "I want to ask you some questions." The doors of the other flats were opening as the neighbors tried to see what was going on without getting themselves involved.

"Why can't I stay here then?" he started to struggle.

Frank took his wrist and twisted his arm up behind his back until he howled. "Because you can't," he replied mildly. When they reached the front door, two other officers were waiting. Frank thrust the boy into their waiting arms, and they quickly deposited him in the back of the ambulance. Frank climbed into the front and settled in for the short ride to Headquarters.

SARAH WAS UPSTAIRS, READING CATHERINE A STORY, when someone started pounding on her front door. Even the most desperate expectant father didn't pound like that, so Sarah told Maeve and Catherine to stay upstairs while she went to see who was there. Sarah's concern evaporated when she saw a woman silhouetted on the glass door, and when she opened it, Minnie Lee nearly collapsed into the room.

"Minnie, what's wrong?" Sarah asked, helping her inside. She wasn't wearing a hat or a coat, and her hair was flying everywhere. She looked as if she'd run all the way here.

"Harry," she gasped as Sarah led her to one of the two stuffed chairs that sat by the front window in her office.

"Is he sick?" Sarah asked, then called Maeve to come down.

"No, no," Minnie said breathlessly, waving away the very idea. "Malloy took him!"

Sarah's heart clenched in her chest, but she couldn't let Minnie see her concern. "Where did he take him?"

"To jail!" Minnie said, her voice breaking on a sob.

Maeve had come clattering down the stairs, Catherine at her heels. Both girls stared, wide-eyed.

"Maeve, will you fix some tea for Mrs. Lee?" Sarah asked, pulling a handkerchief from her pocket and passing it to Minnie. She couldn't help noticing it was the one in which Mrs. Ellsworth had tied the knot. To protect her from evil.

Maeve and Catherine disappeared into the kitchen while Sarah tried to comfort Minnie.

"Did Mr. Malloy arrest Harry?" Sarah asked, remembering that he hadn't actually promised that he wouldn't.

"What does that matter?" Minnie asked in despair. "He took him. You know what they'll do to him!"

"Mr. Malloy won't harm him," Sarah assured her, silently praying it was true. She'd never known him to be cruel. Well, not needlessly cruel, at least. "Why did he say he was taking him?"

"To ask him questions," Minnie said, her tone indicating she didn't believe that for a moment. "Mrs. Brandt, you've got to help me! I went to the Headquarters building, but they wouldn't let me in. There's a man there, he keeps the door . . ."

"Tom," Sarah said, remembering the times he'd opened it for her.

"He said I shouldn't go in. Said it was no place for me!" Minnie explained, outraged. "But my boy's in there!"

"I know," Sarah soothed her. "But he was right. You really shouldn't go in there. It's an awful place."

"You've been there?" she asked in amazement.

"Oh, yes," Sarah said. "But you mustn't worry. Mr. Malloy will let Harry go when he's found out what he needs to know."

"How can you be so sure?" she asked doubtfully.

Sarah realized she couldn't be sure at all.

FRANK GAVE HARRY SOME TIME ALONE IN THE INTERROgation room to consider his sins and to work himself up to a good state of terror. He didn't wait as long as he usually did, though. Harry didn't look like he needed much softening up.

Gino Donatelli accompanied him this time, taking his place by the door while Frank seated himself at the table opposite the boy. Frank felt a small stab of guilt when he saw how small and terrified Harry looked. He was even trembling slightly.

"What did you think about your sister marrying O'Neal?" Frank asked.

The question surprised him. "I . . . She shouldn't of done it."

"Why not?"

Harry needed a few seconds to think that one over. "She . . . she didn't have any right. Papa . . . he already picked her a husband."

"Didn't you think Angel was a little young to be getting married?" Frank asked as if he were merely curious. "Especially to somebody as old as Wong."

"She wasn't going to get married right away. Not until after she finished school," Harry explained. His nervous gaze kept darting to Donatelli, who did look menacing, Malloy noted with satisfaction.

"Didn't you want your sister to be happy?" Frank asked.

"*Happy?*" Harry repeated, as if he'd never heard the word before.

"Yeah, happy. She'd be happy if she married somebody she loved."

"She wasn't going to be happy with Quinn O'Neal," Harry scoffed.

"Is that what you told her when you went to see her?"

He seemed surprised Frank knew this. "Yeah, I did."

"You must've been pretty mad at her."

His face twisted at the memory. He felt guilt, but why? "I was. She didn't have the right."

"You said that before," Frank reminded him. "What do you mean by that?"

Harry glanced at Donatelli again, then back at Frank. The color had risen in his face. "Nothing," he tried.

"*Nothing?*" Frank let his voice harden slightly.

Harry noticed immediately. He straightened in his chair. "I mean, I don't know what it means."

"Yes, you do," Frank said, leaning forward slightly. "Tell me."

Harry's gaze darted around wildly. "It means . . . The Chinese, you have to obey your father. You have to do what he says."

"Do *you* always do what your father says?" Frank inquired.

"Yes . . . no . . . I mean, I try. I have to be a good son."

"Do you?"

"Yes! That's what a good Chinese does!"

"And you're a good Chinese son?"

Harry swallowed. "Yes."

"That's why you always dress like a Chinese," Frank guessed.

Harry nodded. "That's right."

"And why you kept your pigtail when your mother made you cut it off."

He nodded again. "I needed it."

"Why?" Frank asked with interest.

"So I'd look more Chinese," he explained as if he thought Frank should have known.

"That's why you hooked it onto your hat."

"Yes! Then I'd look like the other boys."

"Even though your parents didn't *want* you to look like the other boys."

"But I *am* like them! I'm *just* like them!"

"You don't look like them, though," Frank observed. "If you didn't have on those clothes, you'd look as white as I do."

Harry's face turned scarlet. "But I'm not white!" he insisted. "I'm Chinese!"

"And you wanted to be a good Chinese son," Frank said.

"Yes!"

"So you dressed in Chinese clothes and you wore a pigtail and you did everything your father wanted you to do, like a good Chinese son."

"Yes, I did!" Harry exclaimed excitedly.

"But Angel didn't act Chinese at all, did she?" Frank said.

Uncertainty flickered across his face. "She . . . Yes, she did," he tried.

"No, she didn't. She didn't dress like a Chinese, and she didn't act like a Chinese. She was sneaking out to meet Quinn O'Neal. A good Chinese girl wouldn't do that, would she?"

"No, but—"

"And when her father told her to marry Wong, she should have done it. She should have been a good Chinese girl and obeyed her father, but she didn't, did she, Harry? She didn't because she wasn't a good Chinese girl. She was bad, wasn't she, Harry?"

"No!"

"Yes, she was," Frank insisted, leaning closer, his voice growing louder. "She was bad because she wouldn't obey your father, and she ran away. She ran away with a white man. She ran away with him and she married him and she never had to be a Chinese girl again, did she, Harry? She never had to obey your father again!"

"No!" he shouted, tears flooding his eyes.

"She was free, wasn't she, Harry? And that's why you were so mad. She was free, and you would never be free. You'd be a Chinese man as long as you lived. You would obey your father and do what he said, but she was free and never had to obey again."

"She was bad!" Harry cried, surprising himself.

"Yes, she was," Frank agreed. "She was a wicked girl. She needed to be punished, didn't she, Harry? That's what you went to tell her, isn't it?"

"She didn't have the right to run away!" Harry agreed eagerly, almost relieved to find someone who understood. "I told her she should come home!"

"But she wouldn't, would she?" Frank asked. "She laughed in your face and said you were a fool and that's when you hit her."

"She wouldn't come home!" he confirmed. "But she didn't laugh. She started yelling at me, making fun of my clothes and calling me a coolie and—"

"So you hit her," Frank guessed.

The tears welled again, and this time they spilled over and ran down his cheeks. "I didn't mean to, but she was screaming at me! I had to make her stop!"

"So you hit her, and then you put your hands around her neck, and—"

"*No!* I didn't put my hands around her neck!" he cried in outrage. "I slapped her! I slapped her in the face, and she started to cry!"

"And that's when you put your hands around her neck," Frank tried again, but Harry was having none of it.

"No, no! I slapped her, and she started to cry, and I couldn't stand to see her cry, so I ran away!"

"Don't lie to me, Harry," Frank warned. "Someone saw you."

This surprised him, but he didn't look frightened. "Then they know I never put my hands on her neck! I just slapped her, and when she started crying, I was ashamed, and I ran away."

"When did this happen, Harry?"

"I don't know," he said, trying to remember. "The day after we found out where she was, I guess. My father went to see her that first day, and he told her to come home, but she wouldn't. She said she never had to do what he said ever again. I couldn't believe she said that to him!"

"Why not, Harry?" Frank asked sarcastically. "Is it because you always wanted to, but never were brave enough?"

He flushed again but refused to back down. "It's disrespectful. The Chinese are respectful."

"But Angel wasn't a Chinese anymore, was she? She'd gotten away, but you couldn't, could you? You must've hated her for that."

His tears evaporated in the heat of his anger, and he glared back at Frank, refusing to answer.

"You must've *really* hated her," Frank went on relentlessly. "You hated her so much that you went back to see her—"

"No, I didn't!"

"You went back to see her, and you told her how bad she was, and that's when you—"

"*No!* I told you, I never did that! I never went back! I never saw her again!" He shouted. The tears were starting again. "I never had a chance . . ."

"A chance to do what, Harry?"

"*A chance to say I was sorry!*"

Frank opened his mouth to accuse him again, but someone knocked on the door before he could. Donatelli, as surprised as Frank at the interruption, opened the door. Another officer stood there, a puzzled frown on his face.

"There's a Chinaman upstairs to see you," he told Frank. "He says he killed that Chinese girl."

SARAH ESCORTED MINNIE LEE INTO THE BUILDING where she lived and up the stairs.

"You didn't have to bring me home," Minnie protested, not for the first time. "I still think you should've gone right to the police station."

"I told you, I'll go as soon as you're settled in." She knew going to Headquarters wouldn't do much good. Malloy wouldn't see her until he'd finished with Harry anyway, and if he'd decided to arrest the boy for his sister's murder, she couldn't do anything at all. She didn't want to tell Minnie that, though.

She stopped at Cora's door and knocked. Cora had the baby in her arms when she opened the door, and Cora's face betrayed her anguish. "Minnie!" she cried when she saw her standing behind Sarah. "What happened? Where's Harry?"

"He's still arrested," Minnie said, her voice breaking on fresh tears.

"Come in and sit down," Cora said, stepping aside to let them enter. "Did they let you see him?"

"I couldn't even get inside the building," Minnie said, sinking down onto Cora's overstuffed sofa. "Then I remembered Mrs. Brandt. I thought she might be able to . . ." Her voice trailed off in despair.

"I'm going over there to see Harry, now that Minnie is in good hands," Sarah said. "Has anyone told Mr. Lee yet?"

"George went out right after Minnie left. He was going to get him," Cora said. The baby started to fuss, and she bounced him gently, absently.

Minnie started to cry silently, large tears rolling unheeded down her cheeks. "He couldn't of done it," she murmured. "He couldn't of killed Angel."

"Of course he couldn't," Cora quickly agreed. "He loved her. We all loved her! Now don't you worry yourself anymore. He'll be home soon. You'll see."

"It's all my fault," Minnie moaned. "I should've sent him away. If I'd sent him away, this never would've happened."

"Don't talk nonsense," Cora scolded her gently. "You couldn't send him away. He's your son."

"He was never happy, though. He just couldn't be happy. It's all my fault."

Sarah would have liked to understand what she meant, but there was no time, and it probably wasn't important anyway. "I'll be back as soon as I have something to tell you," she said, moving toward the door. "Stay right here, Minnie, where I can find you."

"I'll take care of her," Cora promised, sitting down on the sofa beside Minnie to comfort her.

Sarah nodded and stepped through the still-open door, but stopped when she saw who was coming up the steps. "Harry?" she asked, hardly able to believe her eyes.

He looked at her in surprise, probably not recognizing her at first.

"Harry?" his mother echoed, jumping off the sofa and hurrying to the door. She fairly pushed Sarah out of the way as she went barreling down the stairs to meet her son. "Thank God! Thank God!" she cried over and over as she wrapped him in her arms and held on fast.

Cora was laughing and crying at the same time as she followed Minnie down the stairs to join the celebration. She patted Harry's back and touched his hair and his shoulder and his arm, as if verifying he was indeed real.

Finally, Minnie calmed down enough to release her son. She held him at arm's length and studied him for a long moment, checking for injuries. "Are you all right?"

Oddly, he looked at Cora before answering. "Yeah," he said uncertainly. "I'm fine."

"Let's get you upstairs then and out of those awful clothes," she said with a disparaging glance at his sackcloth. She took his arm to guide him up, but he balked, wrenching free of her grasp.

"No, I can't!"

"Why not?" his mother asked in surprise.

"I just came to get you. We've got to go back," he said.

"Back where?"

"To the police station," he said stubbornly.

"No, no," his mother insisted. "They let you go, and you don't ever have to go back there again!"

"Yes, I do!" he cried in anguish, looking at Cora again. "We've got to go back there. The only reason they let me go was because George came."

"*George* came?" Cora echoed with a frown. "He came to get you out?"

"No!" Harry wailed. "He came to tell them he killed Angel!"

FRANK STARED AT HIS NEW PRISONER ACROSS THE TABLE in the interrogation room he'd recently shared with Harry Lee. "Your name is George Lee?" Frank confirmed.

"Yes." The young man sat very straight, his face expressionless. He wore the typical Chinese clothing. His shirt was blue silk and covered with beautiful embroidery. He wore his pigtail wound around his head beneath his hat, probably so the street Arabs couldn't get ahold of it to torment him. His face was strangely unlined and amazingly handsome.

"Are you related to Charlie Lee?"

"Yes, he . . . he my father."

He didn't sound too certain about something he should be certain of. Sarah hadn't said anything about Minnie having another child, either. This fellow looked too old to be Minnie's son anyway, and he didn't look like he had any white blood. "Who's your mother?" Frank asked.

He blinked but didn't budge. "Mother in China."

"Did Charlie have another wife in China?" Frank asked, not bothering to hide his disgust.

"Mother in China," he insisted.

"Are you a paper son?" Donatelli asked suddenly, annoying Frank because he knew he wasn't supposed to say anything.

George Lee looked alarmed, but he kept staring at something over Frank's left shoulder.

"What's a paper son?" Frank asked Donatelli.

"A few years back, the government said the only Chinese who could come over here were the sons of men who already lived here. A lot of Chinese suddenly found sons they didn't have before, if you know what I mean."

"*Paper* sons," Frank said in understanding. "So you're Charlie's paper son."

He acted like he hadn't heard the question. "I kill Angel," he said, not for the first time.

"We'll get to that," Frank said, scratching his head. None of this made a lot of sense. "How long have you been Charlie's paper son?"

George seemed to be debating whether to answer or not. He was probably worried about being sent back to China if somebody found out he wasn't really Charlie's son. Maybe he didn't realize that was the least of his worries right now, though.

"Nobody's gonna send you back to China," Frank assured him, although he couldn't be sure. If George had killed Angel, that might be a possible choice of punishments for him. Frank wasn't sure about the laws concerning foreigners. "How long have you been in America?" he tried.

"Four year," he replied without hesitation.

"You've lived with Charlie all that time?"

"Live with wife now," George said.

"You're married?" Frank asked in surprise.

"Yes." Something flickered across his face. Probably thinking about his wife and what this would do to her. She was probably another Irish girl, like Mrs. Lee, too.

"All right, tell me what happened."

"What happened?" he asked uncertainly.

"How you killed Angel," Frank clarified impatiently.

"I go see Angel. Tell her come home. She will not. I kill."

This was probably the shortest confession Frank had ever heard. "When was this?"

"When?" George asked stupidly.

"Yeah, what day. What time."

He had to think this over. "Three day," he decided.

"What time?"

George had to lick his lips while he thought this over. "Not sure," he finally said.

"What did you say to her?"

"I say come home."

"And what did she say?"

"She say no."

Maybe it was because he was Chinese, Frank thought. Maybe he just didn't know all the words in English. "And that made you mad?"

"Yes."

Angel had been killed in the heat of anger. Frank was sure of it. This George fellow didn't seem capable of anger, although he was making Frank pretty mad.

"Why?" Frank asked.

"Why?" George repeated uncertainly.

"Yeah, why did it make you mad?"

"She make father and mother sad."

"But she was married to the Irish boy," Frank reminded him. "You couldn't expect her to leave him and go back home to her parents."

George frowned impatiently. "She should go home," he insisted.

Frank studied him for a long moment. This was all wrong. "Do you always wear your pigtail up like that?"

His hand went to his head protectively. "Yes," he said suspiciously, and then frowned. "Why you ask question? I kill Angel. No more question."

Frank looked at Donatelli, who shrugged helplessly. "Lock him up," Frank told Donatelli. Then he realized that a Chinaman wouldn't fare well among the other felons being confined in the Headquarters jail. If he was a killer, it wouldn't matter, but if he wasn't . . . "But put him in a cell by himself. If you don't, they'll eat him alive."

Donatelli nodded and went over to where George Lee sat.

"I am arrested?" he asked. He didn't look particularly alarmed at the prospect.

"Oh, yes," Frank assured him with a sigh.

But before Donatelli could get him to the door, someone knocked again. Frank signaled for Donatelli to hold up, and when he opened the door, the same officer as before stood there.

"What now?" Frank asked in disgust.

"Mrs. Brandt is here to see you," he said with a smirk.

Somehow, Frank managed not to groan.

Sᴀʀᴀʜ ᴋɴᴇᴡ sʜᴇ ʜᴀᴅ ᴡᴏɴ sᴏᴍᴇ ʀᴇsᴘᴇᴄᴛ ꜰʀᴏᴍ Mᴀʟ-loy's cohorts when she was escorted upstairs to wait in Miss Kelly's office instead of being left to cool her heels among the thieves and prostitutes being brought in on the street level. Even that would have been better than being locked in an interrogation room, as she had been on her first visit here.

Miss Kelly was the first girl secretary in the history of the New York City Police Department, another of Commissioner Roosevelt's innovations. Roosevelt wasn't in his office, but Miss Kelly made her comfortable while she waited for Malloy.

She'd expected a long wait, but Malloy appeared only a few minutes later. He looked angry, of course, but not nearly as angry as she had expected.

"Mrs. Brandt," he said sourly. "What a surprise."

"I need to talk to you about George Lee," she said before he could draw her into an argument about her presence here.

"Why don't you use the commissioner's office?" Miss Kelly suggested. "He won't be in today, and I'm sure he won't mind, since it's Mrs. Brandt," she added.

Sarah's family were lifelong friends with the Roosevelts. "Thank you," Sarah said before Malloy could refuse and led the way.

Malloy closed the door behind them.

"You know I wouldn't have come if it wasn't important," she hurried to explain.

He crossed his arms over his chest and leaned back against the door, silently challenging her to convince him.

"I was at home, minding my own business," she informed him, trying to sound confident instead of defensive, "when Minnie Lee showed up. She was nearly hysterical because you had arrested Harry."

"I didn't arrest him," he said, sounding put upon, although why he should, she couldn't imagine.

"Well, she thought you had. She followed you and tried to get in here, but Tom wouldn't let her."

"I'll have to thank him."

Sarah found his attitude annoying, but she refused to be intimidated. "She only wanted to know what you were going to do to Harry. She was truly frightened, so she asked me if I'd talk to you."

"I already released Harry."

"I know! I knew you wouldn't want me coming down here, so I took Minnie home. As soon as we got there, Harry came in, and he told us George had confessed to killing Angel. Is that true?"

"Yes, it is."

Sarah glared at Malloy, more than annoyed now. "What have you done with him?"

"I locked him up."

"But you can't arrest him!"

He rubbed a hand over his face. "He confessed to a murder, Sarah, so I didn't have much choice. Besides, you only told me I couldn't arrest *Harry*, so how was I supposed to know? Maybe you should give me a list of all the people you don't want me to arrest for killing Angel."

Sarah wanted to smack him. "You can't arrest George

because he's *innocent*. He didn't kill Angel any more than I did!"

"How do you know?"

"I . . . I just know! Don't you see? He saw you taking Harry out, and Minnie told him and Cora that you were arresting him for killing Angel."

"I didn't tell her that!" he said with some exasperation.

"But that's what she thought."

"Who's Cora?"

"She's George's wife. It was her baby I delivered last month."

She thought he flinched slightly, but she couldn't be sure.

"George thought you were going to charge Harry with killing Angel, and he couldn't let Charlie and Minnie lose both their children, so he confessed to protect Harry!"

Malloy didn't look convinced. "Why would he do that? He's got a wife and a new baby."

"Because Charlie brought him to America. He's what they call a paper son to Charlie. That's when—"

"I know what it is."

"Charlie also gave him a job and helped him start his own laundry business. He owes Charlie everything."

"So he decided to pay him back by confessing to his daughter's murder."

"I know it sounds ridiculous, but maybe it's some kind of Chinese honor or duty or something we can't understand. Whatever it is, George didn't kill Angel, and that's the important thing."

Malloy didn't look convinced. For a second she thought he was going to argue with her, but then someone knocked on the door, startling them both.

Malloy was still leaning against it, so he straightened up and opened it. Miss Kelly stood there, her pretty face creased into a frown. "I'm sorry to disturb you, Detective Sergeant, but I was just informed that there's a Chinese man downstairs to see you. He says it's about that Chinese girl who was killed."

12

F RANK TOLD SARAH TO STAY UPSTAIRS, BUT SHE FOL-
lowed him down anyway. At least she had the good sense to
stay back, as if she wasn't with him. The fellow Miss Kelly
had told him about sat on a bench as far from the newly arrested felons as he could get.

He looked like he'd seen some trouble recently, too. His
hat was missing, and his clothes were dirty. Not dirty from
needing to be washed, but dirty from falling down in the
street a few times. His queue was scraggly, with stray hairs
sticking out everywhere, and his face had a streak of dirt
down one cheek and a small cut above the other eye. Both
eyes were as wide as they could get and nothing short of terrified. His gaze kept darting around the room, as if he expected to be set upon at any moment and wanted to be ready.
When he saw Frank, his whole body went limp with relief.

"Mr. Detective Malloy," he exclaimed, scrambling up and hurrying over to meet Frank. "Mr. Detective Malloy, Mr. Detective Malloy," he kept repeating happily.

Frank had the uncomfortable feeling the man was going to throw his arms around him soon, and took a step backward just in case. "Who are you, and what do you want?"

He seemed surprised Frank didn't know him. "I am Ah Woh," he said. "My uncle, he send me to find you."

Frank needed another second to figure it out. "Oh, you're Wong's nephew," he remembered. "Wong wants to see me?"

"Yes, yes!" He nodded vigorously.

Frank looked him over again. Like most Chinese, he'd been immaculate when Frank saw him at Wong's house. "What happened to you?"

The young man's face fell, and he hung his head in shame. "I am worthless."

"Somebody beat you up because you're worthless?"

His expression seemed to confirm it. "Uncle, he send me find you. I go police, but they say you no there. Wrong police."

He must have gone to the precinct house, Frank thought. "Did *they* do this to you?" he asked, pointing to the fellow's ruined clothes.

He shook his head. "They send me new police. Wrong police. They send me new police. Some man, they chase, in street. I fall. They hit. I run away."

It was a pretty typical story. A Chinaman happens into a neighborhood where he isn't known, and the local toughs decide to have a little fun at his expense. What really annoyed him was the way the other cops had given him the runaround. "How did you find me?"

"Man tell me right police. You here," he said simply. "I wait, long time, but you here."

Frank glanced over to the desk sergeant. "You knew I was questioning Chinese men," he growled.

The desk sergeant shrugged unrepentantly. "You were busy, and he looks like a bum."

Frank bit back his instinctive reply, aware of Sarah standing well within hearing distance. He'd deal with the desk sergeant later. He turned back to Ah Woh. "Why did your uncle send you to find me?"

"He say you come. He tell you about dead girl."

"He knows who killed Angel Lee?"

"He not say. He say get you," Ah Woh explained. "You come?" he added anxiously.

Oh, yes, Frank would come. He wanted to know what Wong had discovered. He was the only Chinese man of Angel's acquaintance whom Frank hadn't eliminated as a suspect. Until George had confessed, that is, but Frank wasn't putting too much stock in that story. Then Frank remembered something. "Is the O'Neal girl still there?"

A flicker of distaste passed over Ah Woh's face, but he said, "Yes."

Frank looked over his shoulder to where Sarah stood, straining to hear everything they were saying. "Mrs. Brandt, I have to question Mr. Wong. Could you come along with me to chaperone the young woman there?"

The shock on her face was gratifying. At least he hadn't lost the ability to surprise her. She recovered quickly, though. "Certainly," she said, as proper as you please, and accompanied him and the boy out of the building.

Tom, the doorman, greeted her by name and bade her

good afternoon. She rewarded him with one of those smiles that haunted Frank's dreams. With a sigh, he followed her down the front steps, Ah Woh in their wake.

"I'm not complaining," she said as soon as they were safely out of hearing distance of the newspaper reporters who constantly hovered around Headquarters in search of a story. "But why do you need me to come with you?"

Frank glanced over his shoulder, but Ah Woh was keeping a discreet distance. "To keep that girl busy," he said. "I don't know what her place is in all this, but she isn't going to let Wong tell me anything that she doesn't want me to hear."

"What wouldn't she want you to hear?"

Frank silently debated telling her, but then decided it was inevitable anyway. "I think Wong is involved in Angel's death."

"Do you think he killed her?" she asked in surprise.

"I think it's likely. The killer was a Chinese man, and he's the only one who might have wanted her dead and who also fits the description."

"Surely, he doesn't intend to confess," Sarah said.

"No, but he might have decided to try to pin it on somebody else. That's why I need you to take care of the girl for me. I want to get him alone so I can get him to tell me the truth."

Her frown was disapproving. "How are you going to do that?"

"I don't know yet," he lied. "But I don't want the girl around when I decide."

She gave him one of her looks, which he ignored. Then she asked, "What's the girl like?"

"She's no innocent, that's for sure. If anything, I think

she's got the upper hand on Wong. Seemed like he was doing whatever she wanted."

She gave him a little smile. "A young girl and an older
man," she said smugly. "That's usually the way it is."

Frank grunted in disgust and picked up his pace, making
conversation virtually impossible. It seemed to take forever
to reach Wong's house, but at last they did. Frank and Sarah
stood back and allowed Ah Woh to unlock the front door.

Ah Woh called out something in Chinese to announce
their arrival as they entered the front hallway.

No one answered. The house seemed unnaturally still, as
if no one was home. Maybe Wong had gotten tired of waiting and gone out looking for Frank himself.

Ah Woh called out again, more loudly this time.

"Maybe he's, uh, upstairs," Frank suggested diplomatically. If Wong was busy with the girl, he wouldn't be likely
to come running just because they'd finally shown up.

Ah Woh rubbed his hands on his shirt and looked upward
uncertainly. He probably didn't relish the job of going upstairs and knocking on his uncle's bedroom door. "I look," he
said after a moment and turned toward the door that opened
into Wong's parlor. He pushed it open and cried out in surprise.

Frank rushed over and instantly saw what had shocked
the boy. Wong lay in a heap in the middle of the parlor floor
in a pool of blood. Behind him, Sarah gasped, and he silently
cursed himself for bringing her along.

Ah Woh made a keening sound, half-grief and half-
horror. His slight body swayed, and Frank caught him just
in time to keep him from falling over. He hustled the boy
over to one of the chairs that sat in the hallway and lowered
him into it.

"Is the girl there, too?" Sarah asked, peering into the room.

"I didn't see her," Frank said, hurrying to close the door so she couldn't see the body.

"What's her name?"

"Keely," Frank replied as he pulled the door shut.

"*Keely!*" Sarah shouted. "Keely, where are you?"

Silence greeted her, and the next thing Frank knew, she'd grabbed her skirts and started running up the stairs. Frank took off after her. If the girl was dead upstairs, he didn't want Sarah to be the one to find her.

"*Keely!*" she kept shouting. When she reached the second floor, she started throwing open each door in turn and looking inside. Before Frank could catch her, she came to Wong's bedroom. The huge bed obviously belonged to the master of the house, and a human form made a mound beneath the rumpled bedclothes. Black hair spread across the pillow. "Keely!" Sarah shouted. The form didn't move.

"Sarah!" Frank tried, but she was already at the bed.

"Keely!" she cried, pulling back the covers. The girl was naked, Frank saw in the first instant. In the second, he registered that there was no blood on her. Sarah shook her violently. "Keely, wake up!"

The girl groaned. Sarah shook her again, and Keely made a feeble effort to push her away.

"Is she all right?" Frank asked.

"I don't see any wounds," Sarah said, still shaking the girl. "Keely, can you hear me?"

"Go away," the girl muttered.

"She might be drugged, but she's alive," Sarah said. "Go on downstairs. I'll take care of her."

Frank was only too glad to leave the girl to Sarah's tender

mercies. He fled back to the dead body. At least that was something he knew how to handle.

Sarah slapped the girl's face lightly, and finally her eyes popped open. She looked more mad than anything. "Who are you?" she asked. "What are you doing here?"

"My name is Mrs. Brandt," Sarah told her. "Detective Sergeant Malloy brought me."

"Are you some kind of police lady?" Keely asked with a puzzled frown. She looked like a painting of a wanton, Sarah thought, lying on the bed with her glowing young flesh and her tousled hair.

"No, I'm a nurse. Are you all right?"

The girl was awake now and growing more disgruntled by the minute. "Of course I'm all right," she said indignantly. "Johnny wouldn't hurt me. We're getting married." She suddenly noticed she was exposed and jerked the covers back over her. "Who let you in here, anyways? Was it Ah Woh? He's so stupid! Wait 'til I tell Johnny."

"Keely, when was the last time you saw him? Mr. Wong, I mean?"

She didn't like the question. "I don't know. Today sometime. Before I went to sleep. Why? Where is he?"

"He's downstairs," Sarah said carefully. "When did you go to sleep?"

"I don't know," she said petulantly. "What does it matter? I want to see Johnny."

"Try to remember. Was it after breakfast?"

She was growing alarmed. "I guess so. Johnny brought me some tea, and then I got sleepy. I want to see Johnny." She sat up, holding the covers to her chest.

"I need to tell you something first," Sarah said.

"I don't want to hear it. I want to see Johnny!"

"I'm afraid Mr. Wong is dead," Sarah said.

Keely stared at her for a long moment as various emotions played across her young face. Finally, she said, "No, he's not. I want to see him."

"No, you don't," Sarah assured her. "You'll want to remember him the way he was."

She gave Sarah another incredulous look and then bolted from the bed, dragging a fistful of covers with her. *"Johnny!"* she screamed, nearly bowling Sarah over when she tried to stop her. "Johnny!"

Sarah raced after her, but the girl was too fast. Her bare feet made slapping sounds on the bare wood of the hallway and down the stairs. She made a feeble effort to wrap the covers around her as she ran, but they mostly just dragged behind her. Sarah had to slow down to keep from stepping on them.

Keely stopped when she reached the bottom of the stairs. She glanced at Ah Woh, who still sat where Malloy had left him, staring straight ahead in shock. Then she turned toward the parlor door, which Malloy had closed behind him.

"Johnny!" Keely cried and ran toward the door. She threw it open and stumbled inside, stopping dead when she saw Wong's bloody body. She screamed just as Sarah reached her.

Sarah grabbed for the girl, ready to wrap her arms around her and drag her away, but Keely broke free and lunged for the body. To Sarah's horror, Keely fell to her knees in the pool of blood and flung herself on Wong.

Malloy roared something incomprehensible, and Sarah stared, helpless.

"Johnny, wake up!" Keely was shouting hysterically. "Johnny, don't leave me!" She'd lost her grip on the blanket and was sprawled on the floor completely naked and bloody.

"Do something!" Malloy shouted at Sarah. "Get her out of here!"

Galvanized, Sarah snatched up the nearest blanket and threw it over the girl's naked back. "Come on, Keely," Sarah said, catching her by the arms and hauling her to her feet.

"Johnny!" Keely was still screaming, but more weakly now as the shock began to settle over her.

Sarah wrapped the blanket completely around her and turned her away from the awful sight. "Come with me, Keely," she said firmly, and the girl allowed her to lead her out into the front hall.

Ah Woh seemed to have come out of his initial shock. He was staring at Keely with undisguised loathing. The girl had a smear of blood on her face, and she didn't seem to even notice him sitting there. Sarah led her back upstairs and into the bedroom. She sat her down in an elegant chair in one corner of the room.

"He's dead, isn't he?" Keely said in a small voice.

"Yes, he is." Sarah pulled another cover off the bed and wrapped it around the girl, too. She was in shock, and she might start shivering soon.

Keely reached out to adjust it and saw the blood on her hand. She moaned. "I want to wash it off! I need to take a bath and wash it off!"

"Is there a bathroom here?" Sarah asked.

"Yes, in there." She pointed at a door, and when Sarah opened it, she discovered a lavishly appointed bath with marble floor and fixtures. She turned on the spigots in the tub full blast.

*   *   *

Frank watched in amazement as Sarah took the girl away. He was sure of it now. Keely O'Neal was crazy. He'd never imagined she could care for Wong that much. He'd seen mothers throw themselves on their dead children or wives on their husbands. He'd seen men clinging to their dead wives, too, but that wasn't the kind of relationship Keely and Wong had.

He looked down at the body in disgust. At least he'd had time to examine everything before she got here, because she'd certainly messed it up too badly now to ever guess what had really happened. From what he'd surmised, Wong had been sitting on the sofa. He must have been entertaining his killer. The killer was someone Wong trusted and had no reason to fear, because he'd picked up the fireplace poker and come up behind Wong and crushed his skull. Wong probably hadn't known what hit him. He'd slumped to the floor, dead or unconscious. Probably unconscious, because the amount of blood indicated he'd lain there awhile bleeding before his heart had stopped and the blood flow along with it. One blow was all it had taken. The question now was who had struck it.

Somehow, Frank wasn't surprised to find that Wong had a telephone. He'd already heard the groaning of the pipes as water struggled to reach the floor above, telling him of the luxurious plumbing system. Keely must have thought she was in heaven, living in a place like this, he thought as he picked up the phone and asked the operator to connect him with Police Headquarters.

When Sarah had gotten Keely out of the tub, dried off, and wrapped in a robe that had obviously belonged to Wong, she looked around for some clothes for her to wear. Malloy would want to question her, and then they'd have to take her somewhere, probably back to her family. She couldn't do that in a thin silk robe.

"Where are your clothes?" Sarah asked, looking in vain in the drawers and the clothes press.

"I don't have any," she said, adjusting the robe. "Just what I was wearing when I first came," she added at Sarah's shocked look. "Ah Woh took them to wash, I think. I never needed them after that. Johnny liked me best with no clothes on."

"Well," Sarah said briskly. "I'll ask Ah Woh if he knows where they are. You'll need them now, I think."

"Yeah, I've had enough of wearing Johnny's clothes," she said, looking askance at the robe she was hugging around herself. "What will happen to me?" she asked after a moment.

"Don't worry about that now," Sarah said. "You'll be fine. I'll be right back."

Sarah hurried out, trying not to imagine the days that Keely had spent with Wong. Malloy had said he thought Keely had the upper hand, but how could she have? She may have come voluntarily, but she'd been a virtual prisoner here after that. She didn't even have any clothes! She'd been completely at Wong's mercy. Sarah found herself not quite as upset about his murder as she had been.

Ah Woh had recovered somewhat by the time Sarah found him again. He was pacing in the hallway, keeping an eye on the people who had gathered in the parlor while she'd been busy upstairs. Sarah recognized Officer Donatelli and some of the men from the coroner's office. Sarah asked Ah Woh about Keely's clothes.

He made a face, but he said, "I get." He started for the

back of the house, and Sarah waited in the hallway. She stepped closer to the door to hear what was being said in the parlor. Malloy was instructing Donatelli to take some men and question the neighbors to see if anyone had seen somebody going or coming from the house during the time Ah Woh had been gone.

Then she heard Ah Woh cry out. She reached the kitchen first, but Malloy and his cohorts were right behind her.

"What is it?" she asked, looking around and seeing nothing out of the ordinary.

Ah Woh held up a towel. It was stained with blood.

"Where did you find it?" Malloy asked, pushing past her into the kitchen.

"On floor." He pointed.

"The killer would have had a little blood splashed on him," one of the other men said. "From the force of the blow. Looks like he washed up before he left."

Ah Woh looked at the towel in his hands. Suddenly, his eyes rolled back in his head, and he keeled over in a faint. This time Malloy wasn't quick enough, and the poor fellow fell to the floor with a crash.

By the time Sarah had helped minister to Ah Woh and bring him back to consciousness, and found Keely's clothes, all neatly washed and pressed, she had begun to worry about the girl she'd left alone for so long. She needn't have worried. Keely was back in the bed, fast asleep, when she found her again. If Wong had given her something to put her to sleep, as Sarah suspected, it probably had not worn off completely. Either that or the shock had knocked her out. It did that to some people. They couldn't feel the pain when they slept. Sarah let her sleep until Malloy came knocking. He was ready to question her now.

This time Keely awoke more easily, but when she saw Sarah, her expression crumbled. "It wasn't a dream, was it?" she asked.

"I'm sorry, Keely. It wasn't a dream. You need to get up and get dressed now. Detective Sergeant Malloy has some questions for you."

She let Sarah help her dress, and then allowed Sarah to brush out her hair. Sarah saw some flakes of what she thought was dried blood and wished she'd thought to have Keely wash her hair, too. It was too late for that now, though. She wouldn't mention it to the girl. Besides, she was able to brush nearly all of it out.

"What will he ask me about?" Keely asked when she was finally ready.

"What you saw and heard."

"I didn't see nothing," she protested. "I was asleep."

"Then tell him that," Sarah said. "I'll stay with you, if you like."

"I would," she said pitifully. Sarah's heart went out to her.

FRANK COULD HARDLY BELIEVE THE GIRL WITH SARAH was the same one he'd encountered on his previous visit. Gone was the sly little piece who'd taunted Frank with her sexuality. In her place was a sweet, innocent girl who looked like butter wouldn't melt in her mouth. Her clothes were faded and worn, but so neat and prim that they only made her look more vulnerable.

Frank took Keely and Sarah into the dining room and sat them down at the table. The room was gloomy from the dark mahogany furniture and because the heavy velvet drapes sealed out most of the sunlight.

"Is Johnny still here?" the girl asked in a timid little voice Frank hadn't heard before.

"No, they took him away," Frank said. She seemed relieved at that. "I need to ask you some questions, Keely."

"I don't know nothing," she insisted. "I was asleep. Tell him, missus," she begged Sarah.

"Just answer his questions the best you can," Sarah said.

Keely stuck out her lower lip, like she was pouting, but Frank didn't really care. "Tell me everything that happened today, starting with when you woke up this morning."

She shrugged one shoulder. "I woke up. I mean, Johnny woke me up. He always likes a little poke first thing in the morning."

Frank felt the heat crawling up his neck, and he refused to look at Sarah. He knew this wouldn't embarrass her, but he couldn't help being embarrassed *for* her. "Did you come downstairs for breakfast?"

"No," she said. "Johnny always brings it up to me. I stay in the room all the time." She looked at Sarah. "That's why I never needed no clothes."

Frank didn't dare look at Sarah's expression. "What happened after you had breakfast?"

That shoulder again. "The usual thing. Then we laid around for a while."

"How long?"

"I don't know," she said with a hint of irritation. "I didn't pay no attention."

Frank bit back his own irritation. "All right. Then what happened?"

She wrinkled up her nose as if she was trying to concentrate. "That's when he went down and made the tea, I think.

He brought up a pot of tea to the room. He told me to drink it all."

"Then what happened?"

"I got sleepy, and he told me it was all right to take a nap, so I did."

"Do you usually take a nap like that?"

"I sleep whenever I want," she said. "And wake up whenever I want. I don't have much else to do but keep Johnny happy."

Frank managed not to wince. "How long did you sleep today?"

"Until she woke me up," she said, pointing at Sarah.

Frank hid his annoyance. "Did you hear anything? Did anything wake you up?"

Keely wrinkled her nose again. "I think . . . I thought I was dreaming, but maybe I heard some voices, like somebody shouting or fighting or something."

"And you didn't go see what it was?" he asked.

"I told you, I thought I was dreaming. I didn't really even wake up good."

"The tea may have been drugged," Sarah said.

Frank had been thinking the same thing, although why Wong would drug her, he had no idea. "Had Wong given you stuff that made you sleepy before?"

She considered the question carefully. "Now that you say it, maybe he did. I mean, sometimes I'd get real tired for no reason and go to sleep."

Frank figured Wong had wanted some time away from her, but he didn't say it. "You've been here how long now?"

"I don't know. How many days since you first came?" she replied.

"That was yesterday."

"Five days, then."

Frank nodded. That was what she had told him before. "Did Wong have any visitors while you've been here?"

"Angel's father came," she recalled. "Johnny already told you that."

"Did he come just that once?"

"That's all I know of."

"Anybody else?"

She made a face. "My ma came last night."

"Your mother? What did she want?"

Frank caught a glimpse of the sly smile she'd shown him yesterday. "She wanted me to come home, but Johnny wouldn't let me go. He threw her out."

"Was he keeping you a prisoner here?" Sarah asked in alarm.

"Well, kind of," she allowed, trying for innocence again.

"You came here on your own," Frank reminded her. "And you seemed pretty happy yesterday. You said Wong was going to marry you."

"Well, now, he was standing right there, wasn't he? What was I supposed to say?" she asked indignantly.

"You said it when I woke you up a little while ago, too," Sarah reminded her. "You seemed pretty fond of Mr. Wong."

Keely clearly couldn't make up her mind how she wanted to portray Wong. "He was all right, I guess," she admitted. "He didn't hit me or nothing."

"And you wanted to marry him," Frank reminded her.

"He said he would, and he had to, didn't he? After what he did to me?"

"Why did you come here in the first place, Keely?" Sarah asked.

The girl seemed surprised by the question and not at all certain how to reply. "I . . . It seemed like a good idea."

"Who gave you the idea?" Frank asked.

"I don't remember," she lied.

"I think you do," Frank said. "I think Angel told you about Wong. I think she told you he was rich and that he wanted to marry her. I think you decided that since he couldn't have Angel, he might take you instead."

"What if I did?" she asked petulantly. "Ain't nothing wrong with that."

"And you thought if you moved in here and made Wong happy, that he'd marry you, and you'd have an easy life. Is that what you wanted, Keely? An easy life?"

She stared at him for a long moment, trying to decide how to answer him, and then she burst into tears.

Frank fought the urge to swear as Sarah took the girl into her arms and tried to comfort her. So much for getting anything more out of her now.

Keely sobbed on Sarah's shoulder for a while, until she ran out of steam. Then she pulled away slightly and looked Sarah in the face. "What's going to happen to me now?"

Sarah smiled reassuringly. Frank figured she could calm anybody down with that smile. "Don't worry. We'll take you back to your mother and—"

"*No!*" she cried, rearing back like Sarah had slapped her. "I don't want to go back there! Can't I stay here?"

"Not with Wong dead, you can't," Frank informed her. "I don't know who this place belongs to now, but it's not you."

"Your family will be glad to have you home again," Sarah tried.

"No, they won't! They'll hate me because I ran off with a Chinaman."

"But your mother came to get you last night," Sarah reminded her.

Keely looked a little surprised at this reminder, but she recovered quickly. "My brothers won't want me back, though. Or Iris. I'm afraid of what they'll do!"

Frank could tell Sarah was trying to figure out some way to help the girl. He had to jump in before she offered to take Keely in herself. "You can take her to the Mission," he said.

Sarah liked this idea, even if Keely greeted it with a suspicious frown. "What's the Mission?"

"It's on Mulberry Street, the Prodigal Son Mission," Sarah explained. "It's for girls who don't have anyplace to live. They'll take good care of you there, and you'll be safe."

"I don't know . . ." she hedged.

"You don't have to stay there forever," Sarah said. "Only until you decide what you want to do."

"Or we could take you down to Headquarters and lock you up for safekeeping," Frank said, earning a reproachful glare from Sarah and a hateful one from Keely.

"I'll go to the Mission," she decided unhappily.

"Good," Sarah said. "Do you have anything you'd like to pack?"

"Are we going right now?" Keely asked in surprise.

"The sooner the better," Sarah said. "Surely you don't want to stay in this house after what happened to Mr. Wong."

Keely frowned. "No, I guess not." She rose from her chair and glanced at Frank as if she was afraid he might try to stop her.

No chance of that. Good riddance.

Keely must not have had much to pack up. After only a few minutes, she and Sarah came downstairs again with a small bundle.

"I'll take Keely over and get her settled," Sarah said.

"Then you'll go home and forget about this case," Frank replied.

She gave him one of her smiles, and they started out, but Keely stopped and turned back.

"I been thinking," she said to Frank. "My brothers, they didn't like me being with a Chinaman. Maybe they was the ones killed Johnny."

Frank had been thinking that very thing himself, but he didn't want to say so. Sarah saved him from having to reply. "Don't worry. Mr. Malloy will find out the truth, Keely."

She didn't look very reassured, but she followed Sarah out, leaving Frank to close the door behind them.

When he had, he turned to find Ah Woh standing in the hallway. Frank hadn't heard a single sound out of him. "I'd like to ask you a few questions, if you feel up to it."

Ah Woh nodded slowly, his face a study in grief. He must have cared for his uncle more than Keely had. Frank took him to the dining room, and they sat down at the table.

"Do you know why your uncle sent you to find me today?"

"I tell you, he want talk about dead girl."

"What did he know about Angel's death?"

"I not know. He sad today. He say find you."

"Sad? What do you mean he was sad?"

"No smile. Only frown. Think hard. No eat."

So Wong had known something, something he'd found out since Frank's previous visit. "Did he have any visitors yesterday, besides me?"

"Mrs. O'Neal," he said with distaste.

Like Keely had said. "When was she here?"

"Sky just get dark, she come."

"Did she argue with your uncle?"

"Yes, much shouting. She angry."

"Because Wong wouldn't let her take Keely home," Frank recalled from his conversation with the girl.

Ah Woh frowned. "No, that not why."

"You mean that's not why they were arguing?"

He shook his head.

"Keely said her mother wanted to take her home, but Wong wouldn't let her go."

Ah Woh's young face twisted in anger. "She lie. Mother come, want money."

"Mrs. O'Neal wanted Wong to give her money?"

"Yes, bride-price. She say he should pay for Keely."

Frank remembered Charlie Lee telling him Wong was going to pay him a bride-price for marrying Angel. "But Wong refused?"

"He say he no pay."

"And what did she say?"

"She say . . ." This time Ah Woh's face twisted in pain. "She say he be sorry."

13

As always, Sarah had been greeted warmly at the Prodigal Son Mission. The place might have closed long ago if it hadn't been for Sarah's efforts, so she was something of a celebrity to the girls who had found shelter there. Too many families turned their children out into the streets when they could no longer afford to keep them or simply didn't want to try any longer. The boys could sometimes survive by stealing or working as newsboys or boot blacks, but the girls had few options besides prostitution. The Mission had been founded as a refuge for those girls.

The matron, Mrs. Keller, took Sarah and Keely into her office after the girls had finished greeting her and asking after Maeve and Catherine.

When they were alone, Sarah briefly explained why she had brought Keely to the Mission.

"I want you to know that you are very welcome, Keely," Mrs. Keller said after she had expressed her condolences for Keely's traumatic experience.

"What do I have to do here?" Keely asked suspiciously.

"All the girls have chores, of course. They help with the cooking and cleaning. You can learn to sew, too, if you like. We have some sewing machines upstairs. And we also have educational classes for all the girls."

Keely didn't look very impressed. "You mean like school?"

"Yes, like school," Mrs. Keller said with a smile.

"Do I have to go to them?"

"We'd like for you to give them a try. Having an education can help you make your way in the world."

"How?" she asked skeptically.

Mrs. Keller smiled again. "That will become clearer to you later. We expect you to behave yourself while you're here, too. We don't allow the girls to have gentlemen callers or to meet them elsewhere or to go out in the evenings. We treat each other with courtesy and no fighting is allowed. If you feel you're being badly treated, come to me first, and I'll help you work things out."

Keely looked at Sarah. "How long do I have to stay here?"

Sarah managed not to sigh. "You must know it's dangerous for a girl to be out in the city alone. If you don't go back home to your family and you don't stay here, where would you go?"

Keely had no answer for that.

"I'm sure you'll be happy here, once you get used to it," Mrs. Keller said.

Keely didn't seem to share her confidence.

Mrs. Keller assigned Keely a bed in the dormitory

upstairs, and when Sarah left, Keely was joining the other girls for supper.

She still didn't look very happy, but after all she'd been through today, Sarah couldn't really expect that, she supposed. At least Sarah would be home in time for supper with her own family. The thought quickened her step as she made her way to the Elevated Train Station.

FRANK WAS ALL READY TO HEAD BACK TO THE O'NEAL flat when he remembered that he still had George Lee in custody. While George might deserve to spend a bit more time locked up as punishment for wasting Frank's time with his false confession, his wife certainly didn't deserve to worry any longer.

Frank was gratified to see that George looked much less confident than he had before. In fact, when the officers brought him into the interrogation room, he looked downright scared.

"How are you doing, George?" Frank asked.

George had to swallow before he could say, "Fine."

"Are you? Well, you won't be doing quite so fine after we take you to the Tombs. You know what that is, George?"

George shook his head.

"That's the city jail. You'll be thrown in with all kinds of criminals there—crooks and arsonists and killers. But since you're such a cold-blooded killer yourself, I guess you won't mind, will you?"

George's eyes were wild with terror, but he shook his head again.

Frank leaned back and studied the young man for a few

moments. "Now before I send you down to the Tombs, I want to make sure that I've got everything straight. You killed Angel Lee, is that right?"

"Yes," he said quickly, although his voice broke. He had to clear his throat and try again. "Yes."

"I have to tell you, George, I'm surprised. See, I thought it was John Wong all along."

"Wong?" he repeated stupidly.

"That's right," Frank said. "I've been wrong before, though, and now I know it wasn't Wong because somebody killed him today."

"Killed? John Wong is dead?" he exclaimed in surprise.

"That's right. Somebody killed him. And you know what's really strange? He had already sent for me because he knew who really killed Angel Lee. He was going to tell me, and then somebody killed him. Now who do you think would've done that?"

"I . . . I do not know," George admitted.

"I don't either, at least not yet," Frank admitted right back. "But I know it wasn't you, because you were locked up. Besides, if you were the one who killed Angel, and you killed Wong to keep him from telling me, why would you come down here and confess? That wouldn't make sense, now would it?"

George looked a little confused, but he said "No" with a worried frown.

"Another thing I know is that Harry Lee didn't kill Angel, either."

George looked surprised.

"That's right, George. Harry didn't kill his sister. In fact, I was just about to let him go when you showed up."

George was moving his mouth as if he wanted to say something, but no sound was coming out.

"I've been wondering something, George," Frank confided. "I've been wondering if you knew I was going to let Harry go, would you have come down and confessed to killing Angel?"

"No!" he cried, then caught himself. He looked so miserable, even Frank was moved.

"You didn't kill Angel, did you, George?"

"I . . . I want help Harry," he mumbled.

"So you decided to take the blame so that Harry would go free. So his parents wouldn't lose both their children, is that right?"

"Charlie, he is like father to me," he explained.

"And what about *your* son, George? Who's going to be a father to him if you go to jail for killing Angel?"

His face practically convulsed with pain. "I . . . Charlie take care," he said sadly.

"You aren't doing me any favors here, George," Frank said sternly. "If I lock you up for killing Angel, the person who really killed her goes free. Is that what you want?"

"No!" George said, outraged at the thought.

"Then tell me the truth. Did you kill her?"

"No! No!" he cried in relief. "I not kill. I lie to help Harry."

"You know I could lock you up for doing that," Frank said and let him squirm for a minute or two before adding, "but I've got too much to do today. I need to find the real killer. Now you go home and tell your wife how sorry you are for getting yourself arrested and scaring her half to death."

Frank had to endure an embarrassing amount of gratitude from George before he finally got him released and out of the building and on his way home. Then he set out to find the O'Neal boys.

* * *

Rounding up the O'Neal brothers was probably going to take half the night, so Frank brought several officers with him. He started by posting them outside the building at the bottom of the fire escape and on the inside stairs and in the hallway outside the O'Neal flat. Then he knocked on the door.

Mrs. O'Neal answered it. She didn't look happy to see Frank. "What do you want?"

"I'd like to talk to your boys again," Frank said politely.

"They ain't here," she replied with undisguised satisfaction and started to close the door in his face.

"Mind if I come in to make sure?" Without waiting for an answer, Frank gave the door a shove, sending her staggering backward into the room.

Frank needed only a moment to check the entire flat while Mrs. O'Neal sputtered furiously. Iris and the baby were the only other occupants. The baby appeared to be sleeping, and Iris and Mrs. O'Neal had been sewing men's vests. Several piles of them lay on the kitchen table.

"My boys didn't have nothing to do with killing Angel," Mrs. O'Neal reminded him.

Frank fixed one of his glares on her. "Why did you go to see John Wong last night?"

She gaped at him for a moment. "I . . . I thought you was here to see the boys," she tried.

"I'm asking you a question, Mrs. O'Neal. Why did you go to see John Wong?"

"Might as well tell him," Iris said, not even looking up from her sewing.

Mrs. O'Neal gave her daughter-in-law a black look, which she didn't see because she was concentrating on her work. Finally, Mrs. O'Neal looked back at Frank. "I was looking for my girl."

"Keely?" Frank asked.

"That's right," she said, growing a bit more confident. "I thought he might know where to find her."

"What made you think that?"

"I . . . Somebody told me," she tried.

"Who told you?"

"I . . . I don't remember."

"Was it Angel?"

"Angel? How could it be Angel?" she asked in feigned amazement. "She's dead."

"But she told you where Keely went before she died, didn't she?"

"I told you, I didn't know where Keely was. That's why I wanted to ask Mr. Wong about it."

"Then Angel must have told you *something* about Wong."

She thought this over. "Well, yeah, she did. She allowed as how he knows everything that happens in Chinatown."

"Mrs. O'Neal," Frank said with elaborate patience. "I know Keely was with Wong because I saw her there. I know she went to him because Angel told her that he was rich and Keely was hoping to get him to marry her. Now why did you go to see him last night?"

Her eyes were darting everywhere as she searched her brain for a story that would sound true. "I . . . I wanted to get Keely and bring her home."

"Bring her home!" Iris scoffed with a harsh laugh. "You didn't want her here after she'd been rutting with a Chinaman!"

"Shut your yap, you stupid cow!" Mrs. O'Neal fairly shouted.

Iris was on her feet in an instant, leaning over the table to shout right back. "Stupid cow, am I? You miserable old—"

"*Iris,*" Frank said sharply, to distract her from the looming fight, "why do *you* think she went to see him?"

"She wanted money from him," Iris reported. "For taking Keely."

"He stole my girl!" Mrs. O'Neal exclaimed, having decided to play the aggrieved mother.

"Keely already admitted that she went to Wong of her own free will. In fact," Frank added with some satisfaction, "it was all her idea."

"That ain't true!" Mrs. O'Neal insisted. "She's just a baby. He tricked her somehow."

"How much money did you want from Wong?" Frank asked.

"I already told you—" Mrs. O'Neal began, but Iris interrupted her.

"A hundred dollars!" the younger woman crowed. "I don't know why she'd think Keely was worth that much."

"She's worth a hundred of *you*!" Mrs. O'Neal shouted.

"I guess you were mad when Wong wouldn't pay," Frank guessed.

"That damn heathen!" Mrs. O'Neal sputtered. "He says if I don't like it, I can just take Keely back!"

"I'll bet that made you pretty mad," Frank said.

"Mad enough to spit!"

"So that's why you threatened him."

"I . . ." She realized he'd tricked her. "I never!"

"You told him he'd be sorry he didn't pay," Frank reminded her. "Other people heard you say it."

Mrs. O'Neal sniffed in derision. "Is that why you come? You gonna arrest me for threatening a Chinaman?"

"No, not for threatening one," Frank told her. "For *killing* one."

"Killing?" she echoed in surprise.

"You never said you killed him!" Iris exclaimed in delight. "Is that true? Did she really kill him? You gonna take her away to jail?"

"Shut your mouth!" Mrs. O'Neal screamed and turned back to Frank in alarm. "I never killed no one! He was right as rain when I left him!"

"Yes, he was," Frank agreed, "but somebody paid him a visit today and bashed his head in. Is that what you told your boys to do after he laughed in your face?"

"No!" she cried, clapping her hands to her cheeks. "I never! I never even told them I'd gone!"

"Did they know Keely was with him?"

She stared back at him, pressing her thin lips tightly together in silent refusal to answer.

"Sure they did," Iris replied for her. "We all knew. She didn't let us tell nobody, though. Guess she'd rather let everybody think she ran off to a whorehouse or something."

"How did the boys feel about their sister living with a Chinaman?" Frank asked Iris.

Iris opened her mouth to reply but caught herself. She wasn't real smart, but she'd know better than to implicate her own husband. "They didn't care," she claimed. "They was glad to be rid of her."

"Her mother might've been glad to be rid of her, too," Frank observed, "but that didn't stop her from trying to get something out of it. Is that what they wanted, too? Did they go to see Wong to get the money their mother wanted?"

Now Iris was confused. "They never did that," she said. "Not that I knew!"

"Where were they all day today?" Frank asked.

"I don't know! They go out when they want, and they come back when they please. They don't answer to no one."

"Any idea where they'd be now?"

"No!" Mrs. O'Neal said before Iris could reply. "We got no idea at all. You want 'em, you'll have to find 'em, but they ain't done nothing wrong. Iris is right, I never even told 'em I went to see Wong. That would've shamed them."

Frank sighed. He doubted a hundred dollars in cash would have caused anyone in the O'Neal family a bit of embarrassment. Now he would have to spend the better part of the night trying to find the sons.

He was already out in the hallway when he remembered something else. "Keely needs a place to live now that Wong is dead," he told the girl's mother.

Mrs. O'Neal glared at him. "She'll have to find one on her own. She ain't welcome here no more."

So much for the power of a mother's love, Frank thought.

AFTER SARAH HAD PUT CATHERINE TO BED, SHE WENT back downstairs to find Maeve waiting for her. Catherine had been content with Sarah's explanation that she had taken Mrs. Lee home and found that Mr. Malloy had released her son from jail. Catherine liked stories with happy endings, but Maeve wanted a more detailed account of Sarah's eventful day.

Sarah told her tale, leaving out nothing. Maeve had probably seen more of life than Sarah ever would, so she didn't have to worry about shocking the girl with the description of Wong's murder.

"You think this Keely had feelings for the Chinese man?"

Maeve asked when she'd taken a few minutes to consider the bizarre story.

"If you're asking if she was in love with him, no, she wasn't. I don't think she even knows what that means. She seemed fond of him, though. He treated her well, by her standards, at least, and they were very . . . affectionate," Sarah added discreetly.

"Most girls would want pretty clothes," Maeve observed wryly.

Sarah smiled. "I'm sure she would've started demanding things sooner or later. I think she was concentrating on getting him to marry her first."

"And having no clothes at all would help with that, I guess." Maeve shook her head. "What do you think happened?"

"As near as we can figure, Mr. Wong must have figured out who killed Angel. He sent his nephew to find Mr. Malloy. He must have wanted to keep Keely out of it, so he gave her some kind of drug to put her to sleep."

"She does sound like she'd be the kind to want to horn in on everything."

"Oh, yes," Sarah agreed. "But for whatever reason, she drank something he gave her and was sound asleep when we got there. She said she thought she heard somebody arguing, but she might have dreamed that. I haven't had a chance to talk to Mr. Malloy about the crime, but from what I saw, it looked like someone had hit Mr. Wong over the head with something heavy. I didn't see any signs that he'd been struggling with the person or anything like that, though. Nothing in the room was out of place."

"So if they was shouting, they was being polite about it," Maeve observed.

"I guess so," Sarah agreed.

Maeve shook her head. "Seems kind of strange. Most people, when they're shouting, they're fighting, too."

Maeve's life had been so different from Sarah's. Her heart ached for the girl.

"So you think it's a Chinese what killed Mr. Wong?" Maeve asked.

"If it's the same person who killed Angel, then it would definitely be a Chinese man. Of course, the person who killed Mr. Wong could be someone else entirely. Maybe he had other enemies. And there's the girl, Keely. Her mother wanted her back, and Wong refused. Maybe her brothers decided to have a word with him, and things got out of hand."

"I don't know her brothers, but from what you said . . ."

"What?" Sarah prodded when she hesitated.

"It's just . . . I'd think they wouldn't want her back."

"You mean because she'd taken up with a Chinaman?" Sarah asked.

"Yes. Besides, even if she'd just run away, I expect they'd be glad to be rid of her. One less mouth to feed."

Sarah had imagined the O'Neal boys defending their sister's honor, but Maeve was more likely to be right in her assessment of their character. "Her mother did try to rescue her, at least."

But Maeve shook her head. "That don't seem right either. Did Keely really hear what her ma wanted or did she just go by what Mr. Wong told her?"

"That's a good question," Sarah said. "I don't know. Keely seemed very confident her mother wanted her to come home, though. What else could she have wanted?"

Maeve shrugged a shoulder. "You said Mr. Wong was rich. People like the O'Neals, they wouldn't mind a few extra dollars coming their way, even if it did come from a Chinaman."

"Oh, dear," Sarah said, realizing she hadn't been seeing this situation as clearly as she should. "I wonder if Mr. Wong gave her some money to get rid of her and then told Keely that story about her wanting to take Keely home."

"You said he treated her good. Maybe he didn't want to hurt her feelings."

Was Wong that kind of a man? Sarah had no idea.

"What did Keely think of the Mission?" Maeve asked.

"She wasn't very happy to be there, but I'm sure she'll get used to it."

Maeve gave her a small grin. "Maybe," was all she would say.

FRANK WAS AMAZED THAT THEY'D ONLY HAD TO ROUST half the bars in New York to round up all the O'Neals. Well, half the Irish bars, anyway. It wasn't even midnight. He might get home to sleep yet tonight.

The boys were all drunk to varying degrees, but all three managed to protest their captivity loudly and profanely as they were hauled into Headquarters. Frank ordered them put in individual interrogation rooms again, and the officers who had helped bring them in dragged them away.

In the ensuing quiet, the desk sergeant called to him. "Donatelli's been waiting for you."

Frank vaguely remembered he'd assigned Donatelli to question Wong's neighbors this afternoon to find out if they'd seen anything. It seemed like days had passed since then. "Where is he?"

"Upstairs," he said, referring to the dormitory where

members of the force could catch some sleep if it was too much trouble to go home. "I'll send somebody to wake him."

Frank was waiting at his desk in the detectives' room when Donatelli found him. A day's growth of whiskers marred his handsome face, and his eyes were puffy from lack of sleep, but he was grinning ear to ear.

"You figure out who killed Wong?" Frank asked, allowing himself a glimmer of hope.

"No, but I got some interesting information," he said, pulling up a chair from a neighboring desk and straddling it. "Seems Charlie Lee went to see Wong yesterday."

"Lee? Are you sure?"

"Everybody in the neighborhood knows him. A couple different people saw him, so there's no mistake."

"What time was he there?"

"Midmorning, seems like. He didn't stay long, half an hour or less."

"So somebody saw him leave?"

"The same people who saw him come, mostly. That's how they knew how long he was there."

"What did he look like when he left?"

"He didn't have any blood on him, if that's what you want to know," Donatelli said knowingly. "At least not that anybody noticed. He wasn't running, neither. Of course, Lee's too smart to do something to call attention to himself if he'd just killed a man."

"I don't suppose anybody saw an O'Neal boy," Frank asked sourly.

"No. Didn't see anybody else either."

"Nobody at all? Not even somebody sneaking around, even if they didn't see them going into Wong's house?"

"Not a soul doing anything suspicious. They would've

noticed white men that didn't belong in that neighborhood, at least."

"They probably would," Frank agreed wearily. "I guess I wasted the whole night gathering up the O'Neals."

Donatelli shook his head in sympathy. "So unless the nephew killed Wong before he left that morning to find you, it looks like Charlie Lee has to be the killer."

Frank rubbed the bridge of his nose where a headache was forming. "Let's think about this. Why would Lee kill Wong?"

"Because Wong killed the girl," Donatelli replied helpfully.

"Except he didn't."

"How do you know?"

"Because he sent his nephew to find me. At first I thought he might be guilty and trying to pin it on somebody else, but then he turned up dead, which means the real killer got to him first. So he sent for me because he wanted to tell me something about Angel's death."

Donatelli thought this over for a minute. "Maybe he wanted to confess."

Frank had to resist the urge to smack him across the head. "Do you know how many times a killer's sent for me so he could confess?"

"No," Donatelli replied, eager for the answer.

"Never!" Frank shouted, making the boy jump.

Donatelli shrugged apologetically. "Then why else would Lee have killed him?"

"I don't know," Frank said, "and that makes me mad. You're telling me that Lee has to be the one who killed him, but he doesn't have any reason that we know of. In fact," he continued, thinking aloud, "if Wong knows who killed Angel, Lee's got a good reason to keep him alive."

"Unless it was *Lee* who killed her," Donatelli pointed out.

Frank didn't believe that for a minute, but . . . "Maybe you were right the first time," Frank mused. "We know Wong didn't kill Angel, but Lee didn't know that. Maybe he killed Wong because he *thought* Wong killed Angel."

"That would explain everything," Donatelli said with way too much enthusiasm.

Would Sarah try to talk him out of arresting Charlie Lee, too? He'd have to do it before she found out. Now Frank really was getting a headache. He pushed himself to his feet.

"Where are you going?"

"Upstairs to get some sleep. I'm not going to go to the Lees' place in the middle of the night."

"What about the O'Neals?"

"I'll have somebody lock them up for the night. Do them good. They're drunk, so we'll charge them with that. Besides, I might want to ask them something later, and if I do, I don't want to have to hunt for them all over the city again."

S<small>ARAH HURRIED TO ANSWER THE DOOR BEFORE THE</small> frantic pounding woke the girls upstairs. Pulling her robe more tightly around her, she peered through the glass in the early morning light and saw a woman silhouetted. She opened the door and Minnie Lee practically fell into her arms.

If Minnie had looked bad the last time she'd arrived like this, she looked even worse this morning. She'd dressed in a hurry. Her buttons were done crooked, and her hair pinned up as if a madwoman had styled it.

"He took them both!" she cried, clinging to Sarah as if she needed her support to remain standing. Perhaps she did.

As she had the last time, Sarah helped Minnie into the house, but this time she led her into the kitchen. She didn't want the girls to hear them. Minnie stumbled along with her and finally sank down into the nearest kitchen chair. Sarah set to work making a fire in the stove and putting water on to boil while Minnie sobbed quietly into her handkerchief.

While she waited for the water to heat, Sarah took a chair opposite Minnie. "Now tell me what happened."

"He took them," Minnie repeated.

"Mr. Malloy?"

"Yes," Minnie said, nodding. "He came early, before it was even light. Woke us all up. I was that scared!"

"He took Charlie and Harry both?" Sarah could hardly believe it. Malloy had been so sure they were both innocent of Angel's death. How could they be involved in Wong's?

Minnie took a deep breath and scrubbed the tears from her face. "He come for Charlie at first. He said somebody saw Charlie going to visit John Wong right before he got killed. Did you know somebody killed John Wong?"

"Yes, I did," Sarah said with a shudder, remembering that awful scene. "Did Charlie really visit Mr. Wong yesterday?"

"I don't know! I guess he did, but he never killed John! I'm sure of that."

Of course she'd defend her husband. People often refused to believe their loved ones guilty of crimes, even when confronted with the most irrefutable evidence. Still, maybe Minnie was right. "Do you know why he went?"

Minnie shook her head. "Mr. Malloy asked him, but he never . . ." Her voice broke and she started sobbing again.

"What?" Sarah asked urgently. "What happened?"

Minnie made a valiant effort to regain her composure. "Harry," she managed brokenly.

"Did something happen to him?"

Minnie nodded. "When Mr. Malloy . . . when he starts asking Charlie questions, Harry . . ." She made an incoherent sound and pressed the fingers of one hand against her lips to stop them from quivering. After a few moments, she continued. "Harry, he started shouting and tells him to leave Charlie alone. He says . . ." Minnie's face contorted with pain at the memory, and the words caught in her throat.

But Sarah was pretty sure she knew what Harry had said. "He said he'd killed Mr. Wong, didn't he?" Why else would Malloy have arrested him?

"But he never did it!" Minnie cried. "He couldn't have! He's just a boy!"

Boys killed every day, as Sarah knew too well, but she wouldn't say that to Minnie. "Why would he want to kill Mr. Wong?"

"Because . . ." Minnie had to fight for control again. "Because John killed Angel."

"But I don't think he did," Sarah said in confusion. "And neither does Malloy."

Minnie looked at her in despair. "Harry said he did. He said that's why he killed him."

Sarah rubbed her temples and wondered if there was any chance this was all a bad dream and she'd wake up soon. "All right," she said patiently. "So Harry confessed to killing Mr. Wong, and Mr. Malloy arrested him. Why did he arrest Charlie, too?"

"Because when Harry said he'd killed John, Charlie said that wasn't so because he'd done it himself!"

Malloy must be fit to be tied, Sarah thought. The only good news was that at least one of them was surely innocent.

"This is all my fault!" Minnie wailed as new tears filled her eyes and spilled down her cheeks. "I should've given him away!"

"Given who away?" Sarah asked in confusion.

Minnie shook her head. "It's my punishment. Angel dying, that was my punishment, and now I'm losing Harry, too. I should've given him away!"

"Given *who* away?" Sarah repeated impatiently.

"Harry!" Minnie cried. "I should've given him away! I didn't know what it would be like for him!"

"Are you talking about him going to jail?" Sarah tried, unable to make any sense of it at all.

"No! I . . . Oh, Mrs. Brandt, I did a terrible, wicked thing. It was years ago. I got in a family way with Harry, and the boy, Harry's father, he ran off. I didn't have nobody to take care of me, and Charlie . . . Well, I tricked him. He thought the baby was his, and I never told him any different! People made fun of me for marrying a Chinese, but Charlie was that good to me, so I didn't care, and I got to keep my baby!"

Sarah could only stare at her. No wonder Harry didn't look the least bit Chinese. She'd thought it an accident of nature that he resembled his mother so much more than his father. Everyone else must have thought so, too.

"No one can blame you for that," Sarah told her kindly. "You aren't the first woman to lie about—"

"But I never knew what it would do to Harry," Minnie said, the tears still streaming down her cheeks. "He was almost ashamed because he didn't look Chinese enough, like he was afraid Charlie wouldn't love him because of it! He tried to be just like Charlie. He was even *more* Chinese than Charlie was, even though he hated being different. I saw it in him, but there was nothing I could do, except . . ."

"Except tell him the truth," Sarah finished for her.

"And I couldn't do that, could I?" Minnie asked, her eyes pleading with Sarah to confirm it. "I couldn't break Charlie's heart!"

Sarah reached over and took Minnie's hand. "None of that matters now, Minnie. What matters is saving what's left of your family."

"How can we do that?" Minnie asked in despair.

"By finding out the truth."

14

FRANK WAS BEGINNING TO WONDER IF THE CHINESE were naturally prone to confessing to murders they hadn't committed. He hoped nobody would tell George Lee about Wong's murder until he'd had a chance to at least sort through the current batch of confessions.

Donatelli had gone with him to the Lees' flat earlier, and he was still marveling. "Which one do you think really did it?" he asked Frank for what seemed like the hundredth time. They were sitting in the detectives' room, discussing their strategy.

"I told you, we'll figure it out," Frank snapped.

"But how? And what if we can't? Do we arrest both of them for it?"

Frank gave him a pitying look. "If we can't figure out which one did it, we'll have to let them both go."

"That don't seem right," Donatelli protested.

"Maybe you think it's better to lock up somebody who's innocent instead."

"But the innocent one asked for it," Donatelli reasoned.

"Being stupid still isn't against the law," Frank said. "If it was, we'd have most of New York in custody. And until it is, we've got to let the stupid ones go."

He didn't like it. "Then how do we figure out who did it?"

"*We* don't do anything," Frank told him impatiently. "*I* will interrogate them, and *you* will listen and learn." Frank stood up and headed for the stairs to the basement, Donatelli on his heels.

Harry Lee was pacing around the small room when they opened the door. He stopped abruptly and looked at Frank and Donatelli with undisguised terror. Still, he jutted out his chin defiantly and said, "I killed Mr. Wong. You can let my father go."

"Sit down, Harry," Frank said. "I need to ask you a few questions."

"But I already told you—"

"*Sit down!*"

The boy sat so quickly, he almost upset the chair. His hands lay on the table, closed tightly into fists, and his young face was pale. He was wearing Chinese clothes today, not the ugly sackcloth but a blue silk shirt and black, baggy trousers. His head was bare, and his notorious hat with attached queue was nowhere in sight.

"Tell me what happened," Frank said when he had seated himself across the table from the boy.

Harry swallowed loudly as he worked up his nerve. "I . . . I went to Mr. Wong's house," he began. "After I got back from here, that is. My mother told me to go find my father and tell him George was arrested, but I went to Mr. Wong instead."

"Why?"

"Why what?"

"Why did you go to Wong's house?" Frank asked patiently.

"Because . . . because I knew he was the one who'd killed Angel."

"How did you know that?"

"I told you before, he's got to be the one. He's the only one who hated her enough."

"Why did you go to see him then?"

Harry frowned. He was trying to think. "I . . . I wanted to get him to confess. I knew George didn't do it, and I didn't want him to be in trouble."

"Did you think Wong would confess to a murder just because you asked him real nice and said please?" Frank asked, not bothering to hide his skepticism.

The color rose in the boy's face, but he didn't back down. "He killed her. Admitting it is the honorable thing to do."

"People don't usually do the honorable thing if it's not in their best interest," Frank remarked. "I don't think it was in Mr. Wong's best interest to go to jail."

"That's what *he* said!" the boy claimed. "He wouldn't do it, not even to help George! It made me mad, so I hit him."

"What did you hit him with?" Frank asked.

"The poker," he said without hesitation. "The fireplace poker. I hit him on the head with it."

"You must've been pretty mad."

"I was. He killed my sister!"

"Where were you standing when you hit him?"

"What do you mean?"

"I mean, were you in front of him?"

He blinked while he thought this over. "Yes," he decided. "I was standing in front of him. I told him he was going to hell for killing my sister, and I hit him over the head."

"And he just sat there and watched you?" Frank asked in amazement.

He knew he'd said something wrong, but he didn't know what. "He's a coward," he said. "He was too scared to put up a fight."

"Then what did you do?"

"What?"

"What did you do after you hit Wong over the head."

This question aroused Harry's suspicion, but he couldn't figure out why. "I . . . I ran out. I went home."

"Did you go out the front or the back?"

"I . . . The back. I didn't want anybody to see me."

"I guess that explains why nobody saw you," Frank said, glancing at Donatelli.

"What do you mean?" Harry asked with a frown.

"Just what I said." Frank rose from his chair.

"Are you going to arrest me?" Harry asked almost desperately.

"Sure," Frank lied.

"And you'll let my father go?"

"I'm going to see him right now," Frank assured him. "You wait right here."

As if he had a choice, Frank thought with irony as he waited for Donatelli to lock the door behind them.

"He didn't do it, did he?" Donatelli asked with a trace of disappointment.

"Why not?" Frank asked to test him.

"Wong was hit from behind," Donatelli recalled. "If the

boy had stood in front of him, he would've seen it coming and fought back. He would've put his arm up, at least, to block the blow."

"What else?"

Donatelli thought for a moment. "The killer washed the blood off of him before he went out. The boy didn't know about that. He did know about the poker, though," he added. "How could he?"

"I'm sure everybody in Chinatown knows it by now. Ah Woh knows what happened. Everybody would want to know how Wong was killed, and he doesn't have any reason to keep it a secret."

Donatelli nodded his understanding. "So I guess that means Lee did it."

Frank sighed. "The way this case is going, I wouldn't count on it."

Charlie Lee was sitting very straight in his chair at the table, and when they came in, he stood. He'd dressed in a hurry this morning, but he'd taken some time while he was waiting for them to adjust his business suit and tie his tie and smooth his hair. It was good strategy. How you looked affected the way people treated you. Charlie wanted to be treated well.

"Sit down, Charlie," Frank said. "Make yourself comfortable."

Frank sat in the chair opposite him. When they were both settled, Frank took the opportunity to study him for a moment. His dark eyes were clear, and he returned Frank's gaze boldly. He wasn't afraid, and he was very determined.

"Some witnesses saw you going into John Wong's house yesterday," Frank began.

"That is correct. I visit him," Charlie confirmed.

"Why did you visit him?"

"I . . . I talk to him . . . about Angel."

"What did you talk about?"

Charlie was a better liar than his son but still not very good. "He say he kill Angel."

"He confessed that to you?" Frank asked in amazement.

"Yes," Charlie said confidently. He'd thought this through. "I cannot help. I hit him."

"What did you hit him with?"

"Poker from fireplace."

Frank glanced meaningfully at Donatelli.

"Didn't he try to stop you from hitting him?" Frank asked.

"No. Too fast. He surprise."

Frank nodded his understanding. "I don't guess I can blame you. I'd probably do the same thing if a man told me he killed my child."

Charlie nodded back, satisfied that Frank believed him.

"Then what did you do?"

"What?" Charlie asked suspiciously.

"What did you do after you killed Wong."

"I . . . I go out. Walk home."

Frank glanced at Donatelli again, and this time caught a look of dismay on his handsome face. He bit back a smile and crossed his arms over his chest and leaned back in his chair. "Mr. Lee, you know your son Harry also confessed to killing Mr. Wong."

"I know," Charlie said anxiously. "But he no kill. I kill John. You let Harry go."

Frank didn't move. He continued to stare at Charlie. Charlie bore it well for a minute or two, but eventually, he started to fidget nervously.

"Harry no kill," he repeated, almost plaintively.

"Oh, I know he didn't," Frank said, surprising him. "He couldn't have. He didn't know enough information about how Wong was killed to be the murderer."

Charlie stared at him open-mouthed.

Frank pretended not to notice his astonishment. "The thing that's bothering me is why he'd say he did when he didn't. Do you have any idea?"

Charlie continued to gape for another moment before closing his mouth with a snap and straightening in his chair again. "No," he said simply.

"My guess is that he was trying to protect you." Frank gave him a minute to think this over and realize what a loving sacrifice the boy had made for him. The realization drained Lee's face of color and his eyes glittered with unshed tears.

Then Frank waited for another minute to give him time to realize that if Harry was innocent, he'd confessed to a murder he didn't commit for no reason at all and was now in a lot of trouble. Then he said, "Charlie, I know you didn't kill Wong either. If you keep claiming you did, I'm going to have to lock you up and the real killer will go free. Is that what you want?" Frank was getting tired of explaining this.

"I . . . No!" he exclaimed. "I not want that. Harry really did not kill?" he added.

"No, Harry didn't kill anybody. Now tell me the truth. Why did you go see Wong yesterday?"

This time Charlie decided to cooperate. "He telephone. He tell me come and talk."

This wasn't what Frank had expected. "Wong sent for you?"

"Yes. He say he sorry."

"For what?"

"For Angel," he reported sadly.

"Did he kill her?" Frank asked in amazement.

"No, no," Charlie said, shaking his head vigorously so Frank would understand. "But he know who did."

"And he told you who it was?"

"No, he no say," Charlie reported with a trace of the frustration Frank was feeling. "He say he tell police only. He want tell me he sorry first."

Now Frank was thoroughly confused. "If he didn't do it, why would he be sorry?"

Charlie shook his head again, slowly this time. "I not know. He say it his fault Angel die. He say I understand later."

Frank swore under his breath. The killer must have realized Wong had figured it out and decided to silence him. But who was he and how did he know Wong was going to betray him? And how had Wong figured it out when Frank couldn't? He was missing something, some clue that he should have seen and didn't. That was the only explanation.

"What time was it when you saw Wong?"

"Ten o'clock, maybe," he said uncertainly. "Maybe eleven. Not sure."

So Wong was alive then and dead by three, for what that was worth. If Frank only knew who had visited him after eleven, he might have some useful information.

Someone knocked on the door, making Frank wince. He glanced at Donatelli, who shrugged. "Maybe George confessed," the younger man said with a sly grin and opened the door.

The officer outside said, "Somebody to see you, Detective."

"A Chinese man?" Frank guessed.

The officer scratched his head. "No, two white women. One of them is Mrs. Brandt."

Frank looked at Charlie. "The other one is probably Mrs. Lee." He turned back to Donatelli. "Get the boy. We'll turn them both loose and send them home with her."

Donatelli went out.

Charlie stood, pulling himself up to his full height. "Thank you, Mr. Malloy."

Frank glared at him. "Just don't waste my time again, and keep that boy of yours out of trouble."

Charlie nodded once. "I will."

Donatelli brought Harry into the room. The boy still looked frightened. "Papa!" he exclaimed in surprise when he saw Charlie. "I thought you were going to let him go!" he said to Frank.

"I'm letting you both go," Frank said. "But the next time you lie to me, I'm going to lock you up and forget about you for a couple days."

The boy's gaze darted to Charlie and back to Frank again. "You're letting both of us go?"

"That's right. Your mother is upstairs waiting for you. Take her home and don't come back here."

The boy still didn't understand, but Charlie took him by the arm. "Come," he said and drew the boy out of the room and down the hall. Harry was asking questions, but Charlie silenced him with a stern command, and then they were gone.

Frank rubbed the back of his neck wearily.

"What about Mrs. Brandt?" Donatelli asked.

"What about her?" Frank snapped.

"Nothing, I . . . I guess she'll leave when she sees you let them go," Donatelli tried.

"You don't know her very well then," Frank said. As much as he hated that Sarah was involved in this case, he also felt an overwhelming urge to discuss it with her. Maybe she could help him see what he'd missed. She'd done it before. "Go up and make sure the Lees leave and wait with Mrs. Brandt until I get there. Tell her I'll be with her in a minute and don't let anybody bother her."

"Why don't you just go up yourself?" Donatelli asked with a frown.

"Because Mrs. Lee will make a big fuss if she sees me and start crying and thanking me. Now hurry up. I don't want Mrs. Brandt left alone up there."

Frank waited, trying to figure out where to take Sarah. He thought about the Italian restaurant nearby but decided against it. They might not receive a warm welcome there after what had recently happened. By the time he found Sarah in the lobby upstairs, he'd decided on a neighborhood coffee shop.

Sarah's heart ached when she saw how tired Malloy was. He'd been working way too hard, and the new rash of phony confessions hadn't helped at all. Malloy didn't even speak to her. Anything he said to her here would be noted and repeated and used to tease him, she knew. He motioned toward the door, and Sarah preceded him.

"What about the O'Neal boys?" Donatelli called after them.

"Keep them for a while longer," Malloy called back, and then they were outside.

Tom the doorman wished her a good day, and she thanked him, earning a scowl from Malloy. As soon as they were out of Tom's earshot, she said, "Are you sending me home?"

"Not yet," he replied to her surprise. "Let's get some coffee."

They walked in companionable silence, not wanting to say anything important until they were well away from the resident reporters. In a few short minutes they reached the shop. Malloy ordered coffee, and they waited until the waitress had poured it and left.

"You let both of the Lees go," Sarah said at last.

"They didn't kill Wong," he replied gruffly. "The boy thought the father did it, and the father thought the boy did it. They were trying to protect each other."

"Oh!" Sarah remembered Minnie's story and felt the sting of tears at this evidence of the love they felt for each other. No real father and son could have shown it more clearly.

"What is it?" Malloy asked, reading her emotions too well.

"I was thinking how . . . how love makes people do strange things."

Malloy looked a little surprised, but he didn't say anything, so Sarah took the opportunity to defend herself.

"The reason I'm here is that Minnie came to me again. I guess she thinks I got you to release George the last time and wanted me to help Harry and Charlie. I couldn't just send her home," she added defensively.

He waved away her explanation. "Charlie Lee went to see Wong on the morning he was killed. That's why I brought him in."

"That's what Minnie told me. Why did he go to see him?"

"Wong sent for him. He wanted to tell Charlie he was sorry about Angel. He knew who had killed her, and he thought it was his fault."

"Did he tell Charlie who it was?" Sarah asked in amazement.

"No, he was waiting to tell me."

"But someone killed him before he could," Sarah said. "Are you sure it wasn't Charlie?"

"Positive. He didn't know enough details about the killing."

Sarah considered what she knew about John Wong's death. "But none of this makes sense. It means the killer must have found out somehow that Wong was going to reveal his identity, so he went to Wong's house, and Wong sat there and let him bash him over the head."

"I know. Wong would have fought back, so he must not have known the killer was there," Malloy said. "He must've sneaked in and hidden."

"But who could it be?" Sarah asked in frustration. "You've eliminated all the suspects."

"Which means I missed something. What is it?"

Sarah blinked. He was actually asking for her help! She tried not to act surprised. Or as ridiculously pleased as she felt. "I . . . I don't know. Let's see," she stammered, willing herself to act normally. "It all started with Angel's death, so if we can figure out who might have killed her, we'll know who killed Mr. Wong, too. What do you know about Angel's killer?"

"He was a Chinese man with a pigtail," Malloy said.

"Your witness was too far away to see his face," Sarah recalled. "But she could tell by his clothes that he was Chinese."

"Don't forget the pigtail."

"And by his pigtail," Sarah added. "And Angel knew him well enough to go greet him."

"Which *should* help, but it hasn't so far," Frank groused.

"What color were his clothes?"

"What color?"

"Yes," Sarah said. "The Chinese men wear black trousers, but their shirts are all different colors."

"The witness didn't say what color the killer's shirt was," he said with a frown of annoyance.

"It might not help to know, but it couldn't hurt. Maybe it will help you narrow down your suspect list, at least."

"I don't have any suspects left, remember?" he reminded her crossly.

"Then it's got to be someone else, somebody we haven't thought of yet"

"That's a relief," he said sarcastically. "Now I only have to question every other Chinese man in New York until I find the right one."

"Or figure out how John Wong knew who the killer was," Sarah was happy to remind him.

"Yeah, maybe I could have a séance or something," he said with more sarcasm.

Sarah ignored his barb. "Maybe Mr. Wong's nephew knows something that will help," Sarah mused. "Something must have happened between the time you visited him and the time he was killed that gave Wong the information he needed to figure it out."

"That's true. Ah Woh was pretty upset after we found Wong. Maybe now that he's calmed down, he'll remember something."

"And of course Keely might remember something, too," she added with a grin.

Malloy made a face.

"I could go to see her to save you the trouble," she

offered. "I know you don't want me involved, but I certainly won't be in any danger at the Mission."

"She won't remember anything. She was drugged," he reminded her.

"She wasn't drugged when Wong figured out who the killer is. She might remember something or know who came to see Wong, the same way Ah Woh might."

He shrugged one shoulder. "Go ahead if you don't mind seeing her again."

"Maybe I can convince her to go back home, too."

"Uh, don't bother with that," he said uneasily. "Her mother said she doesn't want her back."

"That's awful!" Sarah exclaimed in outrage.

"The whole family is awful," Malloy reminded her.

Sarah sighed. "I guess I really should go see her, then. She'll need some guidance about what to do next, and she needs to understand that the Mission is the best place for her right now."

"Doesn't she like it there?" he asked knowingly.

"I'm sure she'll get used to it, when she understands she doesn't have much choice," Sarah assured him.

"Good luck," he said with a grin.

"Good luck to you, too," she said more soberly. "Will you let me know what you find out?"

He sobered, too. "Of course."

F RANK WAS PANTING AND SWEATING UNDER HIS CLOTHES by the time he'd climbed up the five flights of stairs to where he had originally encountered the old woman who'd seen Angel's killer. This time he had to knock on the door, and he waited so long for a response that he was starting to fear she had died since his last visit.

At last, a voice asked, "Who's there?"

"Detective Sergeant Frank Malloy," he replied. "I need to ask you a few more questions about that girl's murder."

The door opened at once, and the old woman stood there, her grin revealing toothless gums. "Come on in!" she offered happily. "I guess you ain't found the killer yet or you wouldn't be here."

"No, I haven't, although your information was very helpful. I forgot to ask you something important, though."

"I already told you all I know," she said, hobbling over to the rocking chair that still sat by the window. "But I don't get much company, so go ahead and ask your questions. I'm happy to oblige." She sat down in the chair with a weary sigh.

Frank followed her over to the window and looked out as he had the other day. He'd remembered right. She had a perfect view of the place where Angel had died. "You said the killer was Chinese," he reminded her.

"That's right. Had on them clothes they wear, like I told you."

"Can you describe the clothes he had on?"

"Well, now," she said in surprise. "I'll try. My memory ain't what it used to be, though. Let's see." She screwed up her face as she considered. Frank hoped she was trying to remember and not trying to make something up.

"Had on a hat," she recalled after a moment. "I think I told you that. Had a wide brim."

She hadn't said anything about a brim before. Frank had pictured a bowl-shaped hat, like the one Harry wore that had his old pigtail attached. "What else?"

"The pigtail. Told you that, too."

"Yes, you did," he said encouragingly.

"Trousers was black, and the shirt . . . the shirt is what I remember most. It was red."

Red? "Are you sure?"

" 'Course I'm sure. Wouldn't mistake that, would I? Don't see somebody wearing a red shirt every day, now do I?"

"No, I don't suppose you do," Frank agreed. It wasn't something *he* saw every day, either. He tried to remember *ever* seeing a Chinese man wearing a red shirt.

"Does that help?" she asked hopefully.

"Yeah, it does. Now if you don't mind, would you go over everything you saw again? Right from the beginning."

She didn't mind a bit. Frank doubted anybody paid much attention to her anymore, so having a willing audience was a rare treat. She repeated the story of Angel's murder, but she didn't remember anything new. Satisfied he'd learned everything he could from her, Frank took his leave. Now he just had to find that red shirt.

THE MISSION WAS ONLY A SHORT DISTANCE FROM POLICE Headquarters, so when Malloy left her in search of his witness, Sarah strolled down to pay Keely a visit. Mrs. Keller was happy to call Keely out of her class so Sarah could meet with her.

"Just between us, Keely is going to have a difficult time adjusting to life here," Mrs. Keller confided. "I don't think she ever obeyed a rule in her life, and she . . . Well, she isn't above lying to get herself out of a scrape."

"Do you think she's capable of adjusting?" Sarah asked.

"Oh, she's very bright," Mrs. Keller assured her. "She could learn if she tried."

"Maybe I can help her understand why she needs to," Sarah said. Mrs. Keller didn't give her much encouragement before she went to get the girl.

A few minutes later, Keely came into the front parlor, where Sarah was waiting. She still wore the dress that Ah Woh had washed and pressed so carefully. Her long, dark hair had been carefully brushed and pinned up into a bun on the back of her head. Instead of making her look older, however, it made her look younger and more vulnerable.

"Hello, Keely," Sarah said with a smile.

"Hello," she answered without much enthusiasm, sitting down on the sofa beside her. "If you come to try to get me to go home, you're wasting your time."

Sarah remembered what Malloy had said about her not being welcome there, but she wouldn't mention that to the girl. "No, I came to see how you're doing. You've been through a difficult time, and I don't want you to think no one cares about you."

"Why should *you* care?" she asked skeptically, reaching up to adjust the pins holding her bun in place.

"Because I do," Sarah replied simply. "Do you need anything?"

She didn't look like she believed Sarah, but she said, "I need some clothes." She looked down at her dress in disgust. "I should've made Johnny get me some, but I thought there'd be lots of time for that," she added wistfully.

"You must miss him," Sarah said gently.

Keely made a face, as if her own emotions embarrassed her. "He treated me good. I never knew . . ."

"Knew what?" Sarah asked when her voice trailed off.

"I never knew it could be like that," Keely said with a frown. "I'd been with boys before, but I didn't know it could feel like that. Johnny, he knew how to do things."

Sarah tried not to gape. She hadn't expected such frankness. "Well . . ."

"He was gonna marry me," she said, oblivious to Sarah's discomfort. She was adjusting her bun again. "I made him promise me after we did this one thing that he showed me. I never saw anybody do it like that before."

Sarah wondered how many acts of intercourse Keely had observed, but living in such close quarters with her family had probably provided many opportunities. "Mrs. Keller said you were in class when I arrived," Sarah tried in an attempt to change the subject to something less shocking.

Keely didn't notice. "What'll happen to Johnny's money now that he's gone?" she asked.

Sarah blinked in surprise. "I . . . I don't know. I expect his nephew will inherit it unless he has other family someplace else."

"He don't," Keely said. "He told me. He had a wife in China, but she died, and he didn't have no kids, either. So Ah Woh will get it all?" she asked with interest.

"I suppose he will."

"I guess he'll be wanting a wife then," she mused.

Sarah stared at her, wondering if she could really be thinking about throwing herself at Ah Woh with the renewed hope of getting a rich husband. Somehow she didn't think Ah Woh would be as interested in her as John Wong had been, though. Reminding herself that she'd come here for a reason, Sarah said, "Mr. Malloy thinks that Mr. Wong had figured out who killed Angel."

Keely looked at her in surprise, and Sarah thought she saw a flash of fear in the girl's eyes.

"Don't worry. You're perfectly safe here, Keely," Sarah assured her. "Mr. Malloy wanted me to ask you if Mr. Wong had said anything to you about it."

"No," she said quickly. "He never mentioned it."

"Do you remember if he had any visitors on the day before he died?"

She frowned, and for a moment Sarah thought she wouldn't even answer. "I already told you, my ma came to see him. And that policeman of yours," she said after a moment. "Nobody else. He was with me the rest of the time."

"But no one else?" Sarah pressed her.

"Not that I know of," she said crossly. "Don't forget I was sleeping. Somebody could've come then, and I wouldn't know, would I?"

"Are you sure he didn't say anything about Angel's death? Anything at all?"

"No," she said with certainty, but then she seemed to reconsider. "I mean, now that I think about it, maybe the reason I don't remember is because he was giving me something the whole time I was there, something that made me feel funny."

"The whole time?" Sarah asked in surprise.

"Maybe," she hedged. "But I don't remember much of what happened, like it was a dream or something."

Sarah had the oddest feeling that she was lying about this, but she couldn't imagine why. Maybe Keely was starting to feel guilty about her liaison with John Wong and was trying to find an excuse for her wanton behavior. "So you don't remember anything that might help us figure out who killed Angel?"

"No, I don't remember nothing." Keely fiddled with her

bun again. Obviously, she wasn't used to wearing her hair up, and she finally started pulling out the pins in disgust and shook her head to let the hair fall free. It was braided, one long braid that fell down her back almost to her waist. Sarah was struck again by how young she was—young but toughened by experience.

15

KEELY FIDGETED UNDER SARAH'S GAZE, TUGGING ON the braid. She started wrapping it back into a bun again. "I ain't used to wearing it like this yet," she said, sticking the pins in with extra force, as if that would make it stay. "Mrs. Keller says it's more ladylike."

"It's hard to get used to wearing it up," Sarah said, remembering.

"Do you live around here?" Keely asked, smoothing back a few stray hairs.

"No," Sarah said. "I don't."

"You must live close. The other girls said you come around all the time," she said.

"I live over on Bank Street. It's a few miles from here, in Greenwich Village."

"You married?"

"My husband died a few years ago," Sarah replied.

"I figured you wasn't married. No husband would let you run all over town with a policeman," Keely said with satisfaction. "You got any kids?"

"No," Sarah said, telling a half-lie in her discomfort at the prying questions. She didn't feel like sharing Catherine's story with Keely just now. "Keely, I know you're wondering what will become of you, but you really don't have to worry about anything just now. You're safe here, and you can stay as long as you want."

"I don't like it here," she said flatly.

"I'm sure it's very different than the life you're used to, but at least give it a chance."

"The other girls don't like me," she said. "And I don't like them, neither. Maybe I could be like you. Mrs. Keller said you was a midwife."

"You need special training to be a midwife," Sarah said, seeing an opening to encourage her to remain at the Mission and work on her education.

"Do you have an office or something? Like a doctor?"

"My office is in the front room of my house. I'd be happy to talk to you about it some more, but you'll have to do well in your classes here before you could even consider it."

"Yeah, well, I'll think about it," she said and rose abruptly. "I better get back to my class then."

"I'll ask Mrs. Keller about getting you some clothes," Sarah said, but Keely was already gone.

What on earth was all that talk about becoming a midwife? Sarah wondered. Maybe Keely recognized that Sarah was a possible source of good things and was trying to get on her good side? She felt a bit guilty, attributing such a selfish motive to the girl's actions. Of course, it was too easy to judge her. Sarah had no idea what it was like to grow up as Keely had done, with no hope that her future would be any better than her past.

Maybe Maeve could give her some insights into how to reach Keely. Maybe she'd even bring Maeve down here to talk with her. Anything was worth trying.

F RANK FOUND AH WOH LOOKING BETTER THAN HE HAD the last time he'd seen him. The shock of losing his uncle had passed. His color was good, and his eyes had lost that vacant stare.

"You get killer?" he asked hopefully as he ushered Frank into the house.

"Not yet, I'm afraid," Frank said. "But I need to ask you a few more questions."

"Yes, yes," he said, nodding vigorously. He motioned toward the parlor where Wong had died, and Frank was surprised to see that every trace of the murder had disappeared. The blood-soaked rug was gone, and there was a suspiciously light spot on the floor where extra cleaning had bleached away some of the color along with the bloodstain. Otherwise the room looked perfectly normal.

Frank chose to sit on a chair as far from where Wong had been sitting as possible. Ah Woh perched on a chair nearby, eager to help.

"Did your uncle have any visitors after I left on the day before he died until he sent you to find me the next morning?"

"I tell you, Keely mother," he reminded Frank uncertainly.

Frank doubted Mrs. O'Neal could have helped Wong figure out who killed Angel. "Anybody else? Anybody Chinese?" Frank pressed.

"No," Ah Woh said, shaking his head for emphasis. "I know. No one come."

"Did he go out anyplace?" Frank tried.

"No go out," Ah Woh insisted. "Stay here. With girl."

That didn't make any sense. How could he have figured out who killed Angel if he'd just stayed home with no visitors?

"Are you sure he didn't say anything to you about who he thought had killed Angel?"

Ah Woh scratched his head. "No talk. Tell me find you. That all."

Frank swallowed down his frustration. Snapping at Ah Woh wouldn't help. He tried one more question. "Do you know anybody in Chinatown who wears a red shirt?"

"Red?" he asked doubtfully.

"Yeah, red." Frank looked around the room and found a red vase on the mantle. He pointed to it.

"Ah," Ah Woh said, nodding with understanding. "Uncle have red shirt."

Frank felt his blood quicken. This wasn't what he had expected, but for all he knew, every Chinaman in the city had one. "Can I see it?"

Ah Woh took him upstairs to the bedroom. This room had been cleaned, too. The bedclothes had been stripped, along with all traces of Keely's presence. Ah Woh went to the large chest of drawers and opened the second one from the top. He stared for a long moment, and then started moving the garments in the drawer around when he didn't find what he wanted. When he'd examined everything, he drew back, a puzzled frown on his face.

"Maybe it's in another drawer," Frank suggested.

Ah Woh gave him an uncertain glance, as if such a thing

were impossible, but he closed that drawer and opened the top one, searching that one unsuccessfully as well. Frank watched him search the remaining drawers in the chest, then move to the wardrobe and even look under the bed and in the bathroom, growing more and more agitated until he was almost frantic.

"It not here!" he exclaimed in despair.

"Maybe your uncle threw it away or something," Frank suggested.

"No, no," Ah Woh insisted. "It new."

"It was a new shirt?"

"Yes, new. For wedding."

"The red shirt was for a wedding?" Frank asked, sure he must not be understanding correctly.

"Yes, yes. Chinese wear red for wedding."

"Are you saying Wong hadn't worn the shirt because it was for his wedding to Angel?" If the Chinese only wore red for a wedding, that would explain why Frank had never seen any of them wearing a red shirt.

"Yes! He not wear. Only her."

Now Frank really was confused. "Angel wore the shirt?"

"No, no." Ah Woh shook his head vigorously. "Girl wear."

"Keely wore it?" Frank asked in surprise.

Ah Woh's young face twisted in disgust. "She wear. Dance around."

"Keely put on the red shirt?"

He nodded. "Fix hair," he said, grabbing his queue and waving it. "Wear shirt."

"She braided her hair and put on the red shirt?" Frank asked in amazement.

He nodded again. "She laugh. Run down stairs. Uncle chase." He made a face again. "She want me see."

Yeah, Frank thought. She was the kind of girl who'd want to show herself to a man who couldn't have her. "Did she know the shirt was for his wedding to Angel?"

"Yes. She say . . ." His eyes clouded at the memory.

"What did she say?"

"She say she be Uncle houseboy. I go away," he said bitterly.

Keely also would have thought it was funny to threaten poor Ah Woh. No wonder the boy hated her.

Something stirred in Frank's memory. What had Keely said about dressing up? She'd dressed up the day Angel died. Now he knew she'd dressed up like a *Chinese man* and that she'd been wearing the same color shirt as the killer, a shirt a real Chinese man would only wear on a special day. *And her hair had been braided into a pigtail.*

"Ah Woh," Frank said, fighting hard not to let his excitement show. "Do you remember what happened the day Angel died?"

He nodded uncertainly.

"You told me your uncle was here all afternoon that day."

"Yes, yes," he said, nodding again. "He sleep."

That's what he had claimed the last time Frank asked him, but he'd thought then that he was lying. "He slept all afternoon?"

"Yes!"

"How do you know?"

"He in room with girl. No come out, long time. Very quiet. I look in. He sleep."

"What about her? Did you see her, too?"

The thought about this, trying to remember. "I think . . . I think she with him in bed," he said uncertainly.

"But did you *see* her?"

"No," he finally decided. "Not see. Look in room, very quick. Not see."

"How long do you think your uncle was asleep?"

"Long time," he repeated. Then his eyes grew wide with realization. "Too long!"

Frank had been trying to find out where Wong was that day, and Ah Woh and the girl had given him an alibi. Both said he'd been there all afternoon. He'd never thought to ask where the *girl* had been, because she was the one giving the alibi! He remembered Sarah waking Keely up from her drugged sleep.

"Does your uncle have any drugs here?"

Ah Woh didn't understand the question.

"Something to make a person sleep? Opium maybe," Frank explained.

"No opium," the boy insisted, offended by the question.

"What does he have?"

When Ah Woh shrugged helplessly, Frank started pulling open the drawers in the chest and rummaging through them. He finally found it, a bottle of laudanum, tucked in the back of the bottom drawer. That wasn't unusual. Practically every home in New York would have a supply for treating a variety of ailments. Had Wong used it on Keely yesterday? Or had she been faking? Could *she* have drugged *Wong* the day before so he wouldn't know she went out? Could she have been the one who killed Angel?

Frank didn't even have to think about the answer. Suddenly, it was crystal clear to him. Keely had wanted to marry Wong so she'd be rich and comfortable. She'd claimed him after Angel had abandoned him, but then Angel's father had come to promise Wong he could marry Angel after all. Keely wouldn't have understood that was an empty promise, based on the remote possibility that Angel could get a divorce or annulment from her marriage to Keely's brother. All Keely knew was that Angel was a threat to her.

How easy it would have been to drug Wong, dress in his clothes, braid her hair into a queue, put on a wide-brimmed hat to conceal her features, and travel through the city virtually unnoticed. Angel would have recognized her anyway, even in her disguise, and she would have run to speak with her, just as the old woman had described seeing from her window far above. And Keely was strong enough and angry enough to have wrapped her hands around Angel's throat and squeezed the life out of her.

And that meant she was the one who'd bashed Wong's head in, too. He must have figured it out somehow. He would have remembered how Keely dressed up in his clothes and how he'd lain in a drugged sleep all that afternoon. Keely couldn't let him betray her, so she'd come up behind him and struck the fatal blow. Then she'd pretended she was drugged and didn't hear anything.

Frank realized Ah Woh was staring at him, his eyes full of terror.

"It's all right," Frank assured him. "I think I know who killed your uncle."

FRANK STOPPED OFF AT POLICE HEADQUARTERS TO PICK up a few patrolmen to guard the back door of the Mission. He didn't want to take a chance on Keely slipping away and disappearing into the streets of the city.

Mrs. Keller was surprised to see him but not alarmed. She knew he'd helped Sarah save the Mission. "What brings you here, Detective Sergeant?" she asked pleasantly.

"I need to see Keely O'Neal," he told her.

"She's popular today," Mrs. Keller remarked. "Mrs. Brandt was here earlier to visit her."

Thank heaven Sarah was long gone, Frank thought as he waited in the front parlor for Mrs. Keller to return with the girl. He wondered what lies Keely had told in answer to Sarah's questions.

Frank wasn't sure exactly when he realized something was wrong. Maybe it was because Mrs. Keller had been gone a bit too long. Maybe it was the sound of people moving around in the hallway and someone running upstairs when the house had been so quiet before. He stepped out into the hall and saw Mrs. Keller hurrying back toward him.

"We can't find her," she reported with a worried frown.

"What do you mean, you can't find her?"

"She never went back to her class after Mrs. Brandt left," Mrs. Keller said. "No one has seen her since then."

"She's not upstairs!" a girl called down from the second floor.

"Did you look everywhere?" Mrs. Keller called back.

Frank didn't wait for the answer. He already knew she was gone. Sarah's questions must have spooked her, and she'd decided to disappear. He ran down the hallway to the rear of the house and out the back door. The officers he'd posted there looked at him in surprise.

"Did anybody come out?" he asked.

"Not a soul."

"The girl's missing. Search the yard."

He didn't think they'd find her, but it was foolish not to at least try. Maybe she was still hiding, waiting for dark to escape. Frank went inside and found Mrs. Keller still helping the rest of the girls search the house.

"How long has Mrs. Brandt been gone?" he asked her.

"An hour or so, I'd say. She talked with Keely, and when they were finished and Keely went back to class—or at least I thought she went back to class—Mrs. Brandt asked me about finding some clothes for her. Keely had come with a bundle, and she hadn't said anything about needing clothes, so I didn't think—"

"Detective Sergeant!"

Frank looked up to see one of the officers coming down the hallway toward him. "We found this in the privy," he said, holding up an article of clothing.

"That's the dress Keely was wearing," Mrs. Keller said in surprise. "Why would she have taken it off?"

"So she could dress up," Frank said furiously.

"Dress up as what?" Mrs. Keller asked in surprise.

"As a Chinese man," Frank said, certain he knew exactly what she was wearing. She'd carried her disguise with her in that bundle Mrs. Keller had noticed. That's why Ah Woh hadn't been able to find the red shirt. "She'll be wearing a red silk shirt, one of those fancy ones, and probably black trousers and a wide-brimmed hat." He turned to Mrs. Keller. "Do you have any idea where she might have gone?"

"None at all."

Frank turned to the patrolman still holding the discarded dress. "Go back to Headquarters and round up as many men as you can find. Give them that description and turn them loose in the neighborhood to find out if anybody saw her."

The patrolman's expression mirrored Frank's own lack of confidence in such a search. They'd probably never see Keely O'Neal again. But he hurried to carry out Frank's orders anyway.

* * *

Sarah DECIDED TO WALK HOME INSTEAD OF TAKING THE Elevated Train. Even if she took the train, she'd have to walk quite a ways, and the day was lovely, too lovely to spend squashed into a car with a hundred strangers. Besides, walking gave her time to think.

Malloy was right. They were overlooking something important. She hoped he'd had more luck with his witness than she'd had with Keely. All they had to do was figure out which of the Chinese men Angel knew had killed her and then would have been able to sneak into John Wong's house and kill him, too. If Wong could figure it out, so could they. Or so she thought. By the time she got home to Bank Street, her head hurt from trying.

Catherine came running to meet her, as usual, and jumped up into her arms for a hug. Maeve wasn't far behind her.

"I've been that worried about you, Mrs. Brandt. You've been gone so long!" Maeve exclaimed.

"Have you been worried about me, or have you been wondering what happened?" Sarah teased her, knowing she hadn't been gone all that long. It wasn't even noon yet.

"Well, both," Maeve allowed, blushing slightly. "You can't blame me, though, after the way you and Mrs. Lee left this morning."

"I don't suppose I can," Sarah said, setting Catherine back on her feet.

"I was just making some sandwiches," Maeve said. "Are you hungry?"

Sarah was starving, so they adjourned to the kitchen.

"What happened with that boy Harry and his father?"

Maeve asked as she set about preparing an extra sandwich for Sarah.

Sarah looked at Catherine, judging whether she should speak in front of the child. Catherine seemed more interested in helping Maeve than in what they were discussing, and besides, her news wasn't particularly shocking.

"Mr. Malloy questioned them both and then let them go home," Sarah said.

"Then Mrs. Lee was all upset for nothing," Maeve said.

"Not for nothing," Sarah disagreed. "Having the police come to your house at the crack of dawn and haul away your husband and son is pretty terrifying."

"Why did Mr. Malloy let them go then?"

"Because he didn't think either of them had done anything wrong." Sarah looked at Catherine again. The child seemed engrossed in eating her sandwich, but Sarah knew that she was listening to every word. How could she not? Sarah decided to change the subject. "I stopped by the Mission on my way home to see Keely O'Neal."

"Is she still there?" Maeve asked slyly.

Sarah smiled back. "Yes, but you were right. She doesn't like it very much. She's not used to following so many rules, and she said the other girls don't like her."

"They're always suspicious of a new girl," Maeve said. "Aren't they, Catherine?"

The child nodded solemnly.

"Why is that?" Sarah asked.

"Because you never know what she's really like," Maeve explained, setting a sandwich down in front of Sarah and then taking a seat herself. "Most girls will be scared when they first come, so they keep quiet and keep to themselves until they figure things out."

"How long does that take?"

"A few days, usually. Sometimes longer. That's when you find out what the new girl is really like."

Sarah knew that not every girl who came to the Mission stayed. Some ran away and a very few were asked to leave. "So we still have some time until we know what Keely will do?"

"Yes, but with her, I wouldn't hold out much hope. A girl like that, I'd expect that they'll wake up one morning and she'll have stolen everything she can carry and disappeared."

"Oh, my!" Ordinarily, Sarah would have defended any girl against such an unpleasant prediction, but for some reason, she didn't feel charitable toward Keely.

"That's why the other girls don't act real friendly at first," Maeve continued. "They wait to see if the new girl will turn on them or if she really wants help."

"I'm afraid Keely doesn't really want help," Sarah said with a sigh. "And she can't go home again. You were right about that, too. Her family doesn't want her back after she's been with a Chinese man. The Mission is really the best place for her, so I was hoping you could help me figure out how to reach her."

But Maeve was shaking her head. "She's got to make up her own mind first."

"But couldn't you talk some sense to her?" Sarah argued. "Convince her that her best chance is to stay where she's safe?"

Maeve looked at her in surprise. "You want me to go see her? To try to change her mind?"

"Yes," Sarah said. "You're a perfect example of how a girl can make a success of her life if she tries."

This time Maeve's blush was from pride. "Thank you, Mrs. Brandt."

"I'm only saying what's true," Sarah assured her. "Would you be willing to talk to Keely?"

"I . . . I guess so," Maeve said, "but don't be surprised if it doesn't do any good."

They ate for a few minutes in silence, and then Maeve asked, "If Mr. Malloy let Mr. Lee and his boy go, who's he going after next?"

"He was going to question his witness again, the old lady who saw Angel . . ." Sarah glanced at Catherine, who was listening avidly. "Who saw Angel with the man who hurt her, and get a better description of the clothes the man was wearing. Then he's going to see if Mr. Wong's nephew has remembered anything else."

"It doesn't sound very promising," Maeve observed.

Someone knocked on the back door.

"That'll be Mrs. Ellsworth," Maeve said, jumping up. "She said she'd be over after lunch."

Maeve threw open the back door, and her exclamation of surprise caused Sarah to look up just in time to see a Chinese man lunging for her.

FRANK WAS STANDING ON THE SIDEWALK IN FRONT OF the Mission, directing the search for Keely, when Officer Donatelli wheeled up on a bicycle.

"What are you doing on that thing?" Frank asked, eyeing the cycle with suspicion. The department had started a bicycle squad to patrol the streets, but Donatelli wasn't a member of it.

"It's a good way to get around the city," Donatelli informed him. "It's faster than walking, and you can go between wagons and even up on the sidewalk if you need to, so you never get stuck in traffic. What do you want me to do?"

Frank had pretty much covered all the possibilities. He had every available man questioning people on the six blocks surrounding the Mission. So far, nobody had seen a Chinese man in a red shirt. Probably, Frank thought, they'd just ignored Keely, the way they did all the Chinese they saw. Either way, he was no closer to finding her. He'd even sent someone over to the O'Neal flat, in case she'd taken a chance that her family would hide her, but Keely wasn't there either. He had one last hope.

"Mrs. Brandt was the last person with Keely before she disappeared," Frank told him. "Drive that contraption over to her house and find out what they talked about. Maybe she'll have an idea of where to look for the girl."

Donatelli nodded and took off, pedaling furiously. Frank watched him go with a frown. It might be fast, but only a fool would get on one of those things.

"Mr. Malloy?"

Frank looked up to find Mrs. Keller coming down the front steps of the Mission. An older woman wearing a shabby dress and an enormous apron was with her. They both looked very worried, and the older woman was actually wringing her hands.

"Mr. Malloy, this is Mrs. O'Dell. She's our cook. Tell him what you noticed, Mary."

The older woman's red face grew even redder. "I don't know if it means anything," she wailed.

"Tell him," Mrs. Keller urged.

"Well, just now," she began anxiously, "I went into the kitchen. I figured the girls would be hungry, even with all this excitement, but when I goes to slice the cheese to make them some sandwiches, I can't find my knife."

Frank felt a chill. "Are you sure you didn't misplace it?"

"Oh, no, I looked all over before I ever said a word to Mrs. Keller, I did. It ain't nowhere in the kitchen. I'd swear to that."

"What kind of a knife is it?"

"It's big and sharp," she said a little testily, as if he should have figured that out for himself. "Blade about this long."

Frank managed not to wince when she indicated a blade of about eight inches.

"She probably took it for protection," Mrs. Keller offered.

Frank was sure of it, but Keely's idea of protection was to kill anyone who posed a threat to her. The question was, did she have anyone else on her list of people she wanted to kill?

For a moment, time seemed to stop. Sarah had looked up and seen not Mrs. Ellsworth but a Chinese man standing on her back porch. His hand was raised and holding something, and he'd started to lunge toward Maeve, but he'd caught himself suddenly when Maeve cried out.

In that split second, when they were all frozen, Sarah looked at his face beneath the brim of his hat, and that's when she understood everything.

"*Keely!*" Sarah cried.

Keely's confused gaze darted from Maeve to Sarah, and her face twisted with hatred. The thing in her hand was a knife, Sarah realized in horror, and when she saw Sarah, she drew it back to lunge again. In the same instant, Maeve slammed the door shut with all her strength.

The door caught Keely's arm at the wrist. Keely howled in pain, and the knife went flying. Maeve pulled the door open again, and Keely slumped forward into the opening, grabbing her injured wrist. Merciless, Maeve slammed the door again, this time catching Keely's head and sending her hat flying. The edge of the door split her temple, and when Maeve opened it again, blood began to stream down Keely's face.

Part of Sarah's mind registered that Catherine had fled, leaving her free to worry only about Maeve and Keely. Before she had even formed a coherent thought, she was on her feet and across the room. She grabbed the edge of the door when Maeve would have slammed it again.

"That's enough!" she cried and grabbed Keely by the arm to keep her from slumping to the floor. "Help me get her inside."

"She tried to kill me!" Maeve protested.

"I think she meant to kill *me*," Sarah corrected her. "In any case, she's not going to kill anyone now. Where's the knife?"

Maeve looked around while Sarah helped the dazed girl into the kitchen and down onto a chair.

"I don't see it," Maeve said. "You can't just bring her into the house when she tried to kill us!" she added when she saw what Sarah was doing. "And why is she dressed like that?"

Keely was looking at Maeve in wonder, still clutching her wrist, which Sarah could see now was probably broken. "Who are you?" she asked. Then she looked up at Sarah accusingly. "You said you didn't have any kids."

"We have to tell Mr. Malloy," Maeve informed Sarah. "And you can't leave her here. What if she tries to kill us again?"

"Her wrist is broken," Sarah said, "and I'm not sure she isn't going to pass out from that blow to her head, but if it will make you feel any better, we can tie her up. Go get my mending basket. There's some stockings in it that will do."

Maeve ran out.

"It's broken?" Keely asked, bewildered, staring at her wrist as if she'd never seen it before.

"Maybe," Sarah lied to keep her from panicking. She reached into her pocket and pulled out a handkerchief and pressed it against the cut on Keely's head to stanch the bleeding. "Keely, why did you come here?"

She looked up at Sarah, still dazed. "You saw my braid," she said, as if that was the most obvious reason in the world. "I couldn't let you tell that policeman."

It seemed so logical now. Why hadn't she realized the truth the instant she'd seen Keely's braided hair? The irony was that if Keely hadn't shown up here to kill her, she might never have made the connection. "But how in the world did you find me?"

"You told me the street where you lived," she replied simply. "And then I saw your sign out front."

She was right, of course. Sarah stared at her, taking in the silk shirt and baggy pants that more than adequately concealed her feminine curves. Her dark hair hung down her back in a single pigtail just like the Chinese men wore, and the broad-brimmed hat she'd been wearing would have concealed her features if she kept her head bowed and spoke to no one.

Keely had been the Chinese man that Malloy's witness had seen from so far away. They'd guessed from the way the witness had described Angel's reaction to the man that she'd known him. Of course she had. She would have recognized Keely in her disguise and gone to see what on earth she was up to. Then they'd quarreled, probably over Wong. Angel wouldn't have wanted Keely to marry him. And Keely, in her anger or in fear of losing Wong to Angel, had strangled her. Wong had figured it out somehow, and she'd killed him. Then she'd imagined that Sarah was a threat to her, and she'd come here to kill Sarah, too.

But she hadn't succeeded. Sarah lifted the handkerchief to see if the bleeding had stopped and that's when she noticed the knot in one corner. The knot Mrs. Ellsworth had tied there to protect her. Sarah prided herself in not being superstitious, but she had to admit that this time, at least, it had worked.

Sarah was vaguely aware of someone ringing her front doorbell. She hoped it wasn't a delivery. She couldn't possibly go. Then she heard a familiar voice calling, "Mrs. Brandt! Mrs. Brandt!"

Gino Donatelli burst into her kitchen with Maeve on his heels, and he stopped dead when he saw Keely O'Neal sitting in her kitchen chair with the bloody handkerchief pressed to her face.

"I couldn't believe it when she told me," he said in amazement, gesturing toward Maeve. "Every cop in town is looking for her. She's the one killed the Chinese girl and John Wong, too."

"Mama! Mama!"

The words were soft, almost a whisper, and when Sarah looked down to find the source, she saw Catherine squeezing past Donatelli, who was nearly blocking the doorway into the kitchen.

"Mama," Catherine repeated urgently, looking up at Sarah solemnly. "She won't hurt you now. I hided the knife."

Catherine's sweet face blurred as tears filled Sarah's eyes, and she scooped the child into her arms.

Epilogue

FRANK NO LONGER FELT INTIMIDATED WALKING INTO Felix Decker's office. He might be one of the richest and most powerful men in the city, but he was also Sarah's father. That made him as vulnerable as Frank.

"I didn't get your message until late Saturday night," Frank said by way of excuse for not coming sooner than Monday morning.

"I've been reading about you in the papers," Decker said. Frank imagined he heard disapproval in his tone, but he couldn't be sure. "The press loved the story about the murdered Chinese girl."

Frank could have told him they would have loved to know about Sarah's involvement, too, but he didn't.

"Sit down, Mr. Malloy," Decker said when Frank didn't comment.

Frank took one of the comfortable leather chairs that stood in front of Decker's desk. As always, he marveled at how ordinary Decker's office looked, as if he felt no need to display his wealth or influence with fancy furnishings.

"Your message said you had some information for me," Frank said.

"That's right. I'll admit I didn't believe you when you said you didn't have the time or resources to trace these women yourself. I was afraid you were just trying to delay the investigation."

"Why would I do that?"

Decker considered the question carefully. "I don't pretend to understand your motives, Mr. Malloy. We both know you've already lied about your reasons for wanting to find Dr. Brandt's killer."

"I didn't lie," Frank lied.

Decker smiled slightly. "There are lies of omission."

Frank didn't bother to respond to that. He'd once thought that solving Tom Brandt's murder would give Sarah some peace, but he was no longer certain of that. Decker wanted Sarah to find out her husband wasn't the saintly young doctor she believed him to be so she'd give up her devotion to his memory . . . and his work. Frank just wanted to keep her from being hurt.

"Did you hire Pinkertons to find out about the women?" Frank asked, referring to the detectives employed by Allan Pinkerton's detective agency.

"Yes, but even they had as much difficulty as you predicted you would have. It has taken them all this time to gather the necessary information." Decker pushed a file folder across the desk to him.

Frank picked it up and opened it. Inside he found neatly typed pages of reports on each of three women.

After skimming the reports, he said, "All of them had fathers living at the time Dr. Brandt was murdered."

"Yes, and since your witness claims he heard Dr. Brandt's killer accuse him of ruining his daughter, that means any of the three men could have done it."

Or maybe none of them, Frank thought, but at least it gave them a place to start looking. He closed the folder.

"I have to admit that I might have done the same," Decker said, "if someone had seduced my daughter and driven her insane."

The lack of passion in his voice told Frank he was testing him. "Dr. Brandt didn't seduce any of these women," Frank said, trying not to sound annoyed. "I told you before, they imagined the whole thing. That woman I met, Edna White, she thinks he's still alive and that she meets him at a flat in Chinatown."

"He must have done something to encourage her," Decker argued. "Why else would she remain so devoted to him?"

"All he did was treat her when she was sick and be nice to her."

"And what about these three?" Decker challenged, gesturing toward the folder Frank still held. "One crazy woman could be an accident, but four?"

"These women weren't his patients. But they had the same kind of delusions."

"You told me you found out about them when you were going through Brandt's *patient* files," Decker reminded him.

Frank was having a difficult time holding his temper. "But he wasn't their doctor, and he didn't treat them."

"No, he just sought them out, women who were known to imagine themselves in love with men they hardly knew. Women who believed they had a carnal relationship with these men. I find that strange, don't you, Mr. Malloy?"

Frank tried not to snap at him. "He wanted to find out more about this 'old maid's disease' so he could figure out how to cure Edna White."

"Even if that's true, he managed to make one of these women's fathers angry enough to kill him," Decker pointed out.

"It looks that way," Frank grudgingly agreed.

Decker sat back in his chair and studied Frank for a moment. "What are you going to do now that you have this information?"

Frank wasn't sure. "Commissioner Roosevelt gave me permission to work on the case," he reminded Decker. "So I will."

"One of the families lives outside the city," Decker pointed out. "You have no authority there."

"They might not know that." Frank had lied many times to get the information he wanted. Once more wouldn't bother him.

Decker nodded. "There's something you need to know, Mr. Malloy, but you can't reveal this information to anyone, not even my daughter. Do I have your word?"

Nothing in Frank's life experience led him to believe this would be good news. "Yes, you have my word," he promised, oddly flattered that a man like Decker would consider that promise valid, coming from someone like Frank.

"You may know that our new president owes Commissioner Roosevelt a debt. Even though Theodore had reservations about McKinley in the beginning, he campaigned for him vigorously."

"And politicians always pay their debts," Frank said, understanding the process only too well.

"That's right. He will be giving Theodore a political appointment soon, and when he does . . ."

"Roosevelt will resign from the Commission." Rumors were already circulating.

"Roosevelt is an honorable man," Decker said. "Honorable men are rare and usually despised by those who are not."

"He's made a lot of enemies," Frank agreed.

"Enemies who will no doubt ensure an end to his reforms to the Police Department, among other things."

Frank remembered only too well how the police had operated before Roosevelt had taken office two years ago—the same way it had operated since the first men were issued the leather hats that marked them as law enforcement officers back in the twenties. Men were hired and advanced through the ranks not on merit but by bribing those in charge. Cops investigated crimes only when they were paid a "reward" for doing so. Justice came only to those with the means to pay for it.

"I'd better find Dr. Brandt's killer before Roosevelt leaves then," Frank said. "How long do I have?"

"A few weeks. A month at the most. There's already speculation, so the newspapers may learn about it even sooner."

Frank understood. "Thank you for the information," he said, rising to his feet.

"I didn't do it for you," Decker reminded him. "I want to know what happened, for Sarah's sake."

"So do I," Frank assured him.

*   *   *

Maeve had invited Malloy and his son Brian over for supper. She'd been wanting to show off her cooking skills, and Sarah had suggested these two guests in particular. She wanted an opportunity to speak with Malloy privately, and she knew he wouldn't seek her out. After what had happened with Keely O'Neal, he was more determined than ever to keep Sarah away from him and the crimes he investigated.

The meal was a great success, and Malloy was generous with his compliments, making Maeve blush more than once. Even Brian complimented her. Although the adults weren't quite certain what he was saying with his hand movements, no one could mistake his enormously satisfied grin. Sarah's favorite moment, however, was when Catherine whispered, "Good pie," after she'd taken her first bite.

Malloy had almost choked on his, but when he'd caught Sarah's eye with an unspoken question, he'd taken her hint and pretended nothing untoward had happened. When the meal was over, he'd said, "Maeve, why don't you take the children upstairs? Mrs. Brandt and I will clean up."

Maeve gave him a knowing look that made him blush, and dutifully ushered the children out.

"How long has Catherine been talking?" he asked the instant they were alone.

"Since the day Keely showed up on our doorstep," Sarah told him and pretended not to notice his flinch. She started to clear the table.

"That never should've happened," he said.

"I know. I was so determined not to put myself in danger because I have responsibilities now."

"I've been telling you that for a year," he reminded her.

"I remember," she told him wryly and kept stacking the dishes.

"Are you saying that you're finally ready to listen?"

"Not exactly."

"Then what, exactly?" he asked with the slightest touch of irritation.

"I realized that if I hadn't been trying so hard to protect myself and my family, I probably would have figured out that Keely was the killer much sooner."

"You can't know that," he protested.

"No, I can't, but I also can't be sure it isn't true. In any case, I've also realized that no matter what I do—whether I get involved in solving murders or I just deliver babies that arrive at all hours of the day and night—I'm going to be in some kind of danger every day. None of us knows how long we have to live, Malloy, but if we sit quietly in our houses and try to stay safe, we'll die without ever having lived."

"That's . . . that's crazy!" he insisted.

"I don't think so," she said. "I think it's the sanest thought I've had in a while. And as horrible as it was when Keely showed up here intending to kill me, it shocked Catherine into talking again. I wouldn't trade that for any kind of safety, Malloy."

For the first time she could remember, Malloy was speechless. She didn't want to ruin the moment, so she proceeded to prepare the dishwater, pumping the cold water into the pan and then drawing hot water from the reservoir on the stove and mixing it in. Then she gave Malloy a towel and started washing. Malloy needed no instruction. He dried the dishes as she handed them to him.

After a few minutes of this, he cleared his throat and

said, "I've finally located all of those women your husband was . . . interested in."

She looked at him in surprise. "It's been so long, I . . . I thought you'd given up."

"No, I just needed time to . . . There was a lot of investigating to do, and the families weren't going to cooperate, so I had to do it . . . privately."

Sarah didn't know what that meant, but if he'd wanted to explain, he would have, so she didn't ask. The important thing was that he now had the information he needed. "What are you going to do next?"

"I'm going to question the families. I've got the authority from Roosevelt and now I know where to find them all."

"You know I'll help in any way I can," she said.

He gave her one of his looks. "Yeah, and your mother will help and Maeve will help and even Catherine will help, too," he said sardonically.

"Yes, they will," Sarah informed him just as sardonically. "If that's what it takes. We might even recruit Brian and *your* mother."

That surprised him into a grin before he regained his composure. "Whoever killed your husband probably knows who you are. You can't be involved, Sarah."

She loved it when he called her by her name. For just that moment, they were alone in time and space and connecting in a way she'd never experienced with anyone else. She looked into his dark eyes and saw the fear that made him want to protect her. She saw something else, too, the feelings neither of them dared name. "You'll keep me informed at least, won't you?"

"If I can," he said.

"And if you need anything, anything at all . . ."

"I know, I'll ask for it."

She knew he wouldn't.

"There's one more thing," he said gravely. "We don't have much time."

"What do you mean?"

"Roosevelt won't be around much longer."

"What do you mean? Have you heard something?"

"Not officially, but the rumors say he's going to Washington. When he's gone, I don't know how much longer I'll be allowed to work on this case."

They'd talked about this possibility before. Without Roosevelt and his high-minded reforms, Malloy believed the Police Department would revert back to its former state of corruption. "How long do you have?"

"I don't know."

"Well, then," Sarah said, going back to washing her dishes. "We'll just have to do it quickly, won't we, Frank?"

Author's Note

I'VE LONG BEEN FASCINATED BY THE MYSTERIES OF CHI-natown, so I was thrilled to be able to finally write about them. I have accurately described the way the immigration laws discriminated against the Chinese and how the Chinese managed to prosper through hard work and determination in spite of it.

Please let me hear from you. I will put you on my e-mail list and send you a reminder when the next book in the series, *Murder on Bank Street*, is published. Contact me through my website, victoriathompson.com.